Buffy the Vampire Slayer™

HAUNTED

publisher
MIKE RICHARDSON

editor
SCOTT ALLIE
with MICHAEL CARRIGLITTO

designer
LANI SCHREIBSTEIN

art director
MARK COX

special thanks to
DEBBIE OLSHAN AT FOX LICENSING
AND DAVID CAMPITI AT GLASS HOUSE GRAPHICS

Buffy the Vampire Slayer™: Haunted. Published by Dark Horse Comics, Inc., 10956 SE Main Street, Milwaukie, OR, 97222.
Buffy the Vampire Slayer™ & © 2002 Twentieth Century Fox Film Corporation. All rights reserved.
TM designates a trademark of Twentieth Century Fox Film Corporation. The stories, institutions, and characters in this publication are fictional.
Any resemblance to actual persons, living or dead, events, institutions, or locales, without satiric intent, is purely coincidental.
No portion of this book may be reproduced, by any means, without express written permission from
the copyright holder. Dark Horse Comics® and the Dark Horse logo are trademarks of Dark Horse Comics, Inc.,
registered in various categories and countries. All rights reserved.

PUBLISHED BY
DARK HORSE COMICS, INC.
10956 SE MAIN STREET
MILWAUKIE, OR 97222

FIRST EDITION
SEPTEMBER 2002
ISBN: 1 - 56971 - 737 - 0

1 3 5 7 9 10 8 6 4 2

printed in china

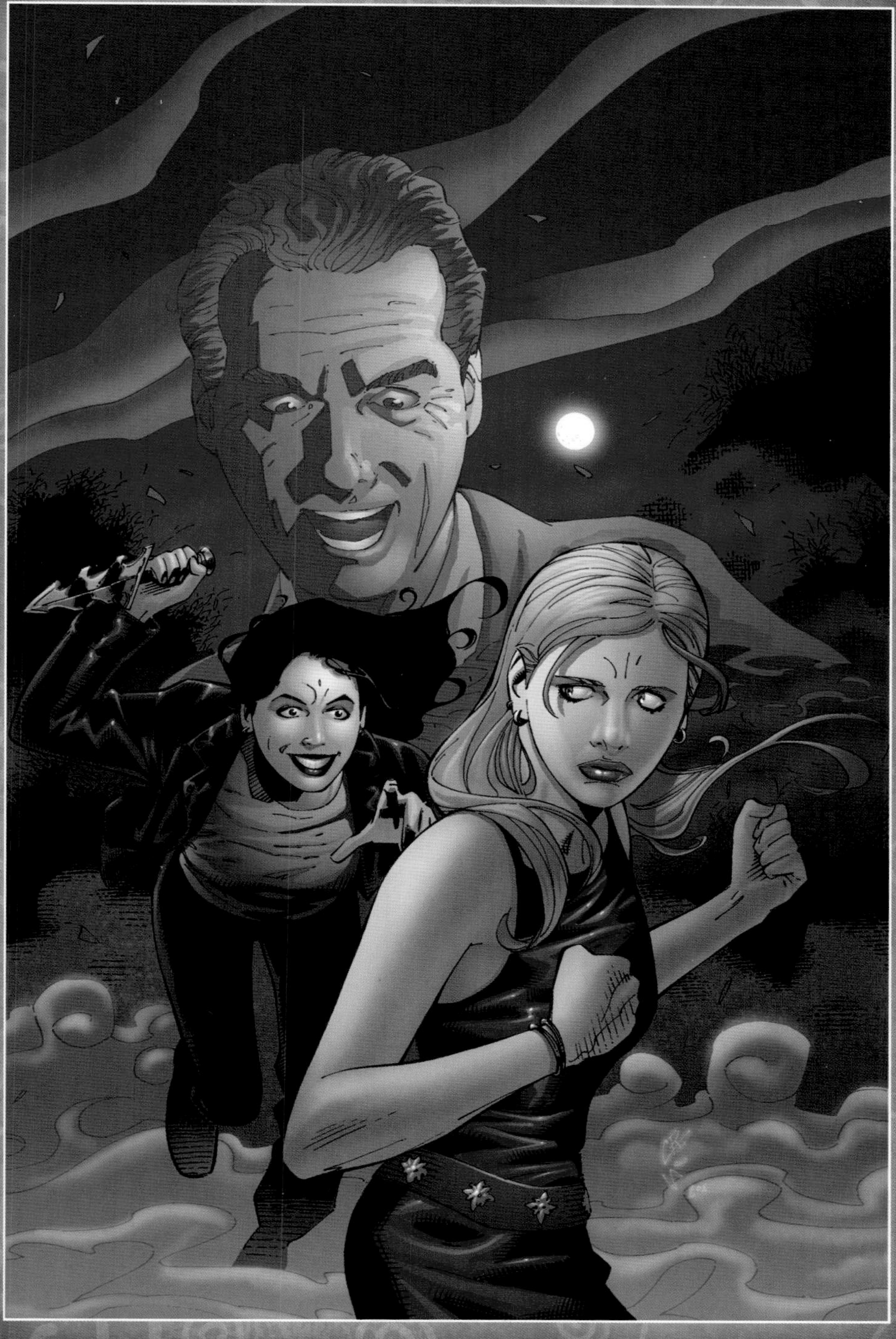

Art by Cliff Richards, Julio Ferreira, *and* Jeromy Cox

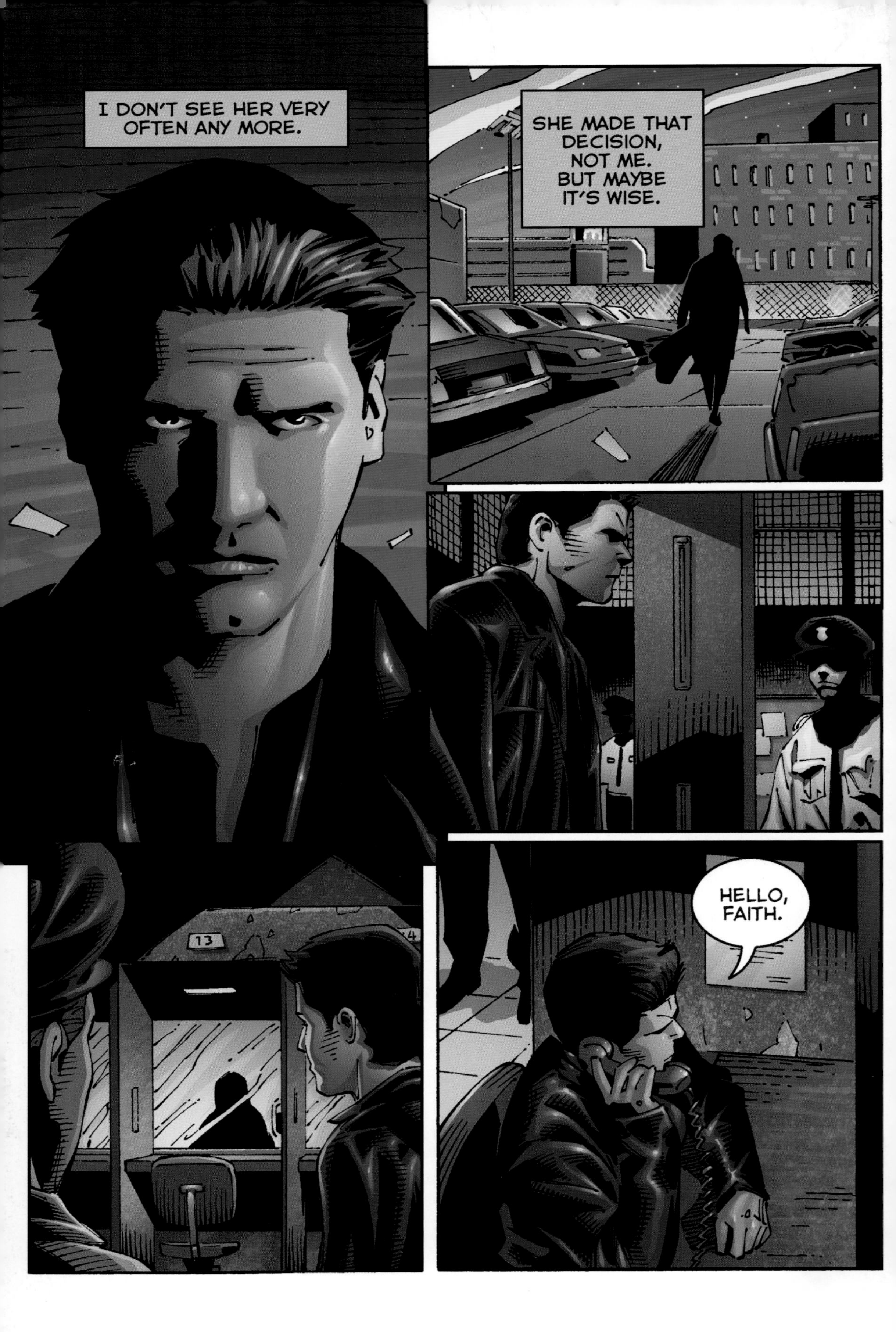
I DON'T SEE HER VERY OFTEN ANY MORE.
SHE MADE THAT DECISION, NOT ME. BUT MAYBE IT'S WISE.
13
HELLO, FAITH.

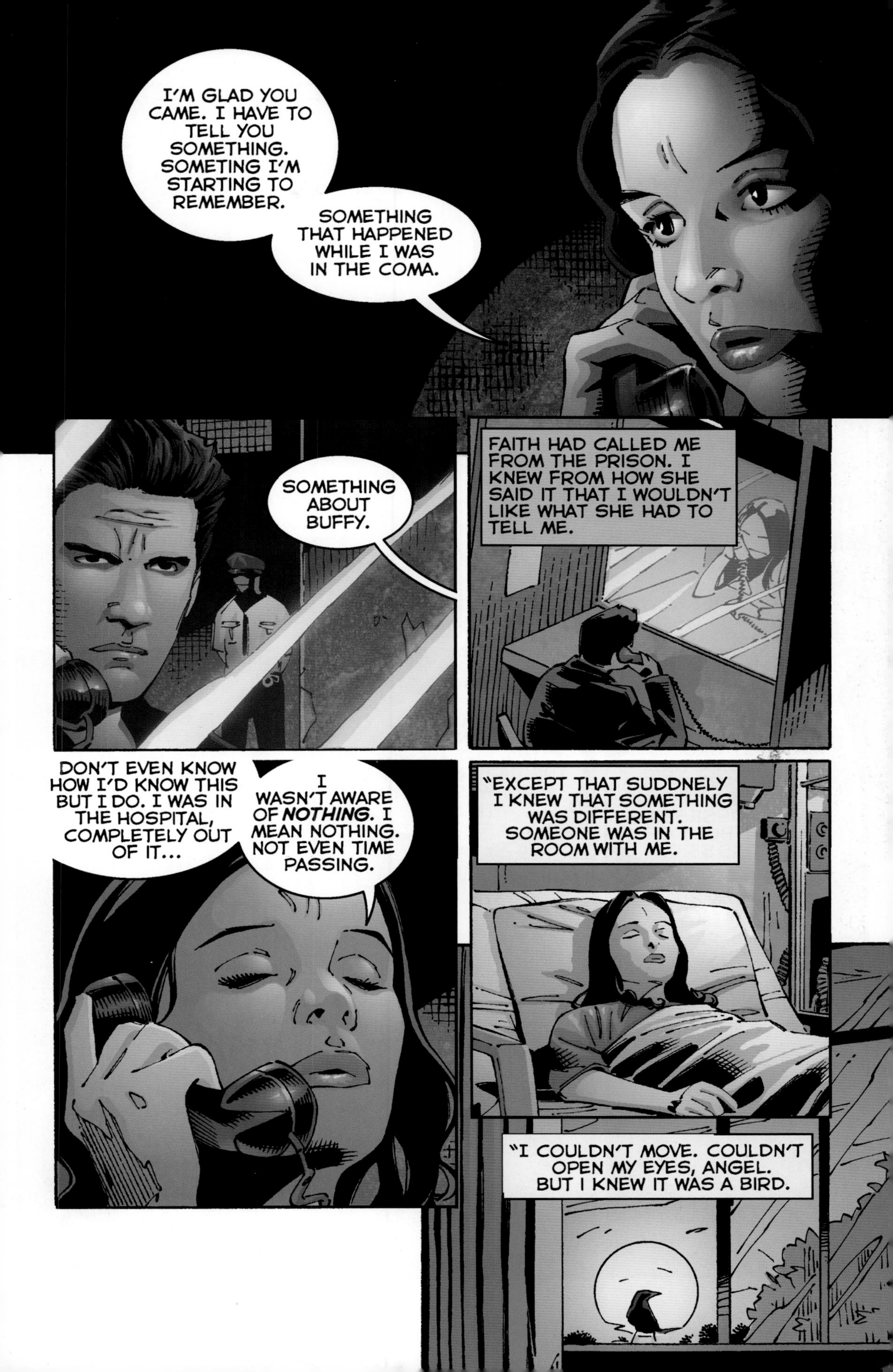
I'M GLAD YOU CAME. I HAVE TO TELL YOU SOMETHING. SOMETING I'M STARTING TO REMEMBER.
SOMETHING THAT HAPPENED WHILE I WAS IN THE COMA.
SOMETHING ABOUT BUFFY.
FAITH HAD CALLED ME FROM THE PRISON. I KNEW FROM HOW SHE SAID IT THAT I WOULDN'T LIKE WHAT SHE HAD TO TELL ME.
DON'T EVEN KNOW HOW I'D KNOW THIS BUT I DO. I WAS IN THE HOSPITAL, COMPLETELY OUT OF IT...
I WASN'T AWARE OF ***NOTHING***. I MEAN NOTHING. NOT EVEN TIME PASSING.
"EXCEPT THAT SUDDNELY I KNEW THAT SOMETHING WAS DIFFERENT. SOMEONE WAS IN THE ROOM WITH ME.
"I COULDN'T MOVE. COULDN'T OPEN MY EYES, ANGEL. BUT I KNEW IT WAS A BIRD.

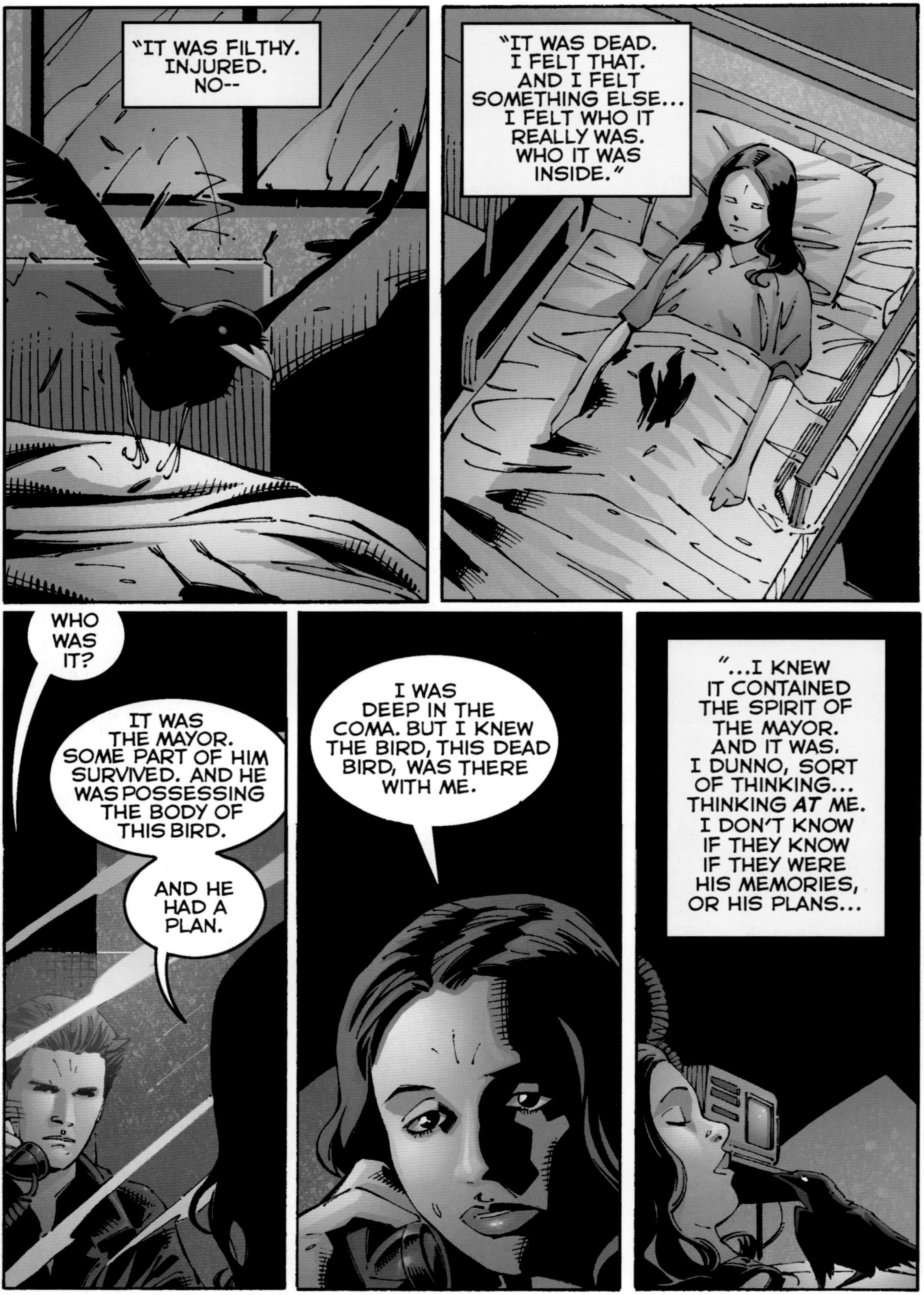
"IT WAS FILTHY. INJURED. NO--
"IT WAS DEAD. I FELT THAT. AND I FELT SOMETHING ELSE... I FELT WHO IT REALLY WAS. WHO IT WAS INSIDE."
WHO WAS IT?
IT WAS THE MAYOR. SOME PART OF HIM SURVIVED. AND HE WAS POSSESSING THE BODY OF THIS BIRD.
AND HE HAD A PLAN.
I WAS DEEP IN THE COMA. BUT I KNEW THE BIRD, THIS DEAD BIRD, WAS THERE WITH ME.
"...I KNEW IT CONTAINED THE SPIRIT OF THE MAYOR. AND IT WAS, I DUNNO, SORT OF THINKING... THINKING *AT* ME. I DON'T KNOW IF THEY KNOW IF THEY WERE HIS MEMORIES, OR HIS PLANS...

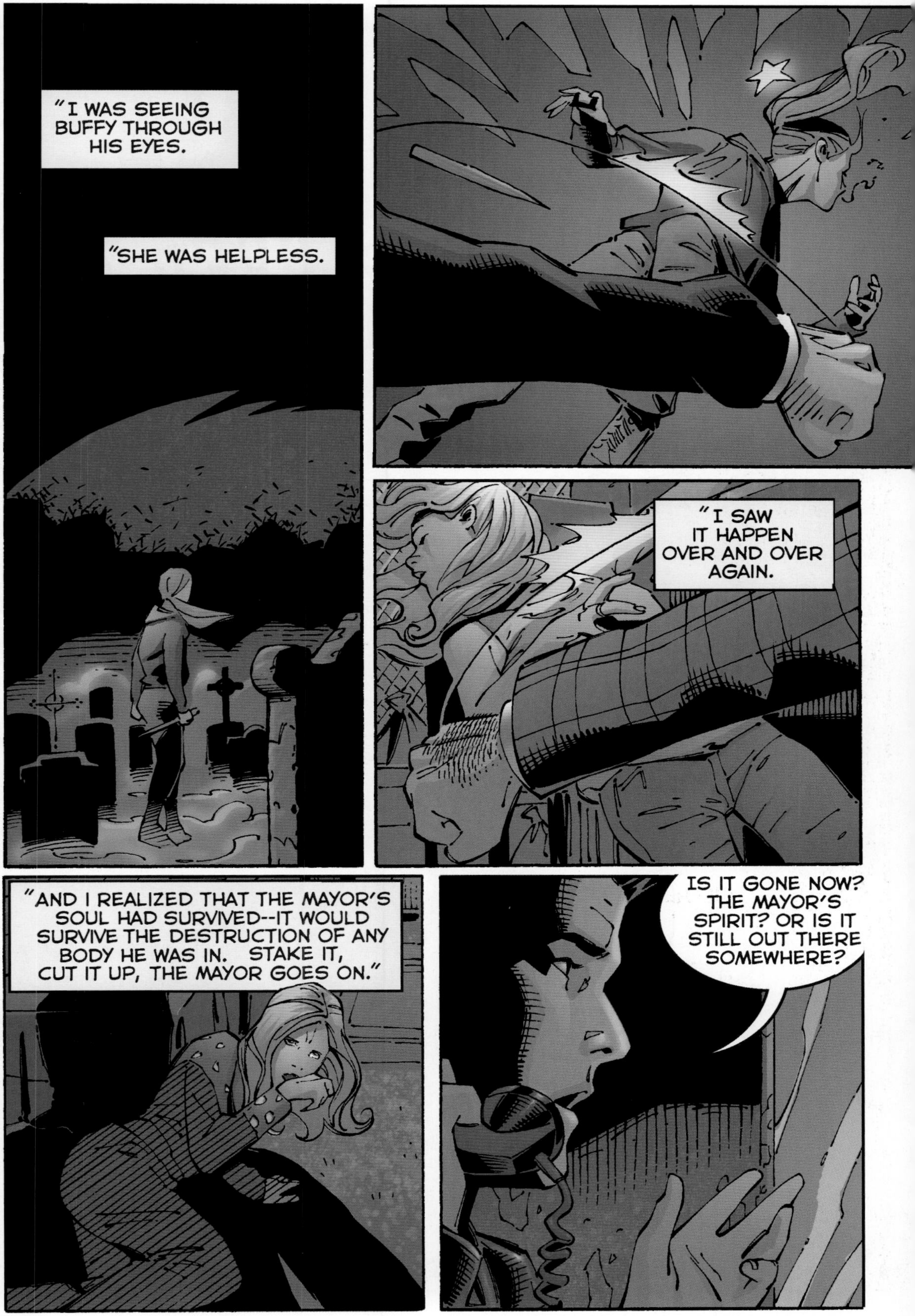
"I WAS SEEING BUFFY THROUGH HIS EYES.
"SHE WAS HELPLESS.
"I SAW IT HAPPEN OVER AND OVER AGAIN.
"AND I REALIZED THAT THE MAYOR'S SOUL HAD SURVIVED--IT WOULD SURVIVE THE DESTRUCTION OF ANY BODY HE WAS IN. STAKE IT, CUT IT UP, THE MAYOR GOES ON."
IS IT GONE NOW? THE MAYOR'S SPIRIT? OR IS IT STILL OUT THERE SOMEWHERE?

Buffy THE VAMPIRE SLAYER™

GOT NO IDEA, ANGEL. NO IDEA AT ALL.

HAUNTED

based on the television series created by
JOSS WHEDON

writer **JANE ESPENSON**

penciller **CLIFF RICHARDS**

inker **JULIO FERREIRA**

colorist **JEROMY COX**

letterer **CLEM ROBINS**

This story takes place after Buffy the Vampire Slayer's third season.

Dark horse comics®

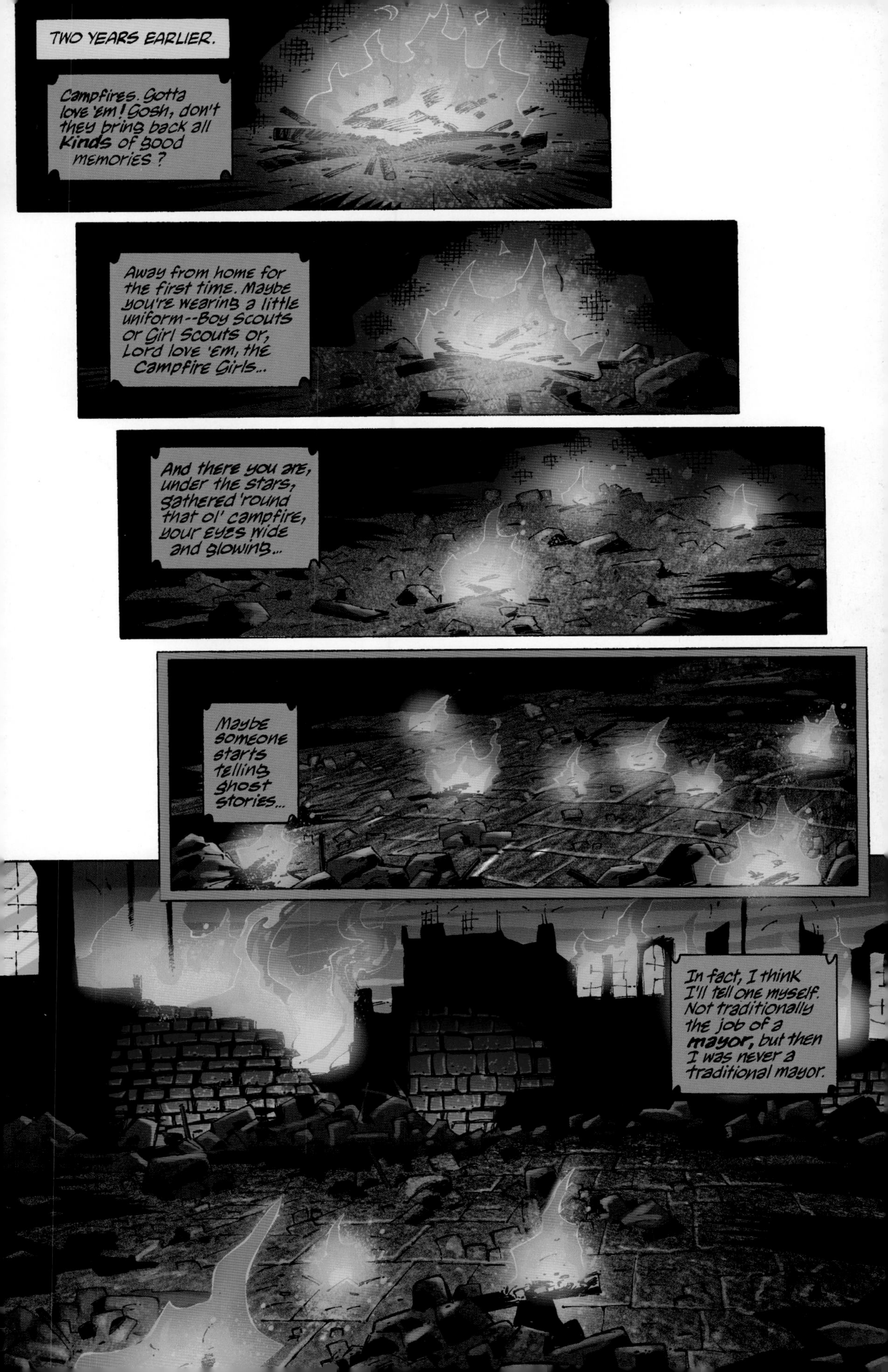
TWO YEARS EARLIER.
Campfires. Gotta love 'em! Gosh, don't they bring back all kinds of good memories?
Away from home for the first time. Maybe you're wearing a little uniform--Boy Scouts or Girl Scouts or, Lord love 'em, the Campfire Girls...
And there you are, under the stars, gathered 'round that ol' campfire, your eyes wide and glowing...
Maybe someone starts telling ghost stories...
In fact, I think I'll tell one myself. Not traditionally the job of a mayor, but then I was never a traditional mayor.

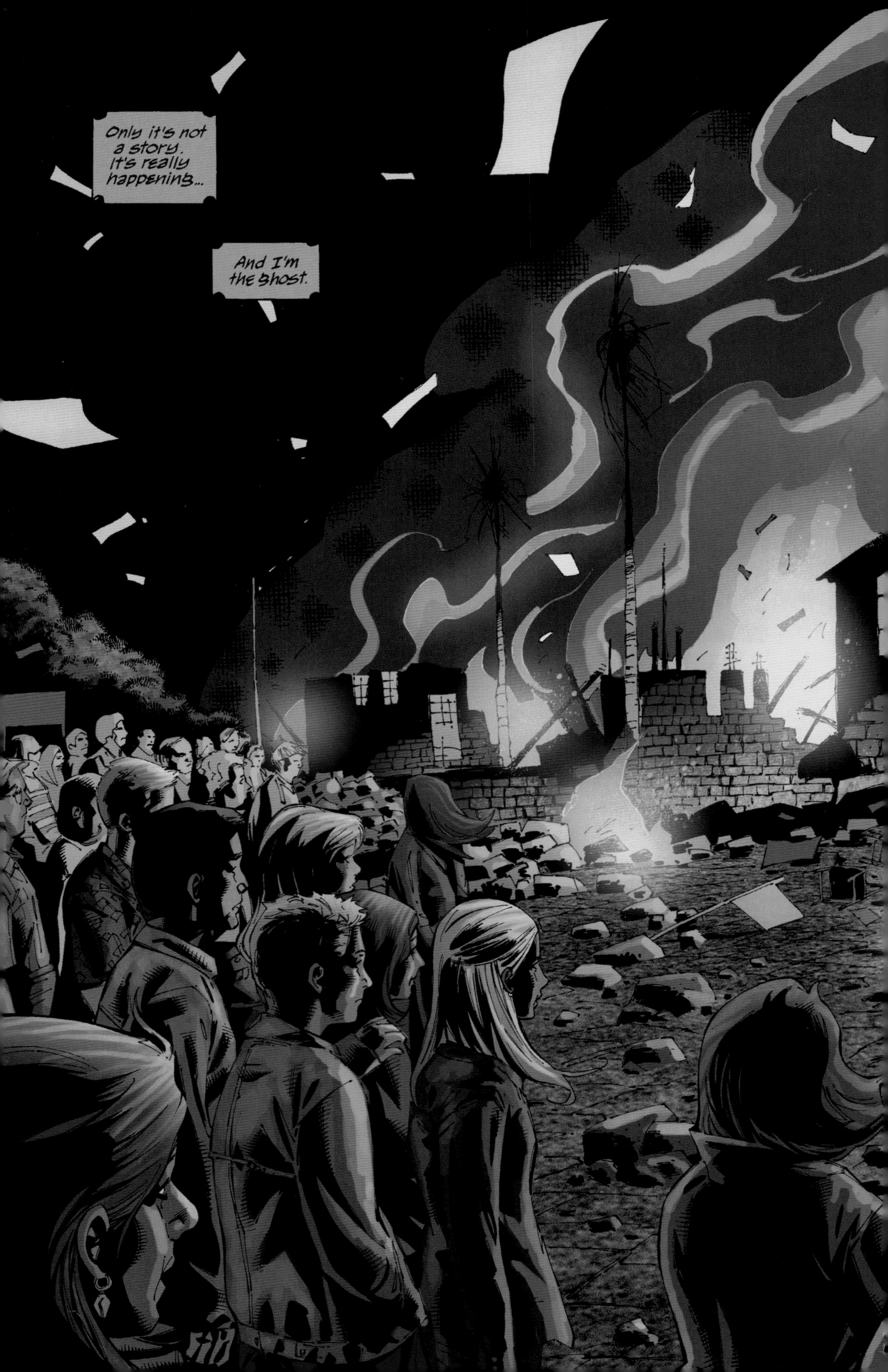
Only it's not a story. It's really happening...
And I'm the ghost.

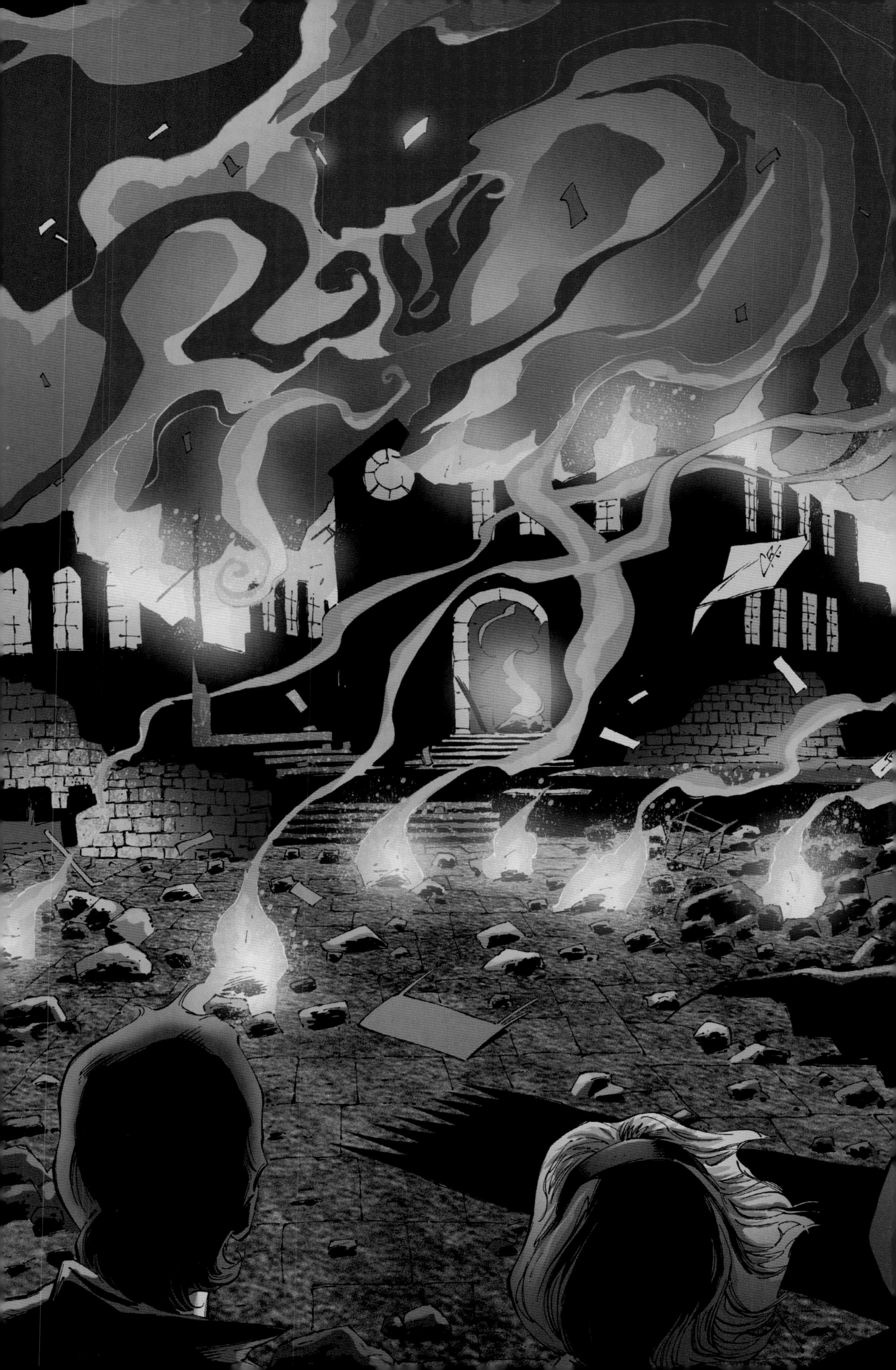

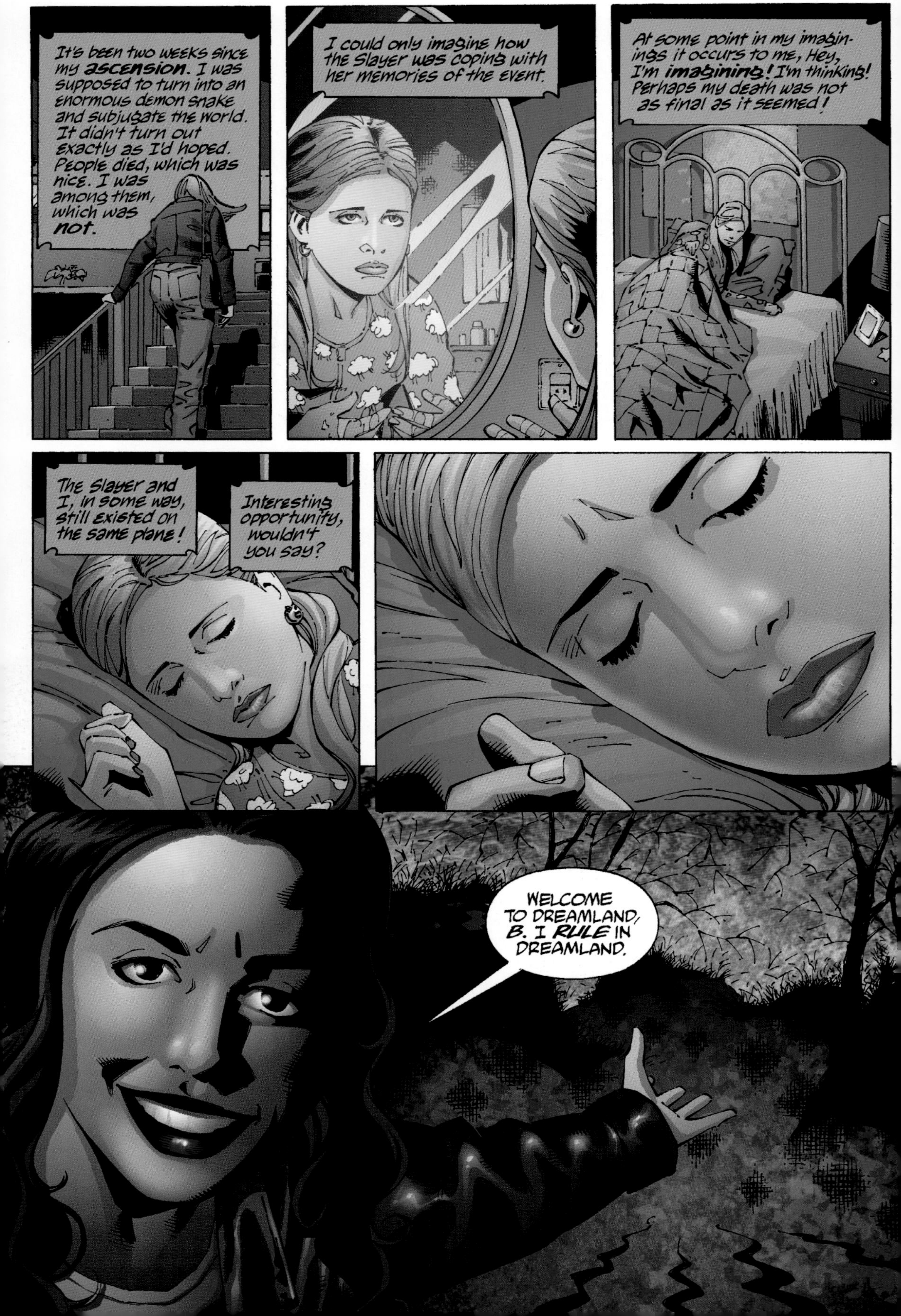

It's been two weeks since my ascension. I was supposed to turn into an enormous demon snake and subjugate the world. It didn't turn out exactly as I'd hoped. People died, which was nice. I was among them, which was not.
I could only imagine how the Slayer was coping with her memories of the event.
At some point in my imaginings it occurs to me, Hey, I'm imagining! I'm thinking! Perhaps my death was not as final as it seemed!
The Slayer and I, in some way, still existed on the same plane!
Interesting opportunity, wouldn't you say?
WELCOME TO DREAMLAND, B. I RULE IN DREAMLAND.

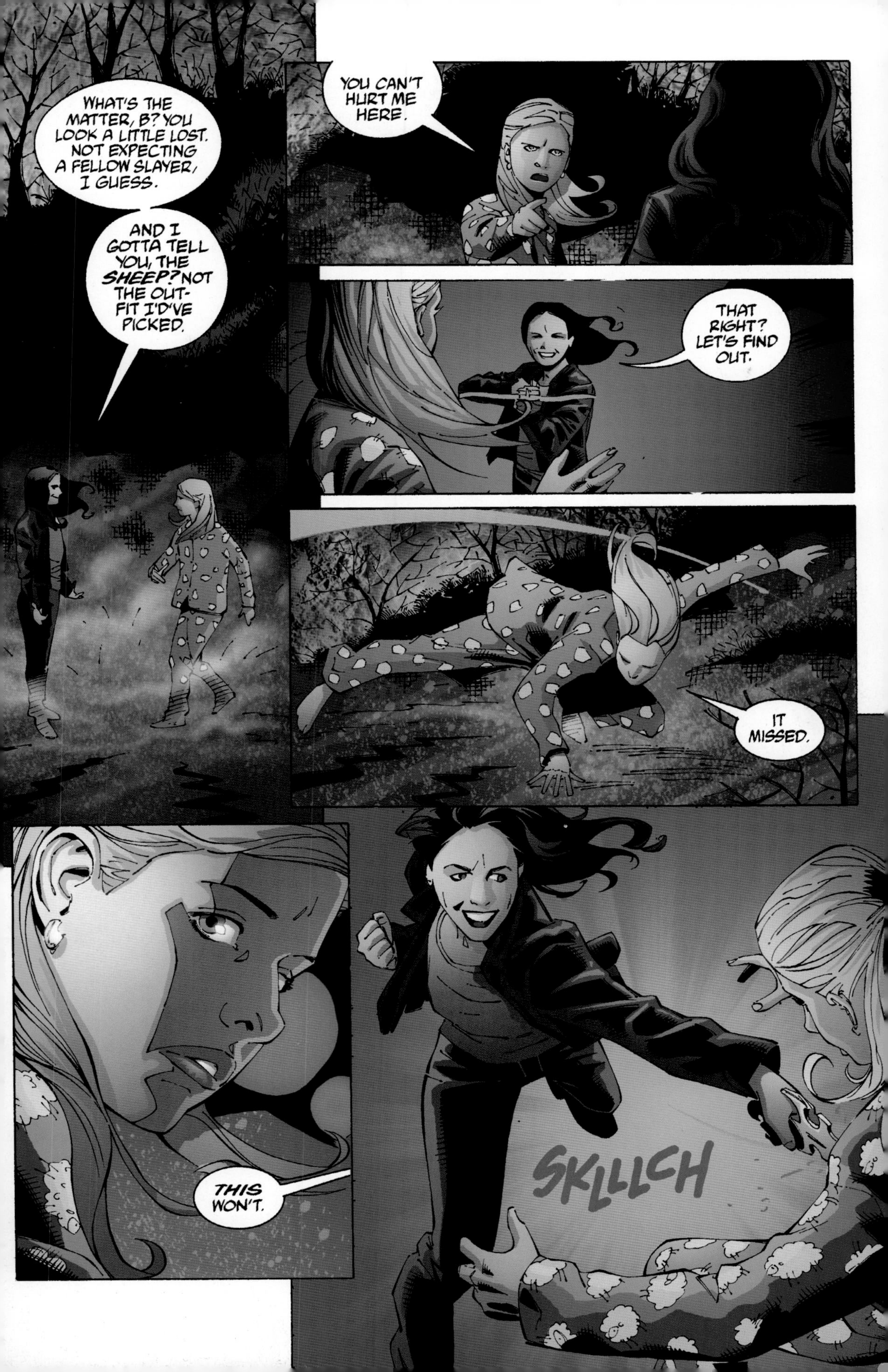
WHAT'S THE MATTER, B? YOU LOOK A LITTLE LOST. NOT EXPECTING A FELLOW SLAYER, I GUESS.
AND I GOTTA TELL YOU, THE *SHEEP?* NOT THE OUTFIT I'D'VE PICKED.
YOU CAN'T HURT ME HERE.
THAT RIGHT? LET'S FIND OUT.
IT MISSED.
THIS WON'T.
SKLLLCH

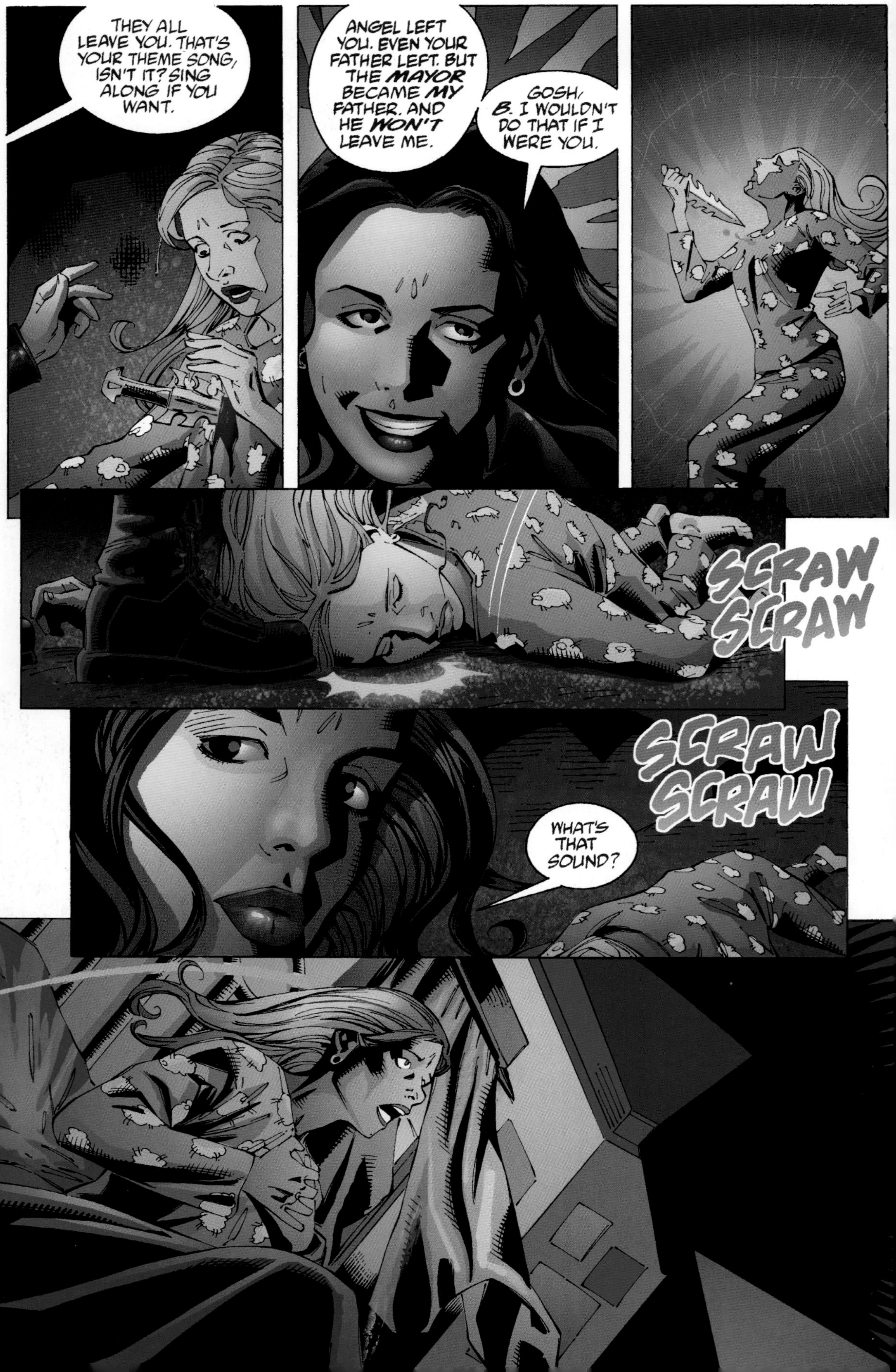
THEY ALL LEAVE YOU. THAT'S YOUR THEME SONG, ISN'T IT? SING ALONG IF YOU WANT.
ANGEL LEFT YOU. EVEN YOUR FATHER LEFT. BUT THE MAYOR BECAME MY FATHER. AND HE WON'T LEAVE ME.
GOSH, B. I WOULDN'T DO THAT IF I WERE YOU.
SCRAW SCRAW
SCRAW SCRAW
WHAT'S THAT SOUND?

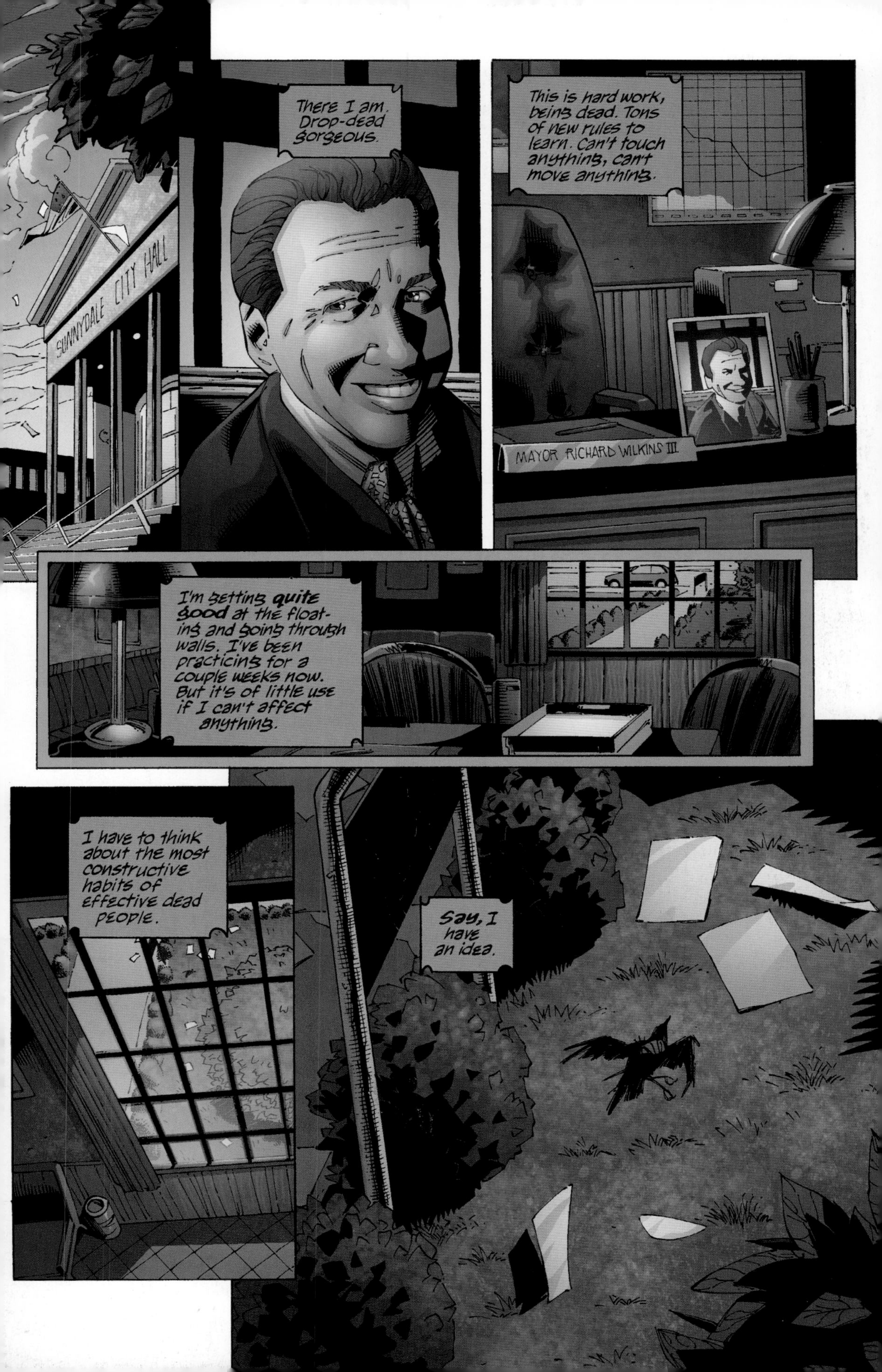
SUNNYDALE CITY HALL
There I am. Drop-dead gorgeous.
This is hard work, being dead. Tons of new rules to learn. Can't touch anything, can't move anything.
MAYOR RICHARD WILKINS III
I'm getting **quite good** at the floating and going through walls. I've been practicing for a couple weeks now. But it's of little use if I can't affect anything.
I have to think about the most constructive habits of effective dead people.
Say, I have an idea.

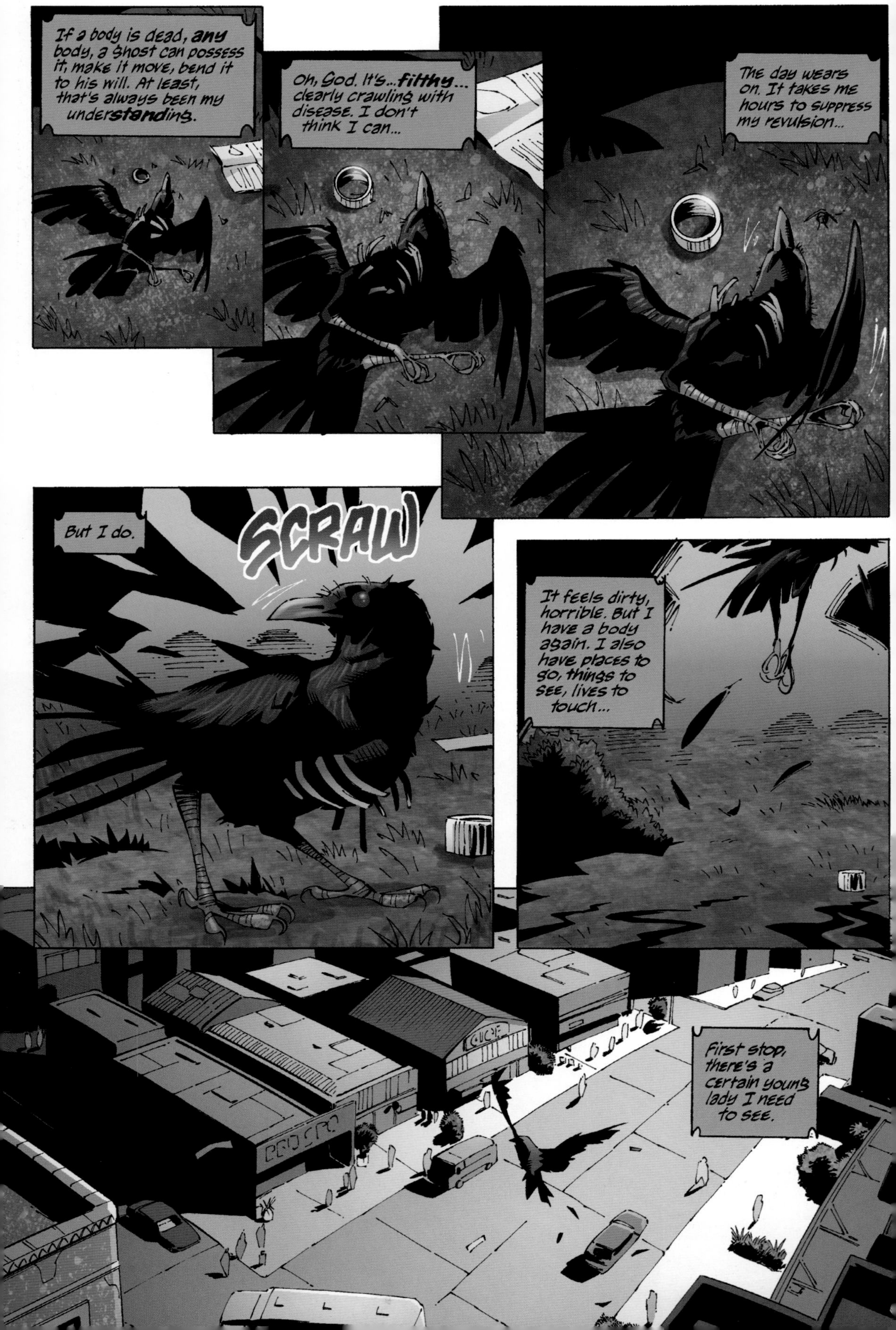
If a body is dead, any body, a ghost can possess it, make it move, bend it to his will. At least, that's always been my understanding.
Oh, God. It's...filthy... clearly crawling with disease. I don't think I can...
The day wears on. It takes me hours to suppress my revulsion...
But I do.
SCRAW
It feels dirty, horrible. But I have a body again. I also have places to go, things to see, lives to touch...
First stop, there's a certain young lady I need to see.

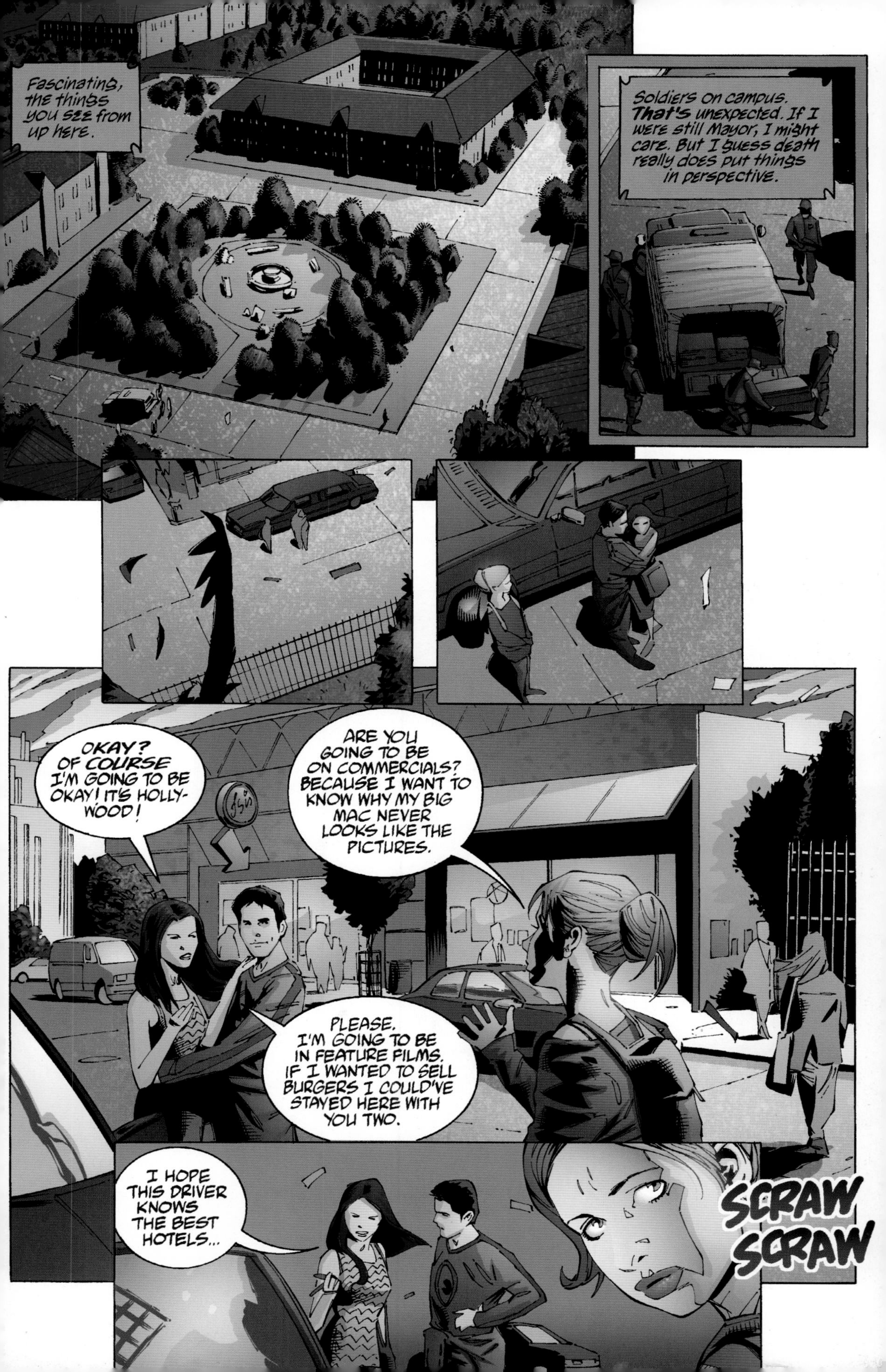
Fascinating, the things you see from up here.
Soldiers on campus. That's unexpected. If I were still Mayor, I might care. But I guess death really does put things in perspective.
OKAY? OF COURSE I'M GOING TO BE OKAY! IT'S HOLLY-WOOD!
ARE YOU GOING TO BE ON COMMERCIALS? BECAUSE I WANT TO KNOW WHY MY BIG MAC NEVER LOOKS LIKE THE PICTURES.
PLEASE. I'M GOING TO BE IN FEATURE FILMS. IF I WANTED TO SELL BURGERS I COULD'VE STAYED HERE WITH YOU TWO.
I HOPE THIS DRIVER KNOWS THE BEST HOTELS...
SCRAW SCRAW

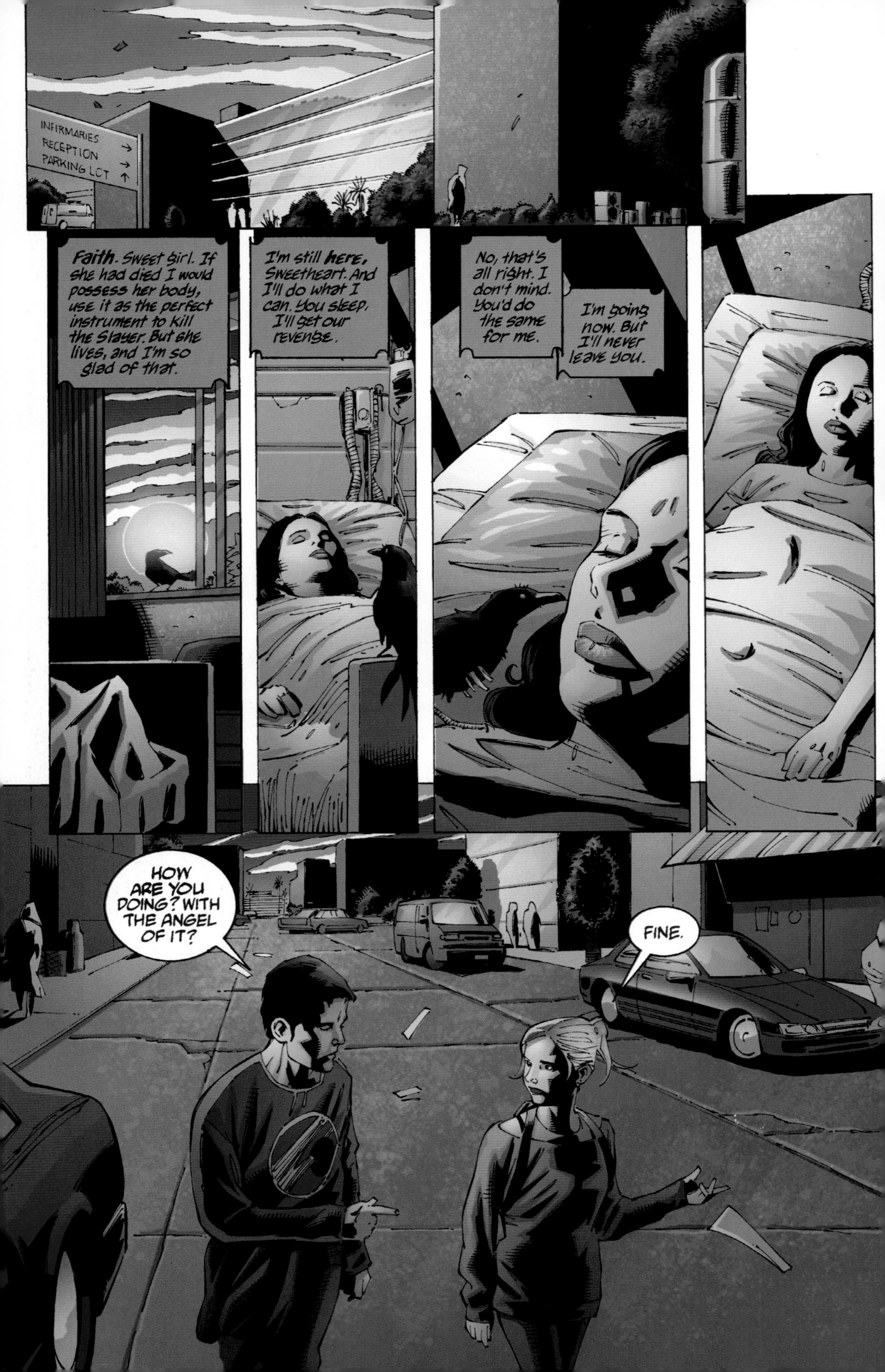
INFIRMARIES
RECEPTION
PARKING LOT
Faith. Sweet girl. If she had died I would possess her body, use it as the perfect instrument to kill the Slayer. But she lives, and I'm so glad of that.
I'm still here, Sweetheart. And I'll do what I can. You sleep, I'll get our revenge.
No, that's all right. I don't mind. You'd do the same for me.
I'm going now. But I'll never leave you.
HOW ARE YOU DOING? WITH THE ANGEL OF IT?
FINE.

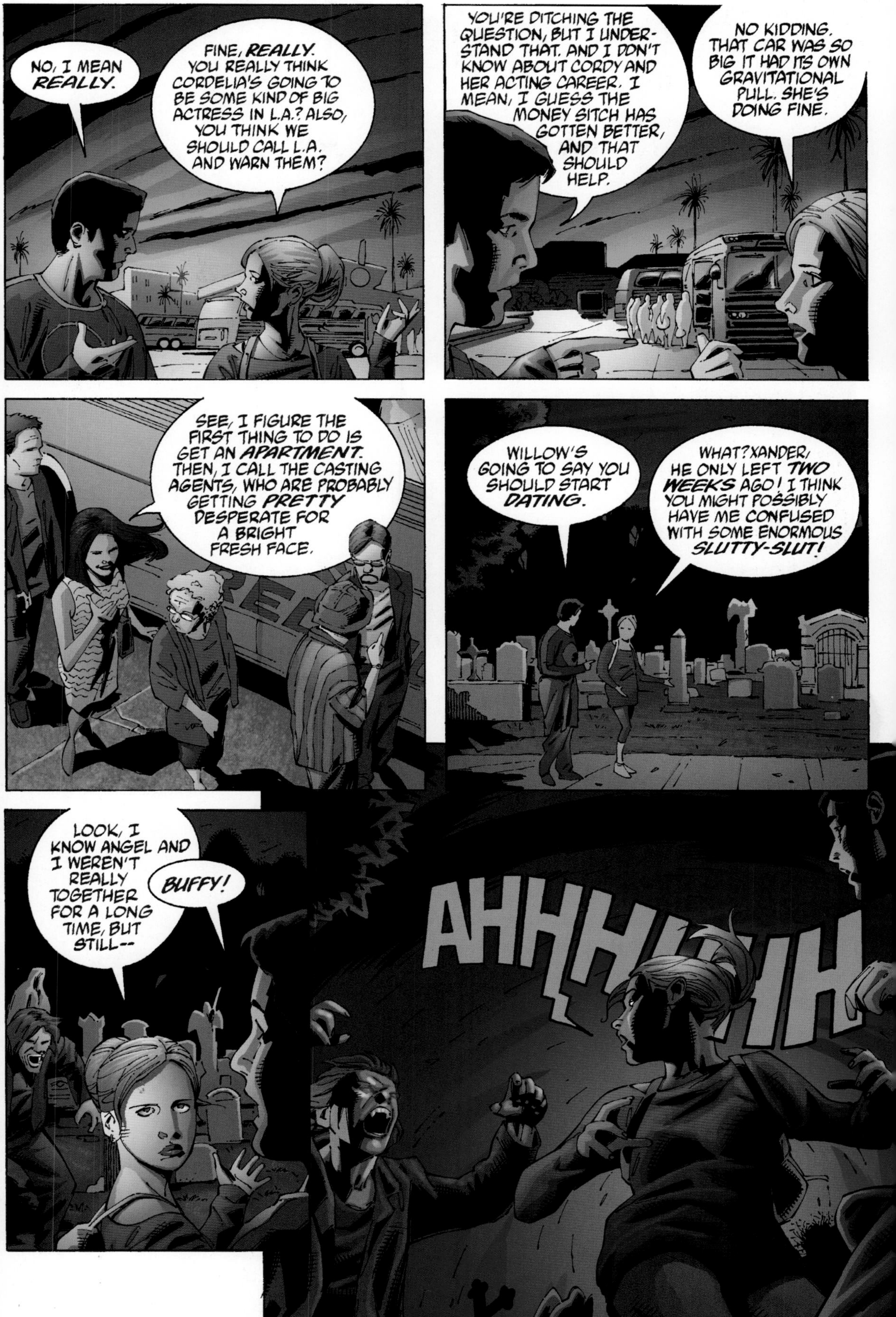

NO, I MEAN REALLY.
FINE, REALLY. YOU REALLY THINK CORDELIA'S GOING TO BE SOME KIND OF BIG ACTRESS IN L.A.? ALSO, YOU THINK WE SHOULD CALL L.A. AND WARN THEM?
YOU'RE DITCHING THE QUESTION, BUT I UNDERSTAND THAT. AND I DON'T KNOW ABOUT CORDY AND HER ACTING CAREER. I MEAN, I GUESS THE MONEY SITCH HAS GOTTEN BETTER, AND THAT SHOULD HELP.
NO KIDDING. THAT CAR WAS SO BIG IT HAD ITS OWN GRAVITATIONAL PULL. SHE'S DOING FINE.
SEE, I FIGURE THE FIRST THING TO DO IS GET AN APARTMENT. THEN, I CALL THE CASTING AGENTS, WHO ARE PROBABLY GETTING PRETTY DESPERATE FOR A BRIGHT FRESH FACE.
WILLOW'S GOING TO SAY YOU SHOULD START DATING.
WHAT? XANDER, HE ONLY LEFT TWO WEEKS AGO! I THINK YOU MIGHT POSSIBLY HAVE ME CONFUSED WITH SOME ENORMOUS SLUTTY-SLUT!
LOOK, I KNOW ANGEL AND I WEREN'T REALLY TOGETHER FOR A LONG TIME, BUT STILL--
BUFFY!
AHHHHHH

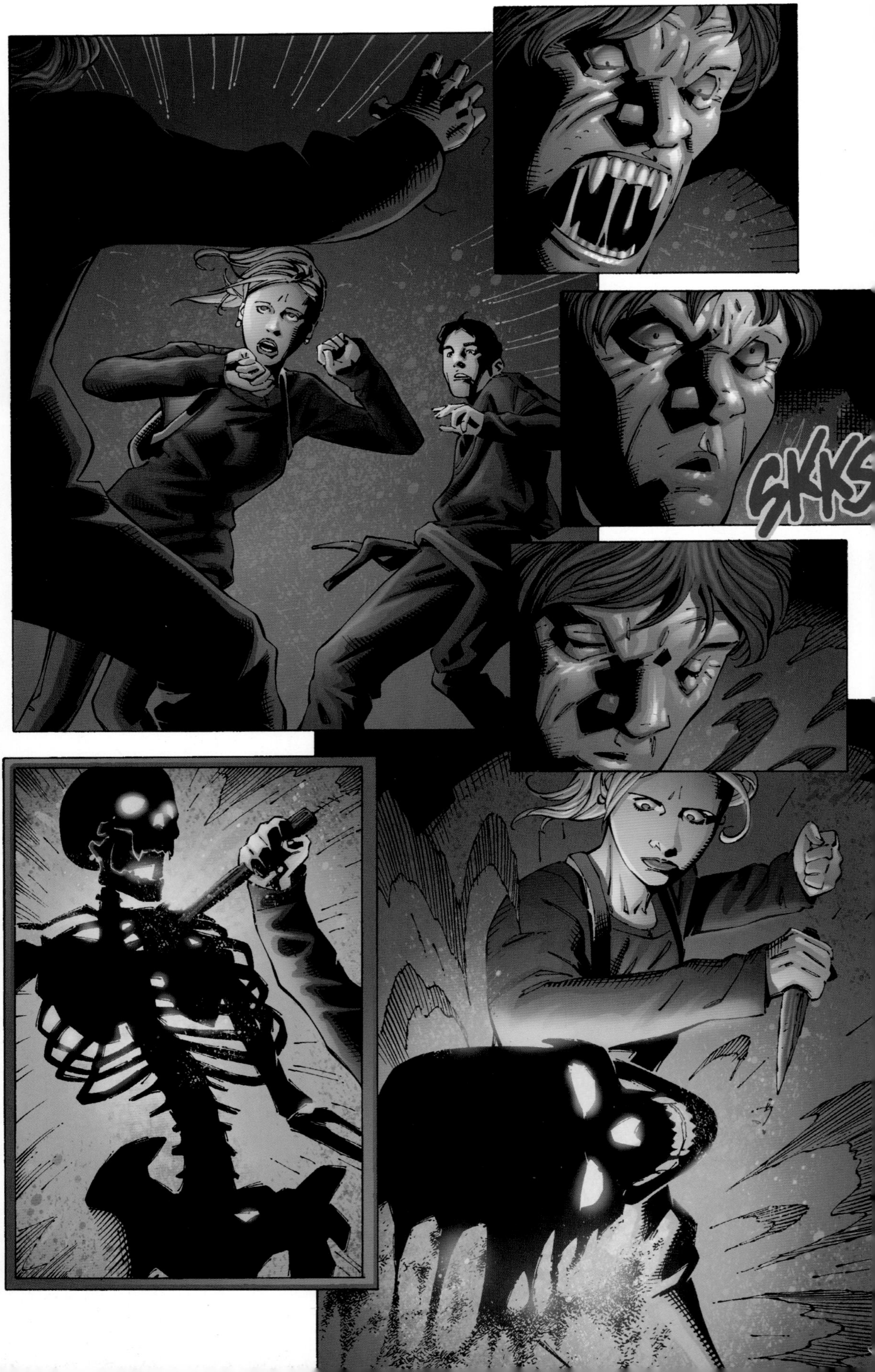
SKKS

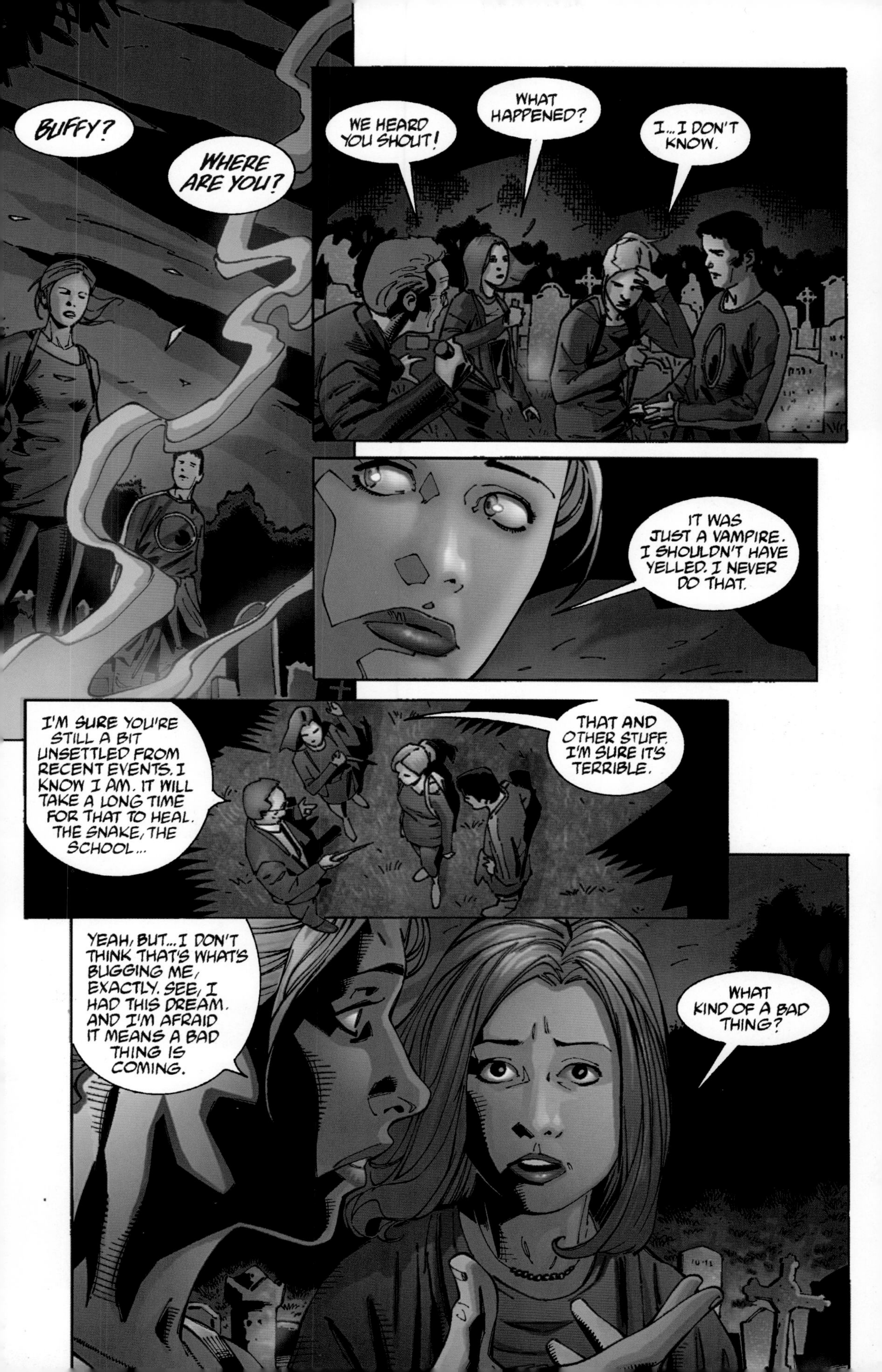
BUFFY?
WHERE ARE YOU?
WE HEARD YOU SHOUT!
WHAT HAPPENED?
I... I DON'T KNOW.
IT WAS JUST A VAMPIRE. I SHOULDN'T HAVE YELLED. I NEVER DO THAT.
I'M SURE YOU'RE STILL A BIT UNSETTLED FROM RECENT EVENTS. I KNOW I AM. IT WILL TAKE A LONG TIME FOR THAT TO HEAL. THE SNAKE, THE SCHOOL...
THAT AND OTHER STUFF. I'M SURE IT'S TERRIBLE.
YEAH, BUT... I DON'T THINK THAT'S WHAT'S BUGGING ME, EXACTLY. SEE, I HAD THIS DREAM. AND I'M AFRAID IT MEANS A BAD THING IS COMING.
WHAT KIND OF A BAD THING?

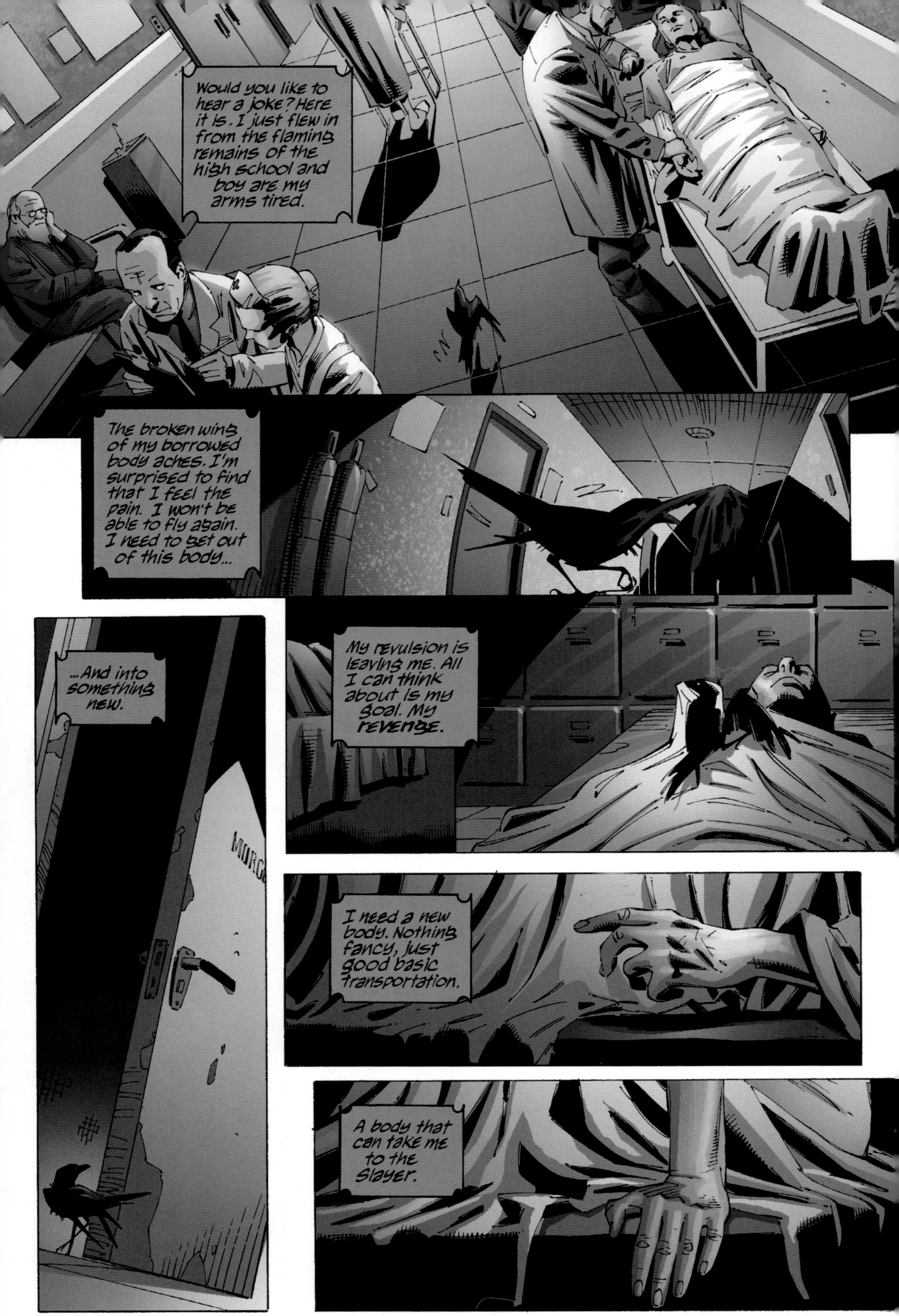
Would you like to hear a joke? Here it is. I just flew in from the flaming remains of the high school and boy are my arms tired.
The broken wing of my borrowed body aches. I'm surprised to find that I feel the pain. I won't be able to fly again. I need to get out of this body...
...And into something new.
MORG
My revulsion is leaving me. All I can think about is my goal. My revenge.
I need a new body. Nothing fancy, just good basic transportation.
A body that can take me to the Slayer.

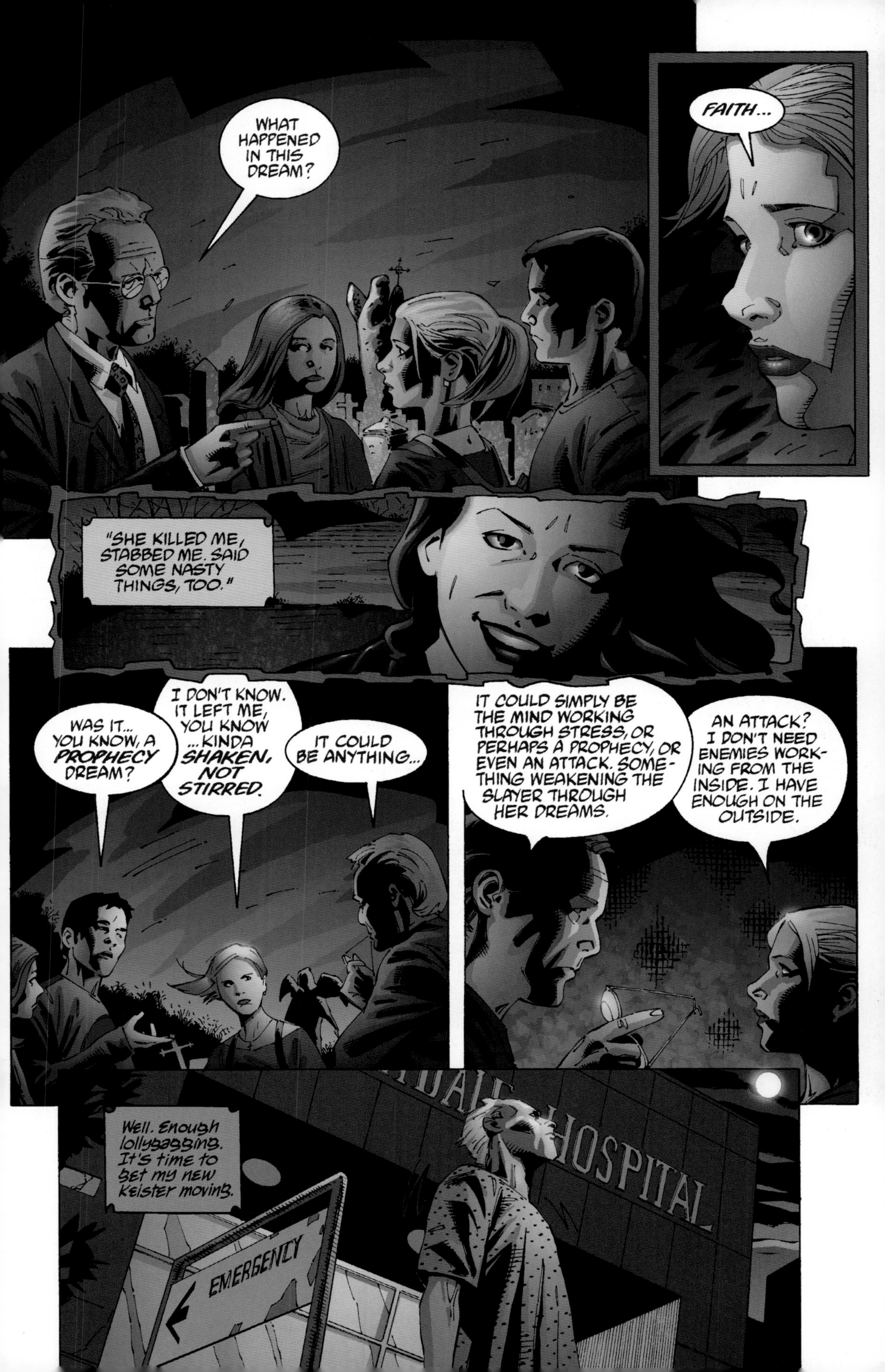
WHAT HAPPENED IN THIS DREAM?
FAITH...
"SHE KILLED ME, STABBED ME. SAID SOME NASTY THINGS, TOO."
WAS IT... YOU KNOW, A PROPHECY DREAM?
I DON'T KNOW. IT LEFT ME, YOU KNOW ...KINDA SHAKEN, NOT STIRRED.
IT COULD BE ANYTHING...
IT COULD SIMPLY BE THE MIND WORKING THROUGH STRESS, OR PERHAPS A PROPHECY, OR EVEN AN ATTACK. SOMETHING WEAKENING THE SLAYER THROUGH HER DREAMS.
AN ATTACK? I DON'T NEED ENEMIES WORKING FROM THE INSIDE. I HAVE ENOUGH ON THE OUTSIDE.
Well. Enough lollygagging. It's time to get my new keister moving.
HOSPITAL
EMERGENCY

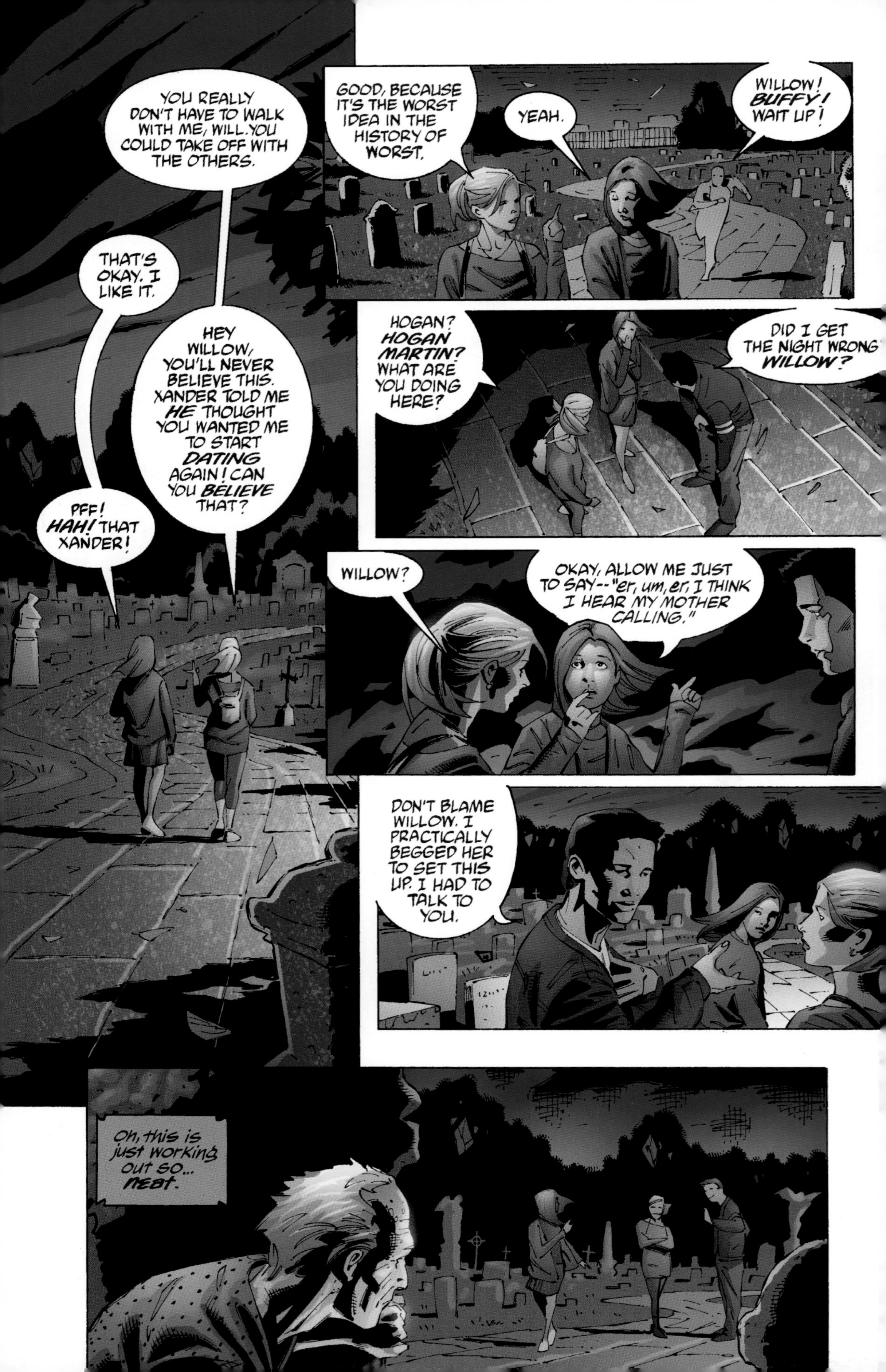
YOU REALLY DON'T HAVE TO WALK WITH ME, WILL. YOU COULD TAKE OFF WITH THE OTHERS.
THAT'S OKAY. I LIKE IT.
HEY WILLOW, YOU'LL NEVER BELIEVE THIS. XANDER TOLD ME *HE* THOUGHT YOU WANTED ME TO START *DATING* AGAIN! CAN YOU *BELIEVE* THAT?
PFF! *HAH!* THAT XANDER!
GOOD, BECAUSE IT'S THE WORST IDEA IN THE HISTORY OF WORST.
YEAH.
WILLOW! *BUFFY!* WAIT UP!
HOGAN? *HOGAN MARTIN?* WHAT ARE YOU DOING HERE?
DID I GET THE NIGHT WRONG *WILLOW?*
WILLOW?
OKAY, ALLOW ME JUST TO SAY--"*er, um, er,* I THINK I HEAR MY MOTHER CALLING."
DON'T BLAME WILLOW. I PRACTICALLY BEGGED HER TO SET THIS UP. I HAD TO TALK TO YOU.
Oh, this is just working out so... *neat*.

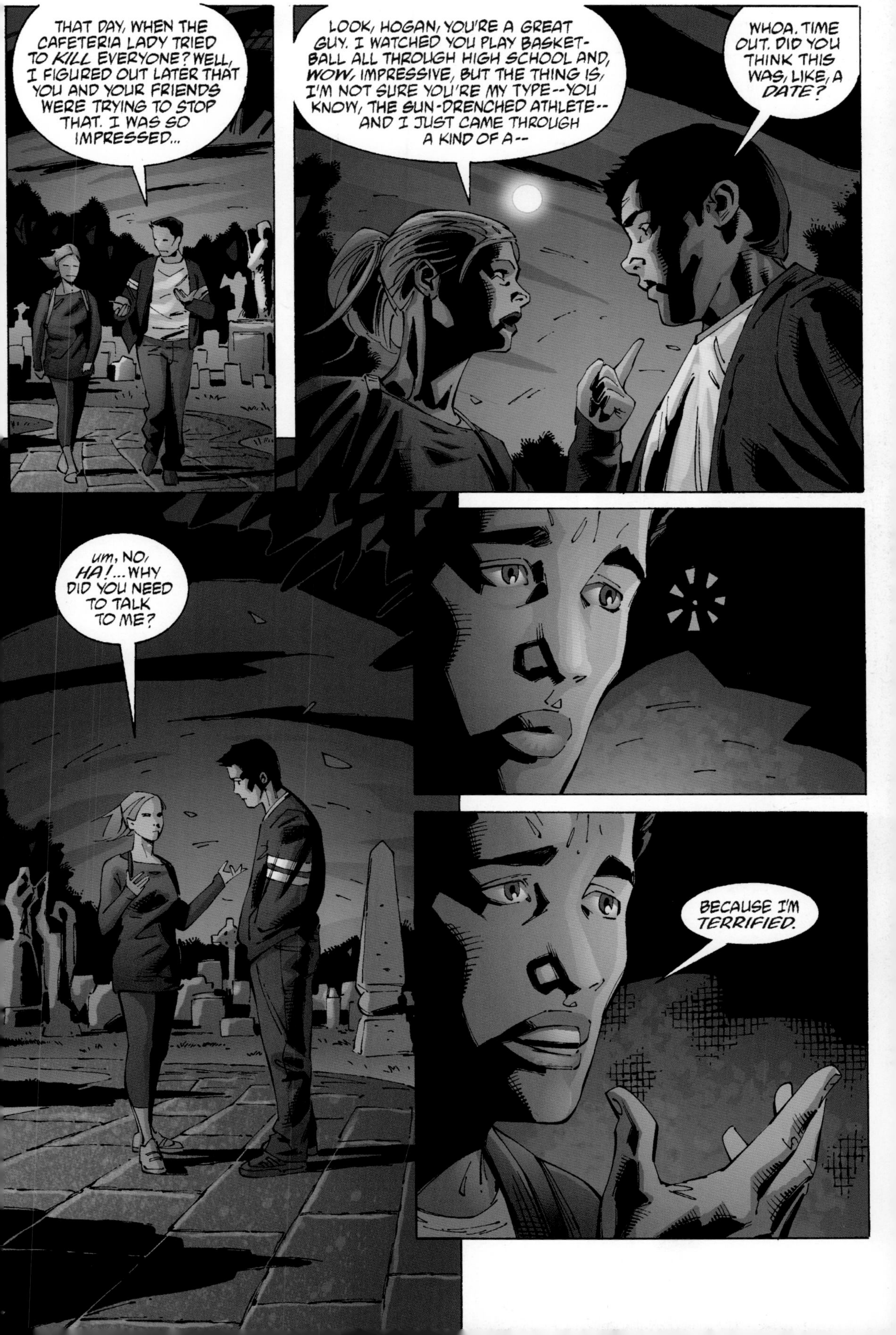
THAT DAY, WHEN THE CAFETERIA LADY TRIED TO KILL EVERYONE? WELL, I FIGURED OUT LATER THAT YOU AND YOUR FRIENDS WERE TRYING TO STOP THAT. I WAS SO IMPRESSED...
LOOK, HOGAN, YOU'RE A GREAT GUY. I WATCHED YOU PLAY BASKET-BALL ALL THROUGH HIGH SCHOOL AND, WOW, IMPRESSIVE, BUT THE THING IS, I'M NOT SURE YOU'RE MY TYPE--YOU KNOW, THE SUN-DRENCHED ATHLETE--AND I JUST CAME THROUGH A KIND OF A--
WHOA. TIME OUT. DID YOU THINK THIS WAS, LIKE, A DATE?
um, NO, HA!...WHY DID YOU NEED TO TALK TO ME?
BECAUSE I'M TERRIFIED.

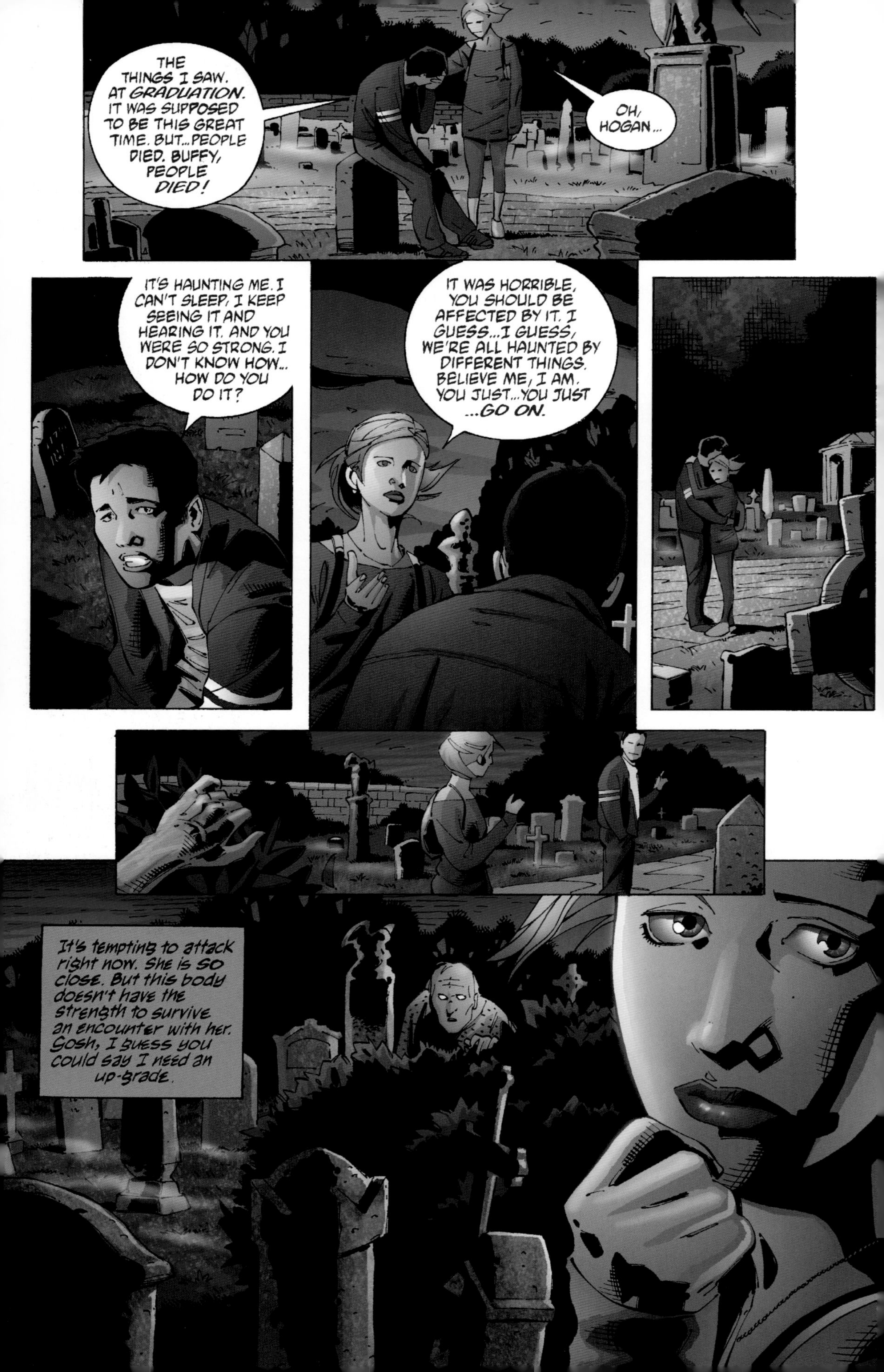
THE THINGS I SAW. AT GRADUATION. IT WAS SUPPOSED TO BE THIS GREAT TIME. BUT...PEOPLE DIED. BUFFY, PEOPLE DIED!
OH, HOGAN...
IT'S HAUNTING ME. I CAN'T SLEEP, I KEEP SEEING IT AND HEARING IT. AND YOU WERE SO STRONG. I DON'T KNOW HOW... HOW DO YOU DO IT?
IT WAS HORRIBLE, YOU SHOULD BE AFFECTED BY IT. I GUESS...I GUESS, WE'RE ALL HAUNTED BY DIFFERENT THINGS. BELIEVE ME, I AM. YOU JUST...YOU JUST ...GO ON.
It's tempting to attack right now. She is so close. But this body doesn't have the strength to survive an encounter with her. Gosh, I guess you could say I need an up-grade.

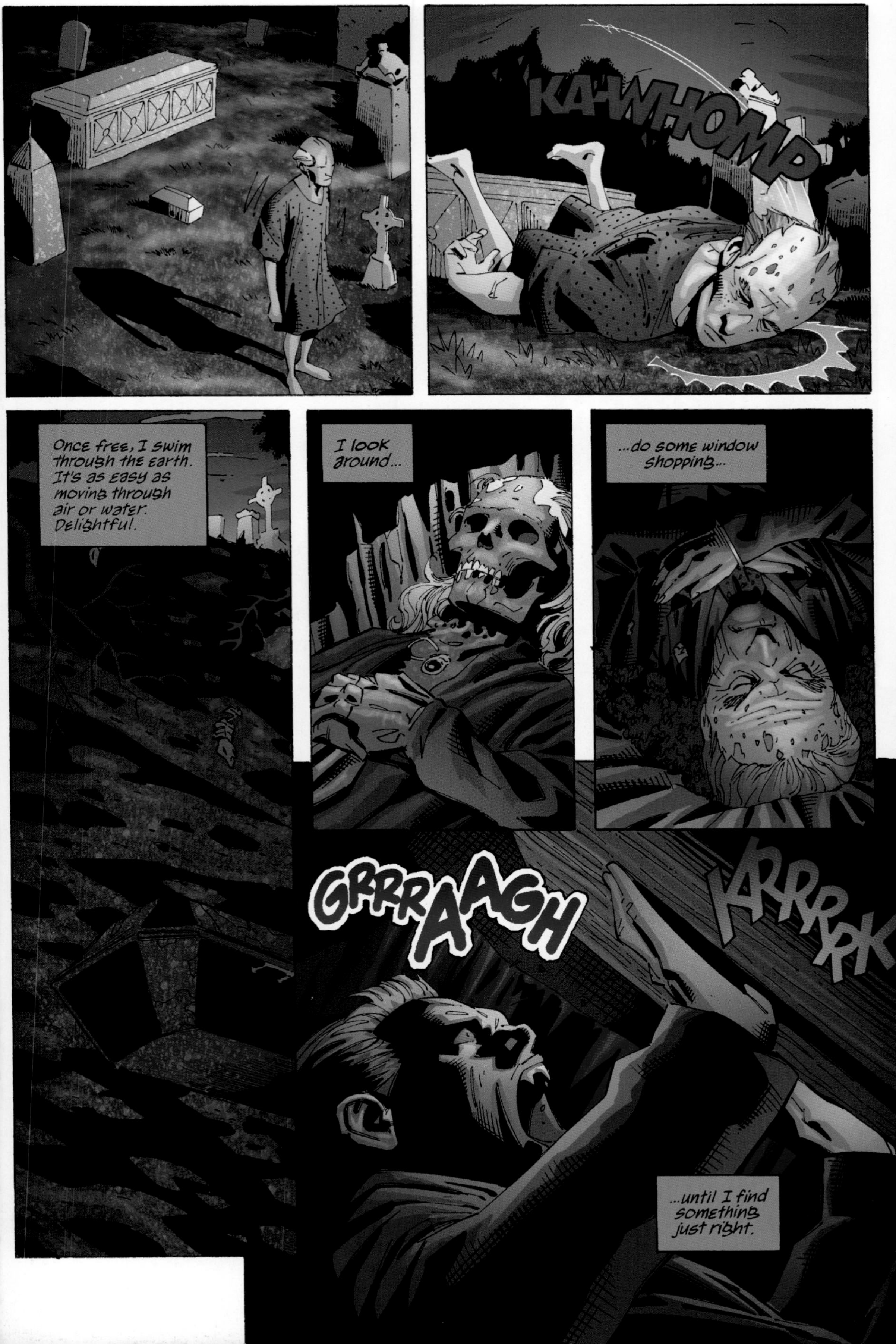
KA-WHOMP
Once free, I swim through the earth. It's as easy as moving through air or water. Delightful.
I look around...
...do some window shopping...
GRRRAAGH
KRRRRK
...until I find something just right.

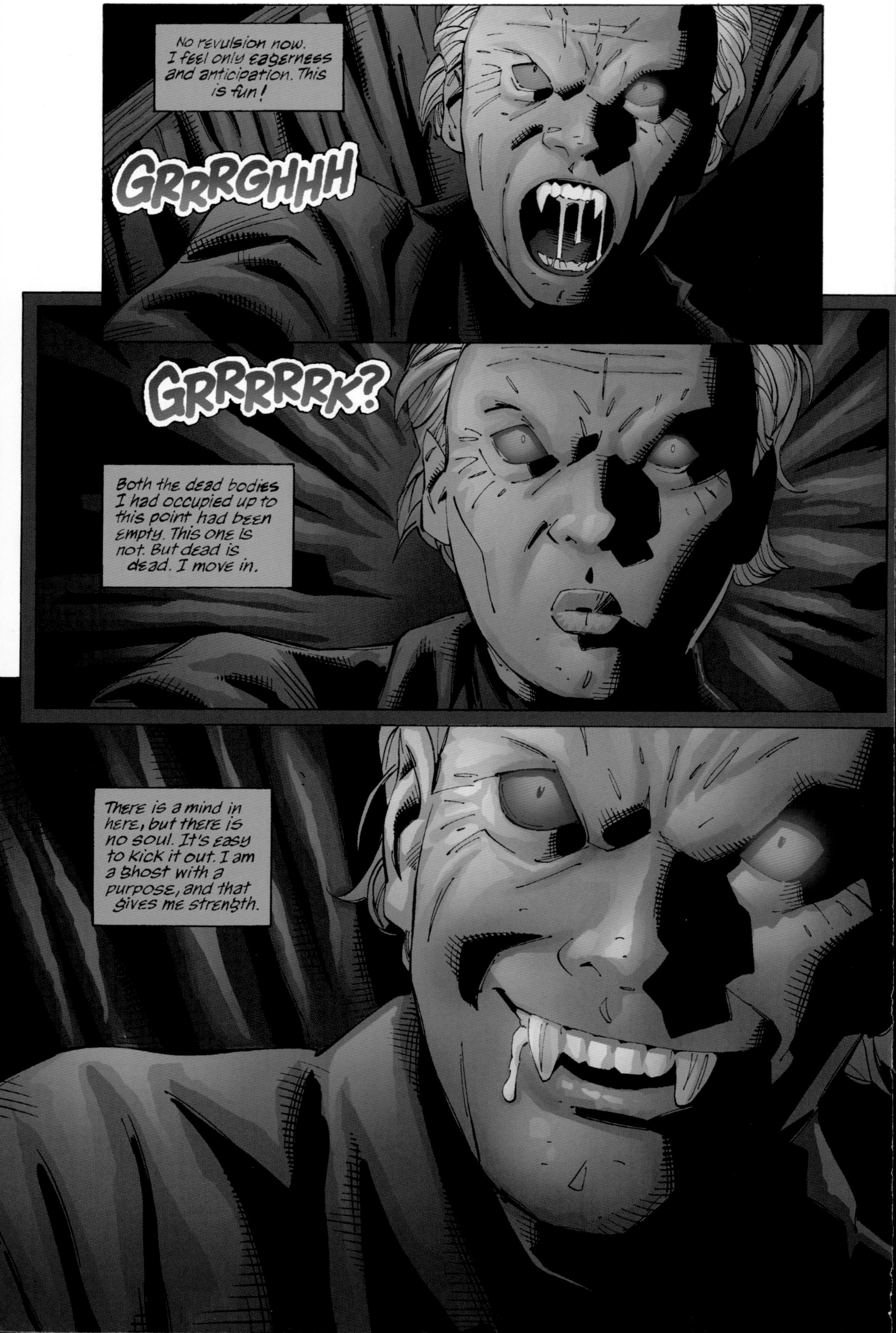

No revulsion now. I feel only eagerness and anticipation. This is fun!
GRRRGHHH
GRRRRRK?
Both the dead bodies I had occupied up to this point had been empty. This one is not. But dead is dead. I move in.
There is a mind in here, but there is no soul. It's easy to kick it out. I am a ghost with a purpose, and that gives me strength.

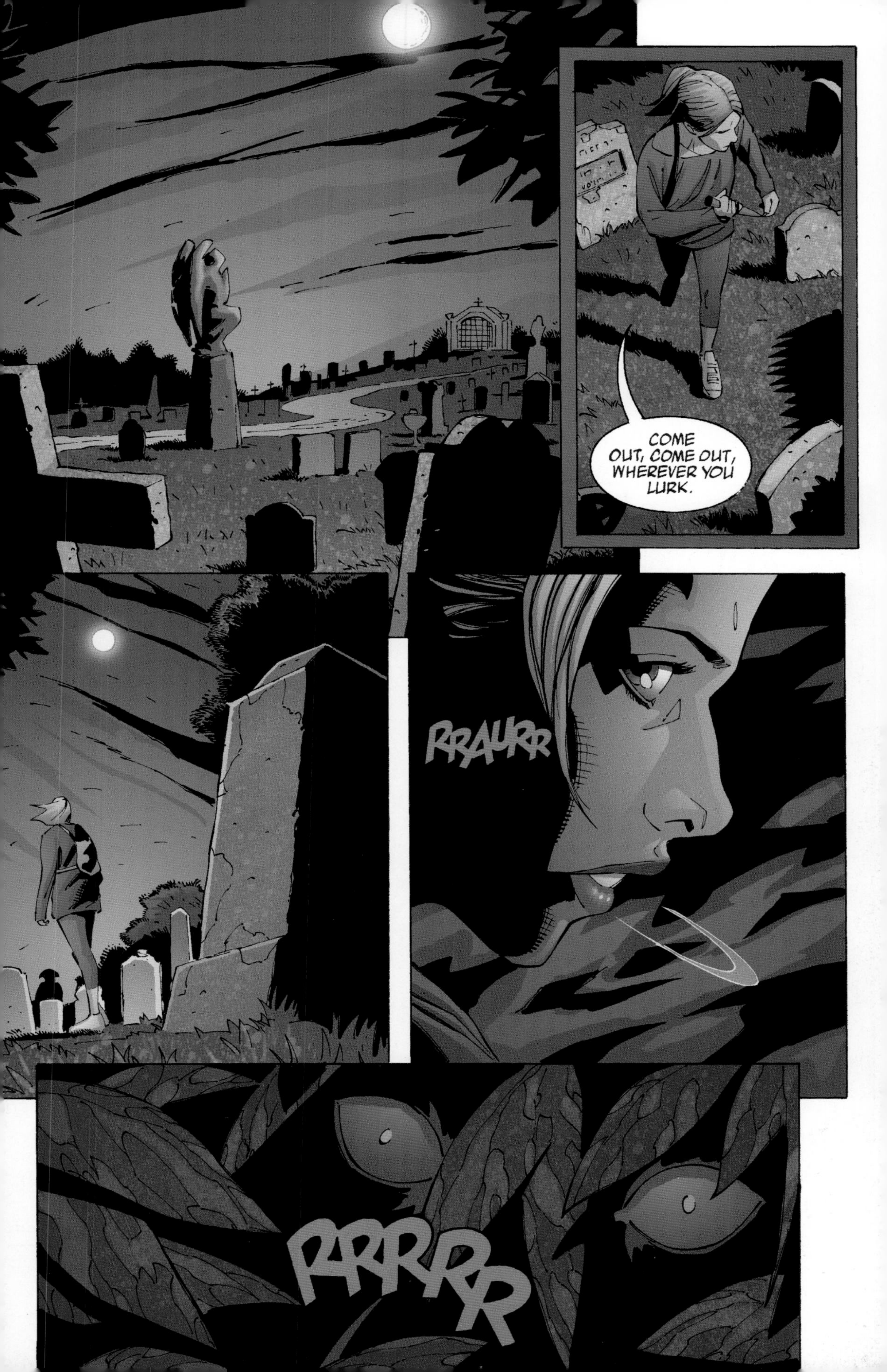
COME OUT, COME OUT, WHEREVER YOU LURK.
RRAURR
RRRRR

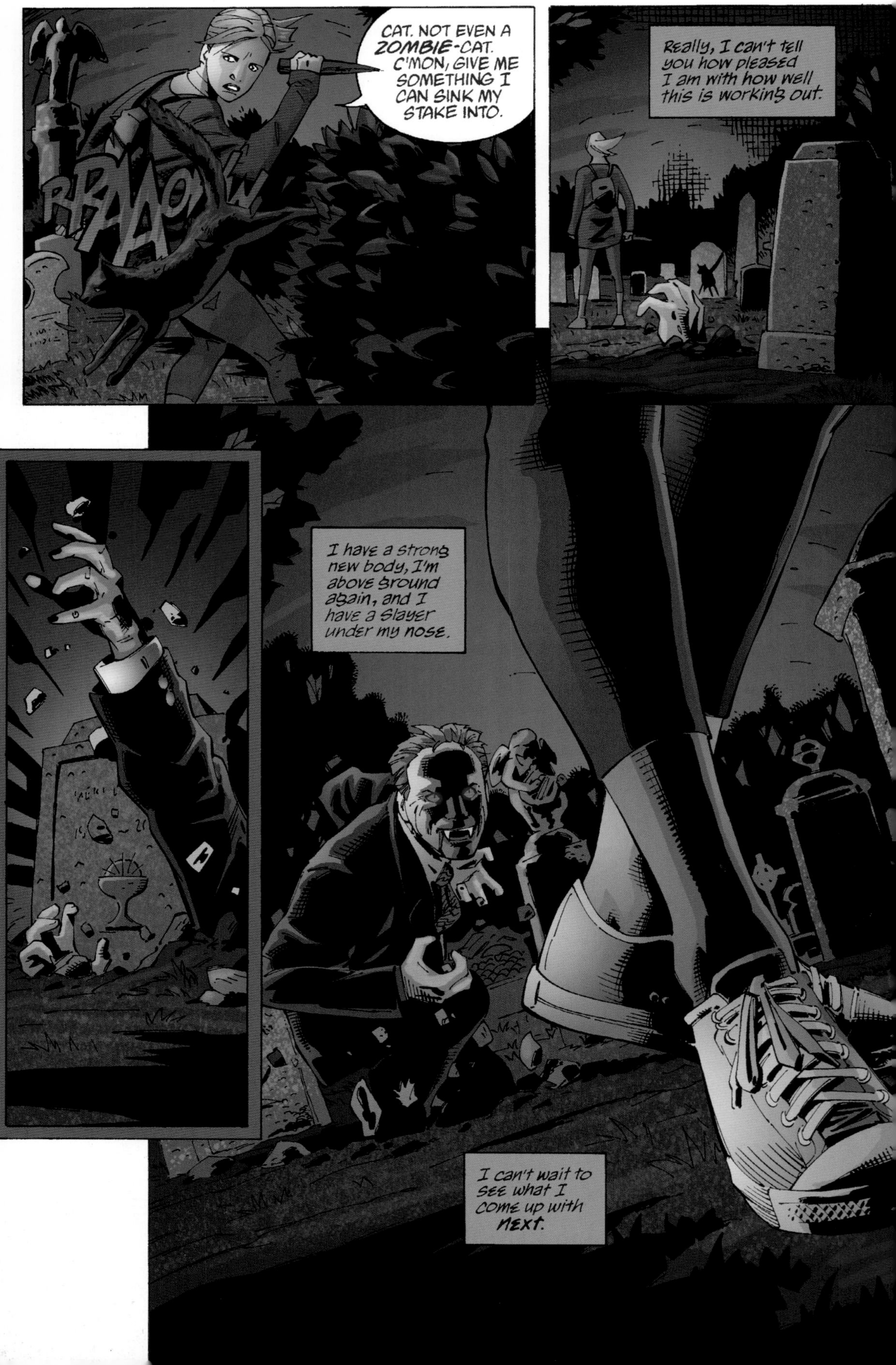

CAT. NOT EVEN A ZOMBIE-CAT. C'MON, GIVE ME SOMETHING I CAN SINK MY STAKE INTO.
RRAAOW
Really, I can't tell you how pleased I am with how well this is working out.
I have a strong new body, I'm above ground again, and I have a Slayer under my nose.
I can't wait to see what I come up with next.

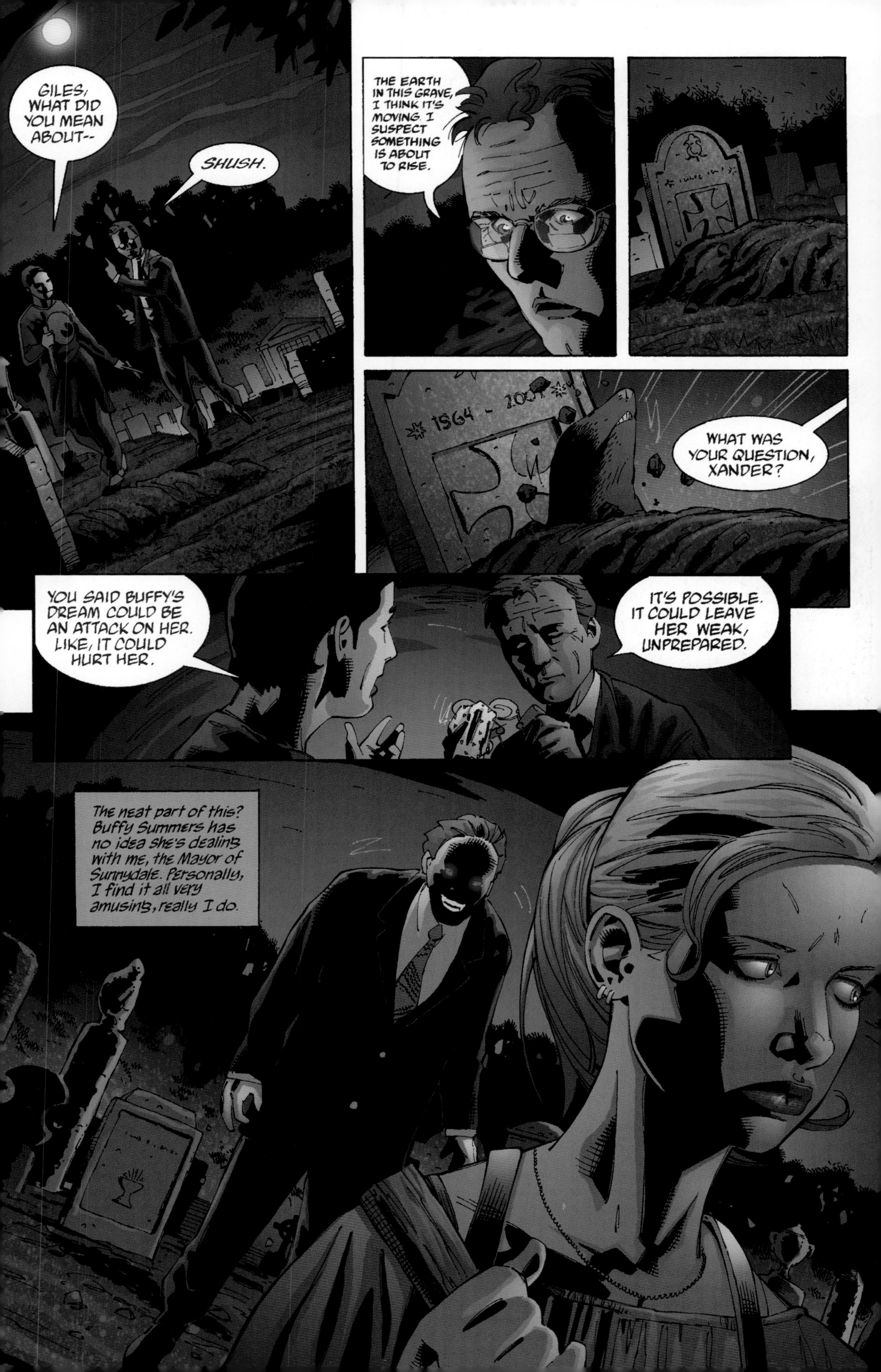
GILES, WHAT DID YOU MEAN ABOUT--
SHUSH.
THE EARTH IN THIS GRAVE, I THINK IT'S MOVING. I SUSPECT SOMETHING IS ABOUT TO RISE.
1864 - 2001
WHAT WAS YOUR QUESTION, XANDER?
YOU SAID BUFFY'S DREAM COULD BE AN ATTACK ON HER. LIKE, IT COULD HURT HER.
IT'S POSSIBLE. IT COULD LEAVE HER WEAK, UNPREPARED.
The neat part of this? Buffy Summers has no idea she's dealing with me, the Mayor of Sunnydale. Personally, I find it all very amusing, really I do.

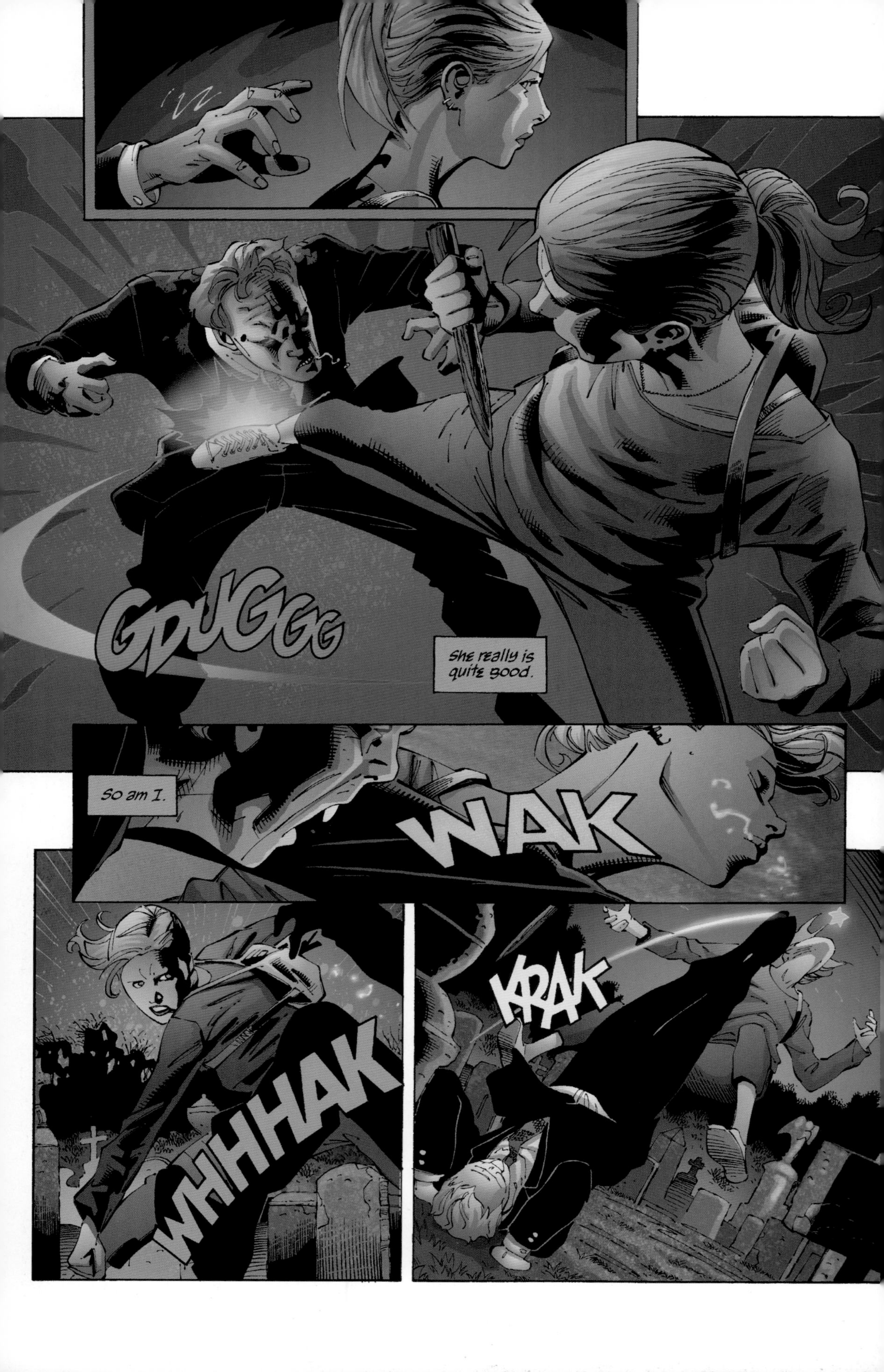
GDUGGG
She really is quite good.
So am I.
WAK
WHHHAK
KRAK

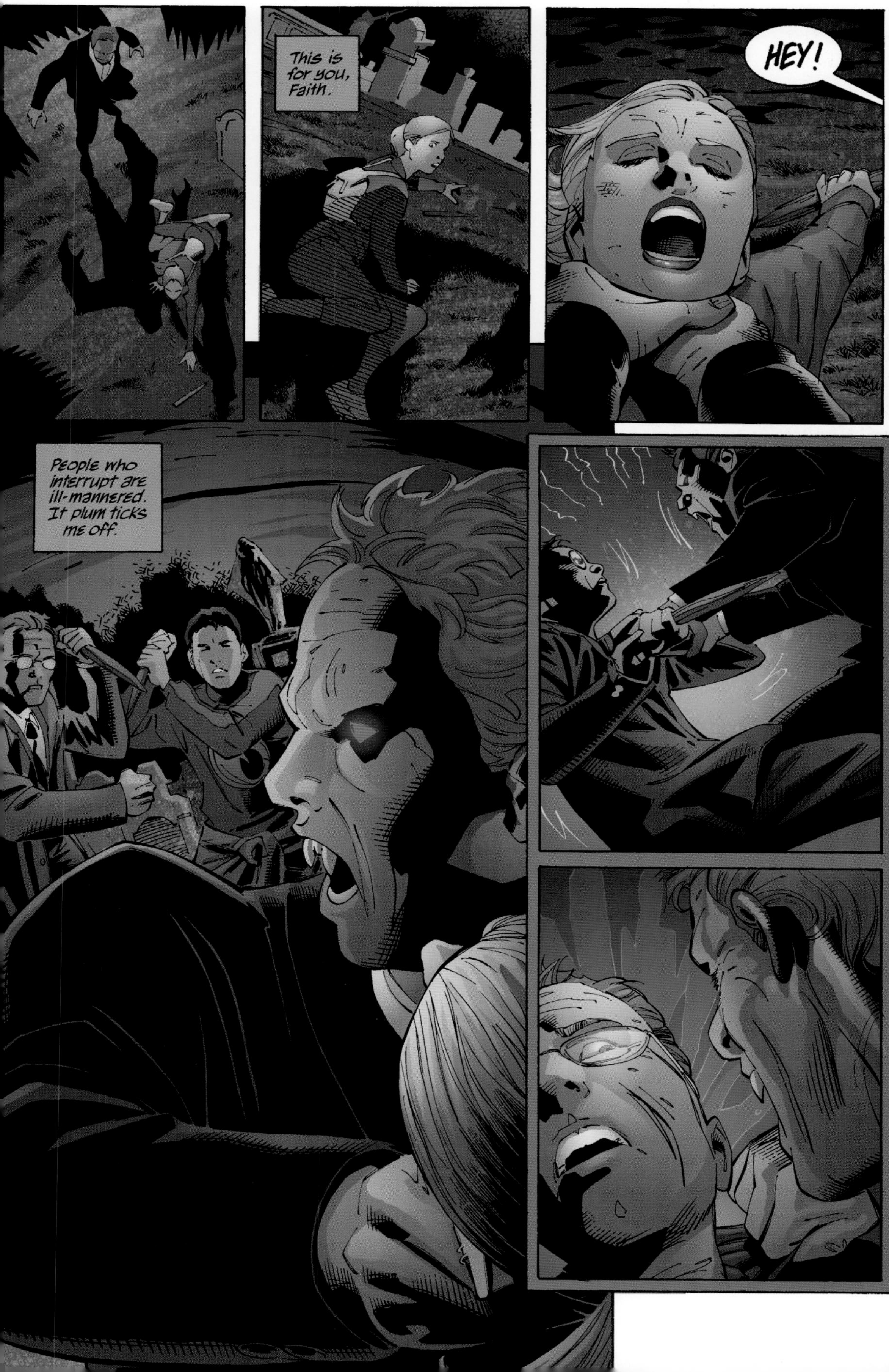
This is for you, Faith.
HEY!
People who interrupt are ill-mannered. It plum ticks me off.

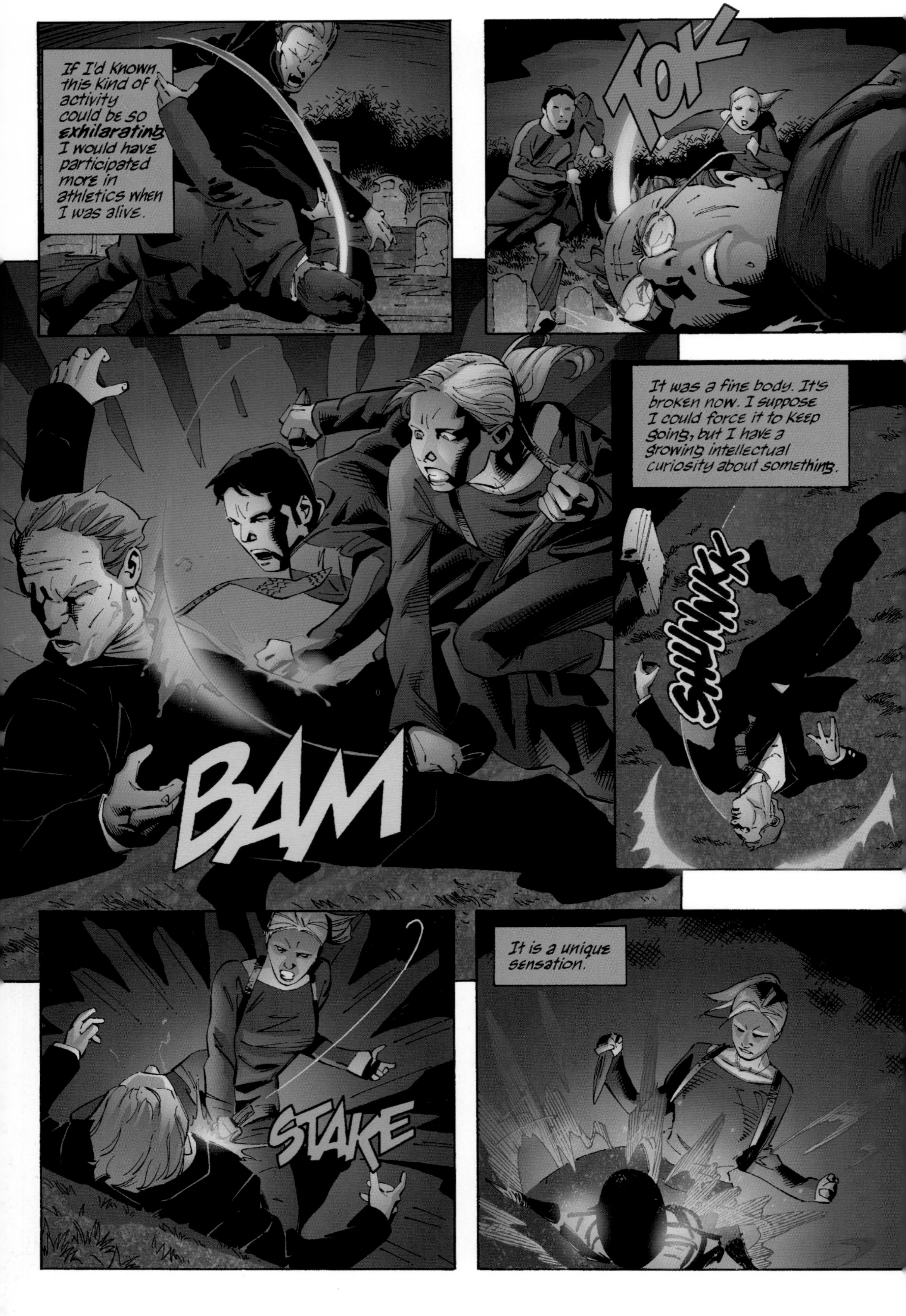
If I'd known this kind of activity could be so **exhilarating** I would have participated more in athletics when I was alive.
TOK
It was a fine body. It's broken now. I suppose I could force it to keep going, but I have a growing intellectual curiosity about something.
BAM
SHUNKK
STAKE
It is a unique sensation.

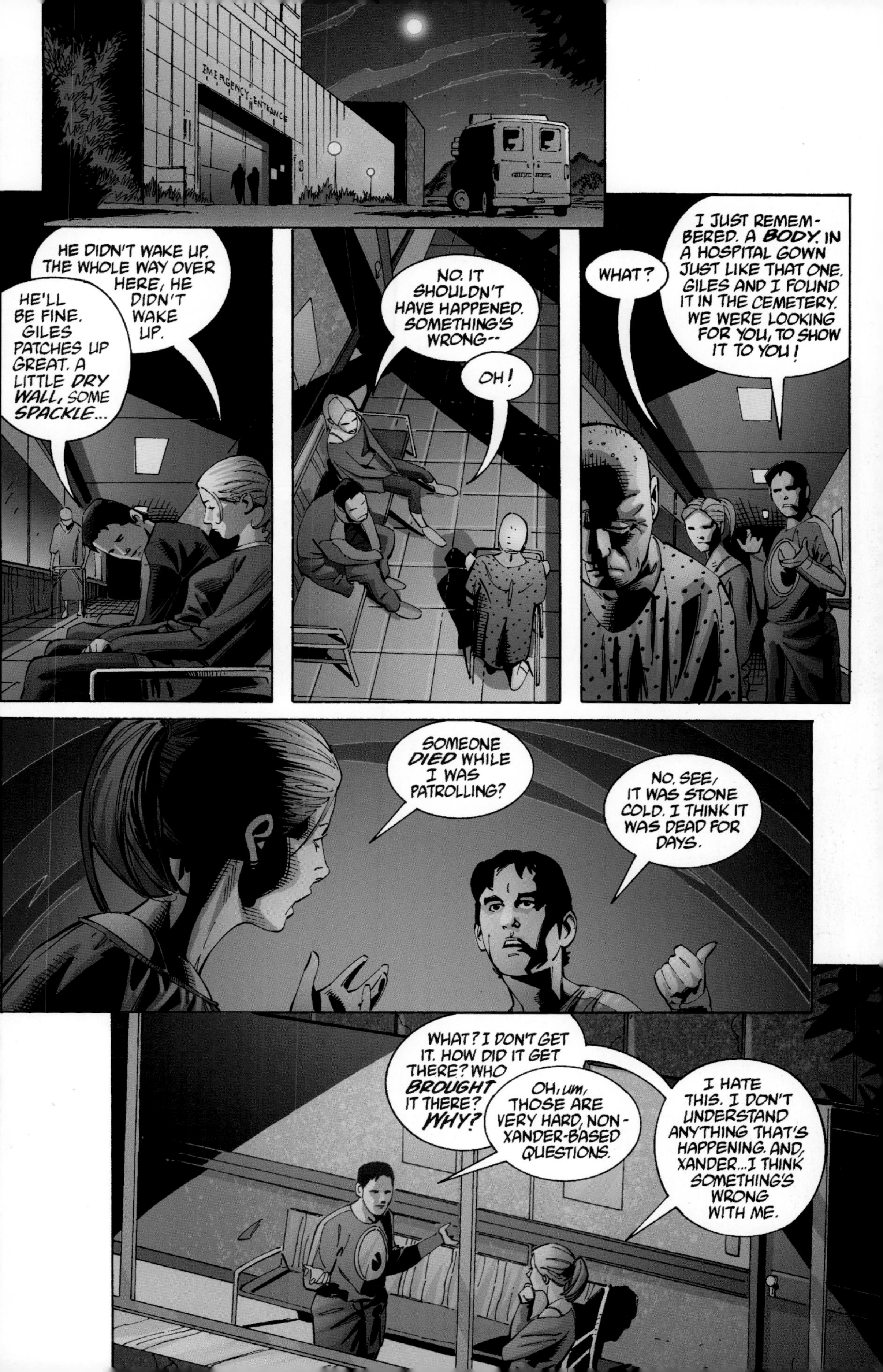
EMERGENCY ENTRANCE
HE DIDN'T WAKE UP. THE WHOLE WAY OVER HERE, HE DIDN'T WAKE UP.
HE'LL BE FINE. GILES PATCHES UP GREAT. A LITTLE DRY WALL, SOME SPACKLE...
NO. IT SHOULDN'T HAVE HAPPENED. SOMETHING'S WRONG--
OH!
WHAT?
I JUST REMEMBERED. A BODY. IN A HOSPITAL GOWN JUST LIKE THAT ONE. GILES AND I FOUND IT IN THE CEMETERY. WE WERE LOOKING FOR YOU, TO SHOW IT TO YOU!
SOMEONE DIED WHILE I WAS PATROLLING?
NO. SEE, IT WAS STONE COLD. I THINK IT WAS DEAD FOR DAYS.
WHAT? I DON'T GET IT. HOW DID IT GET THERE? WHO BROUGHT IT THERE? WHY?
OH, UM, THOSE ARE VERY HARD, NON-XANDER-BASED QUESTIONS.
I HATE THIS. I DON'T UNDERSTAND ANYTHING THAT'S HAPPENING. AND, XANDER...I THINK SOMETHING'S WRONG WITH ME.

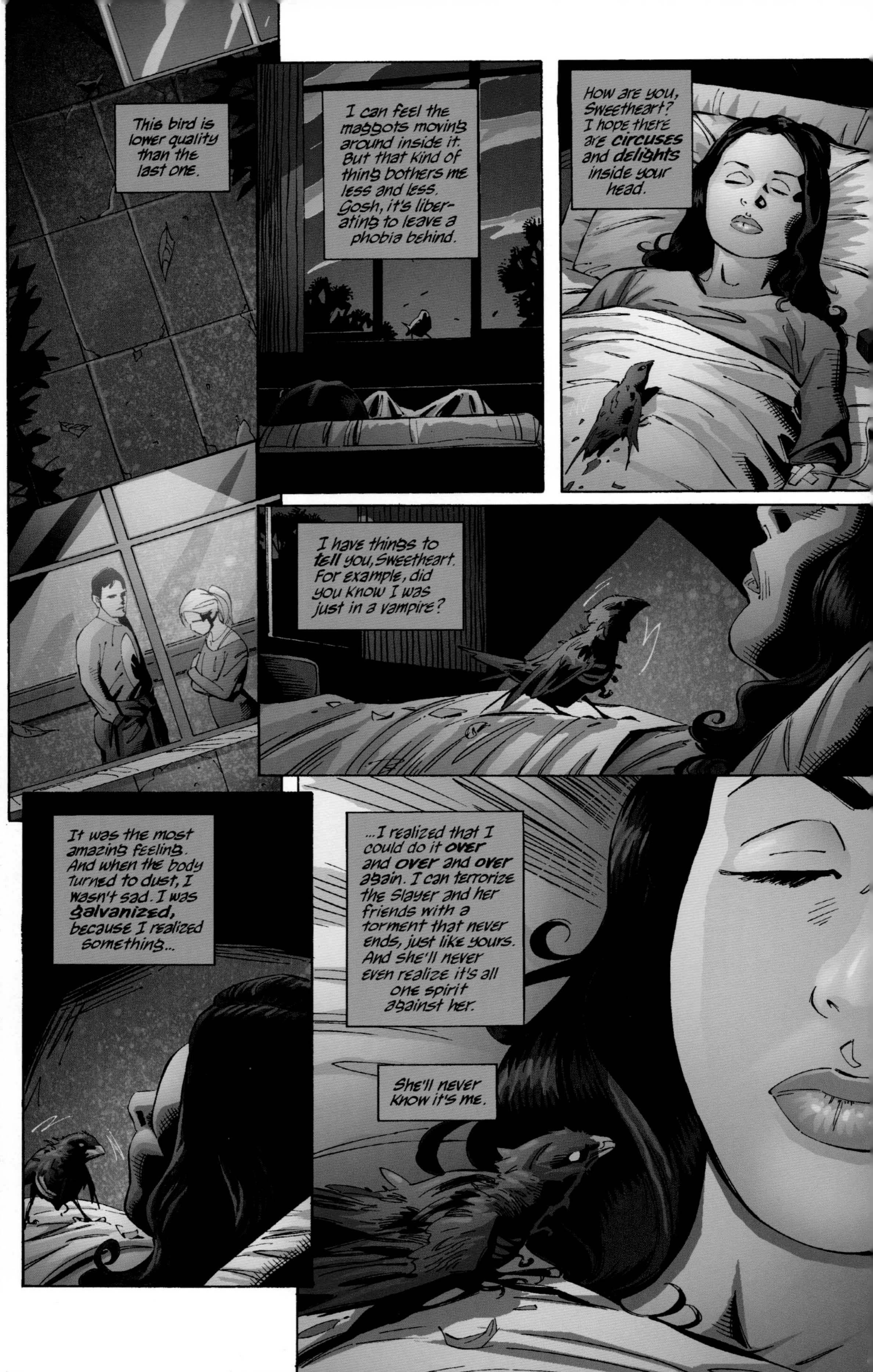
This bird is lower quality than the last one.
I can feel the maggots moving around inside it. But that kind of thing bothers me less and less. Gosh, it's liberating to leave a phobia behind.
How are you, Sweetheart? I hope there are **circuses** and **delights** inside your head.
I have things to **tell** you, Sweetheart. For example, did you know I was just in a vampire?
It was the most amazing feeling. And when the body turned to dust, I wasn't sad. I was **galvanized,** because I realized something...
...I realized that I could do it **over** and **over** and **over** again. I can terrorize the Slayer and her friends with a torment that never ends, just like yours. And she'll never even realize it's all one spirit against her.
She'll never know it's me.

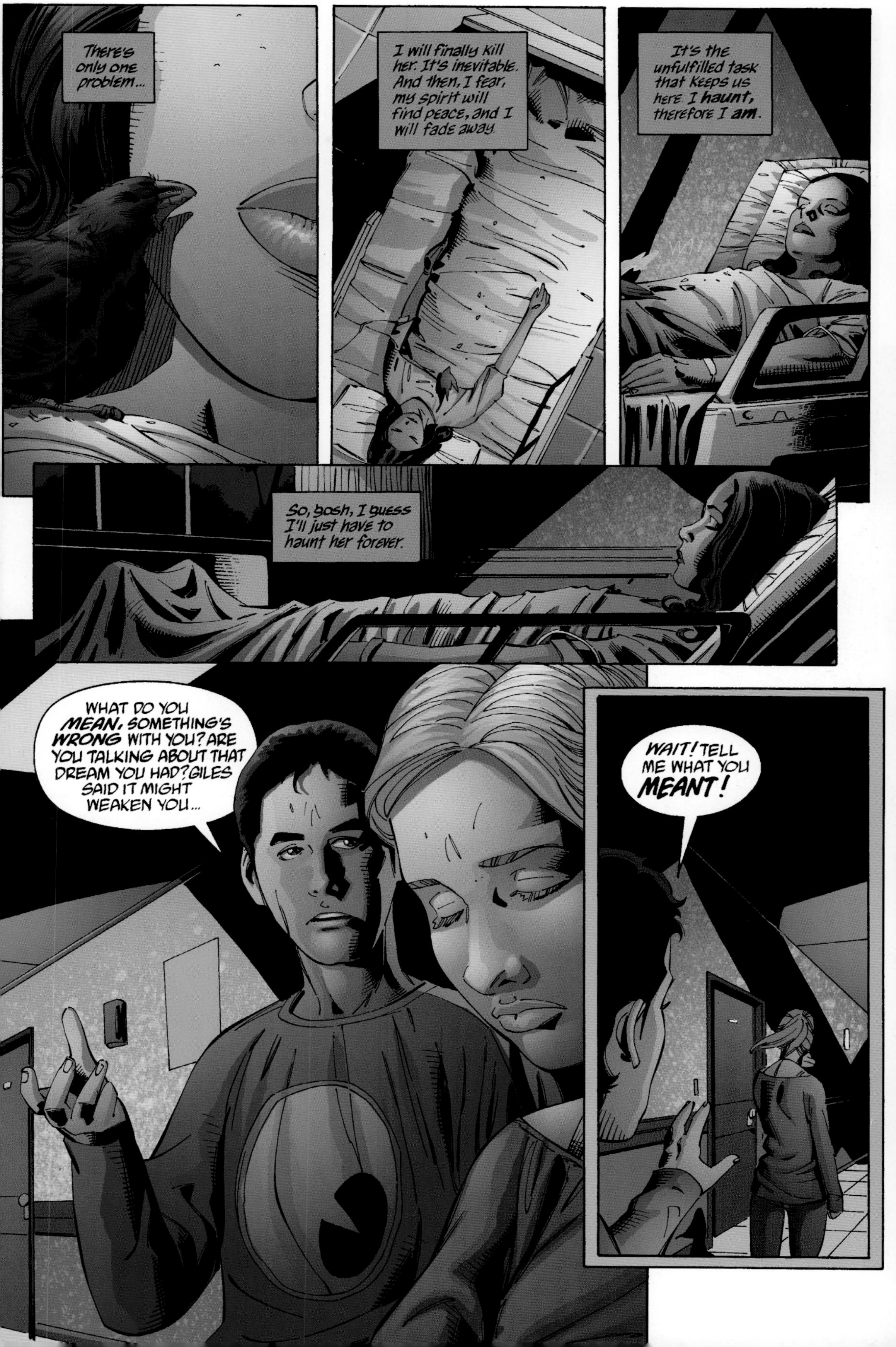
There's only one problem...
I will finally kill her. It's inevitable. And then, I fear, my spirit will find peace, and I will fade away.
It's the unfulfilled task that keeps us here. I haunt, therefore I am.
So, gosh, I guess I'll just have to haunt her forever.
WHAT DO YOU MEAN, SOMETHING'S WRONG WITH YOU? ARE YOU TALKING ABOUT THAT DREAM YOU HAD? GILES SAID IT MIGHT WEAKEN YOU...
WAIT! TELL ME WHAT YOU MEANT!

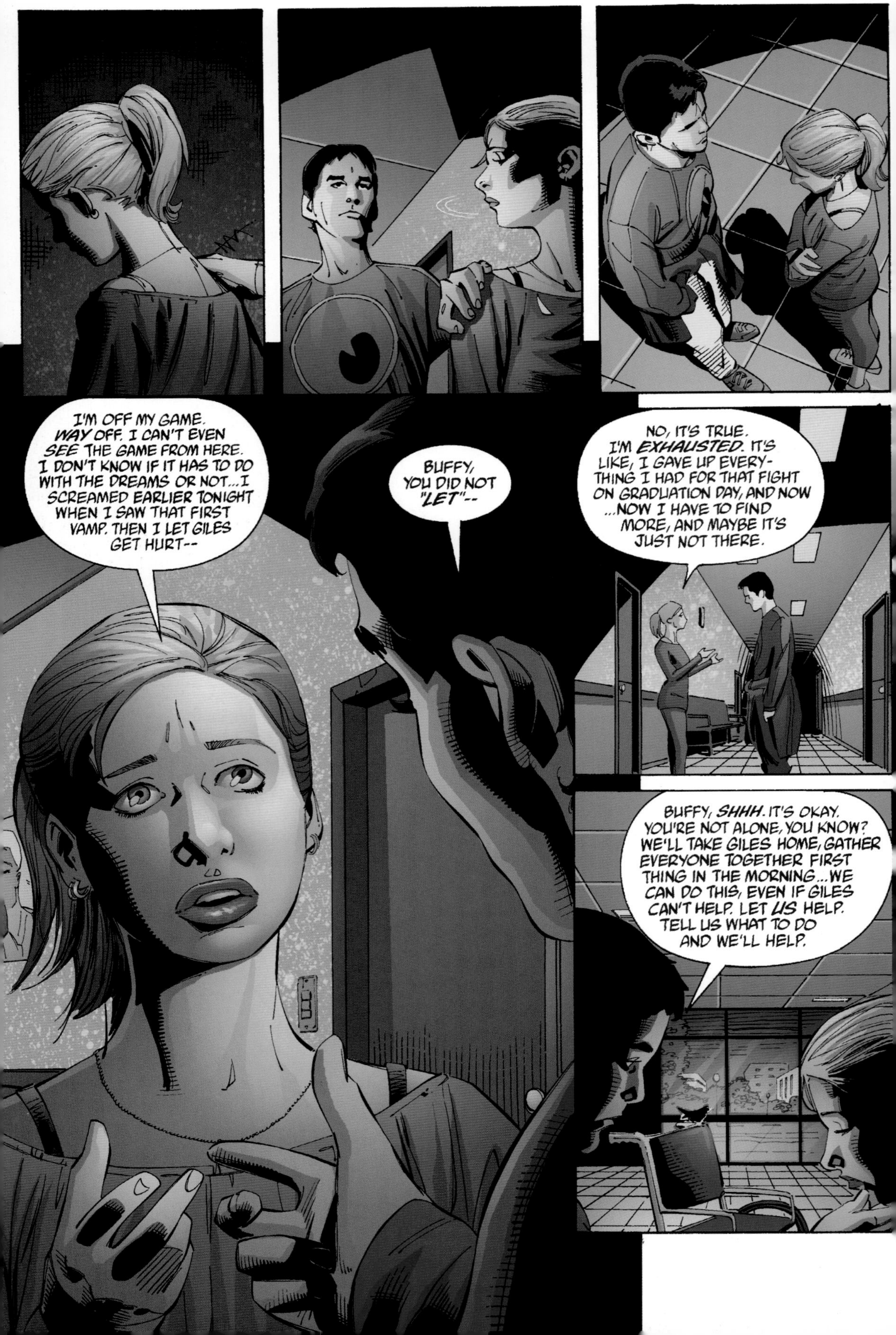

I'M OFF MY GAME. *WAY* OFF. I CAN'T EVEN *SEE* THE GAME FROM HERE. I DON'T KNOW IF IT HAS TO DO WITH THE DREAMS OR NOT... I SCREAMED EARLIER TONIGHT WHEN I SAW THAT FIRST VAMP. THEN I LET GILES GET HURT--
BUFFY, YOU DID NOT *"LET"*--
NO, IT'S TRUE. I'M *EXHAUSTED*. IT'S LIKE, I GAVE UP EVERY-THING I HAD FOR THAT FIGHT ON GRADUATION DAY, AND NOW ...NOW I HAVE TO FIND MORE, AND MAYBE IT'S JUST NOT THERE.
BUFFY, *SHHH*. IT'S OKAY. YOU'RE NOT ALONE, YOU KNOW? WE'LL TAKE GILES HOME, GATHER EVERYONE TOGETHER FIRST THING IN THE MORNING... WE CAN DO THIS, EVEN IF GILES CAN'T HELP. LET *US* HELP. TELL US WHAT TO DO AND WE'LL HELP.

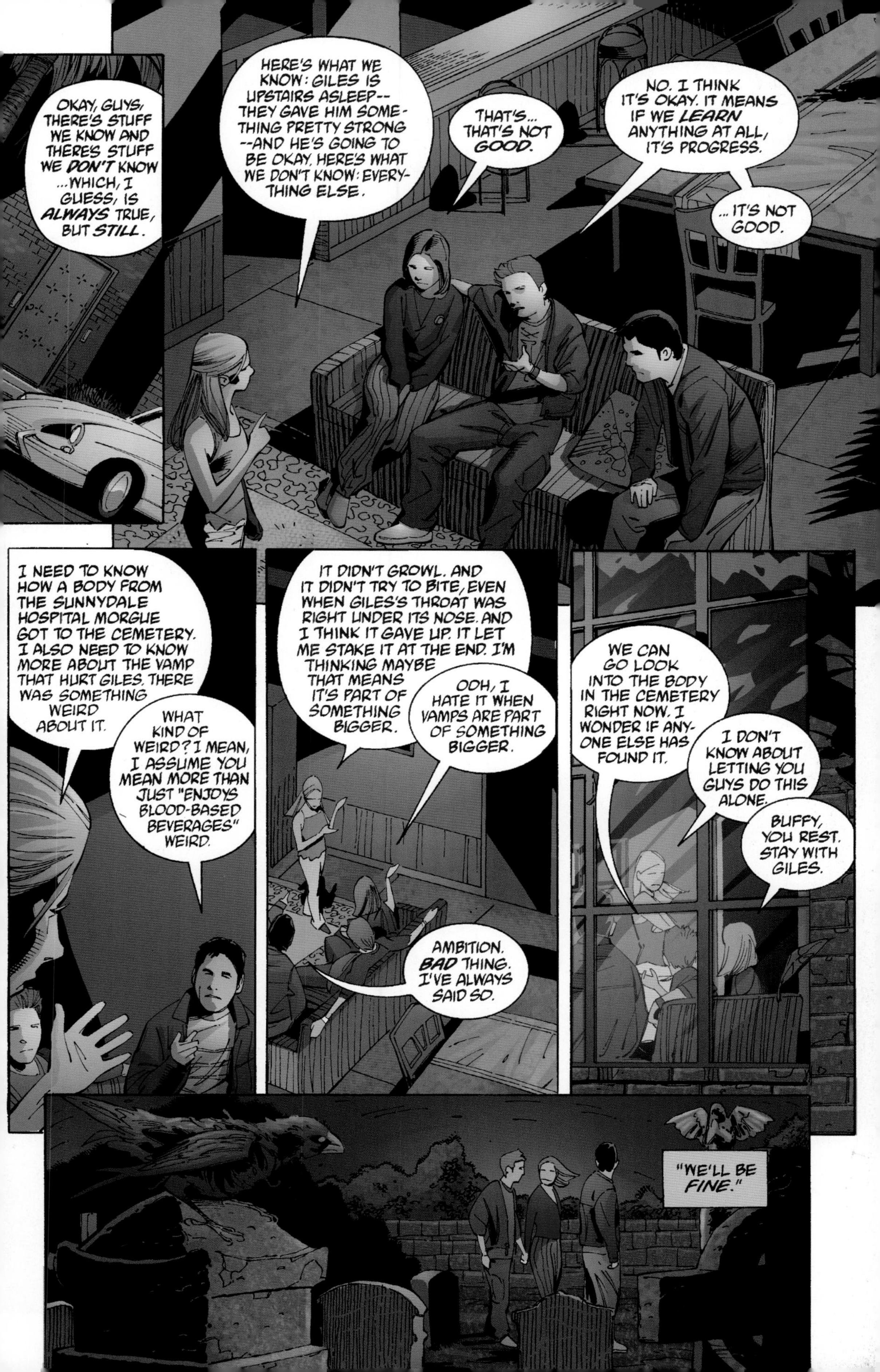
OKAY, GUYS, THERE'S STUFF WE KNOW AND THERE'S STUFF WE DON'T KNOW ...WHICH, I GUESS, IS ALWAYS TRUE, BUT STILL.
HERE'S WHAT WE KNOW: GILES IS UPSTAIRS ASLEEP-- THEY GAVE HIM SOMETHING PRETTY STRONG --AND HE'S GOING TO BE OKAY. HERE'S WHAT WE DON'T KNOW: EVERYTHING ELSE.
THAT'S... THAT'S NOT GOOD.
NO. I THINK IT'S OKAY. IT MEANS IF WE LEARN ANYTHING AT ALL, IT'S PROGRESS.
... IT'S NOT GOOD.
I NEED TO KNOW HOW A BODY FROM THE SUNNYDALE HOSPITAL MORGUE GOT TO THE CEMETERY. I ALSO NEED TO KNOW MORE ABOUT THE VAMP THAT HURT GILES. THERE WAS SOMETHING WEIRD ABOUT IT.
WHAT KIND OF WEIRD? I MEAN, I ASSUME YOU MEAN MORE THAN JUST "ENJOYS BLOOD-BASED BEVERAGES" WEIRD.
IT DIDN'T GROWL. AND IT DIDN'T TRY TO BITE, EVEN WHEN GILES'S THROAT WAS RIGHT UNDER ITS NOSE. AND I THINK IT GAVE UP. IT LET ME STAKE IT AT THE END. I'M THINKING MAYBE THAT MEANS IT'S PART OF SOMETHING BIGGER.
OOH, I HATE IT WHEN VAMPS ARE PART OF SOMETHING BIGGER.
AMBITION. BAD THING. I'VE ALWAYS SAID SO.
WE CAN GO LOOK INTO THE BODY IN THE CEMETERY RIGHT NOW. I WONDER IF ANYONE ELSE HAS FOUND IT.
I DON'T KNOW ABOUT LETTING YOU GUYS DO THIS ALONE.
BUFFY, YOU REST. STAY WITH GILES.
"WE'LL BE FINE."

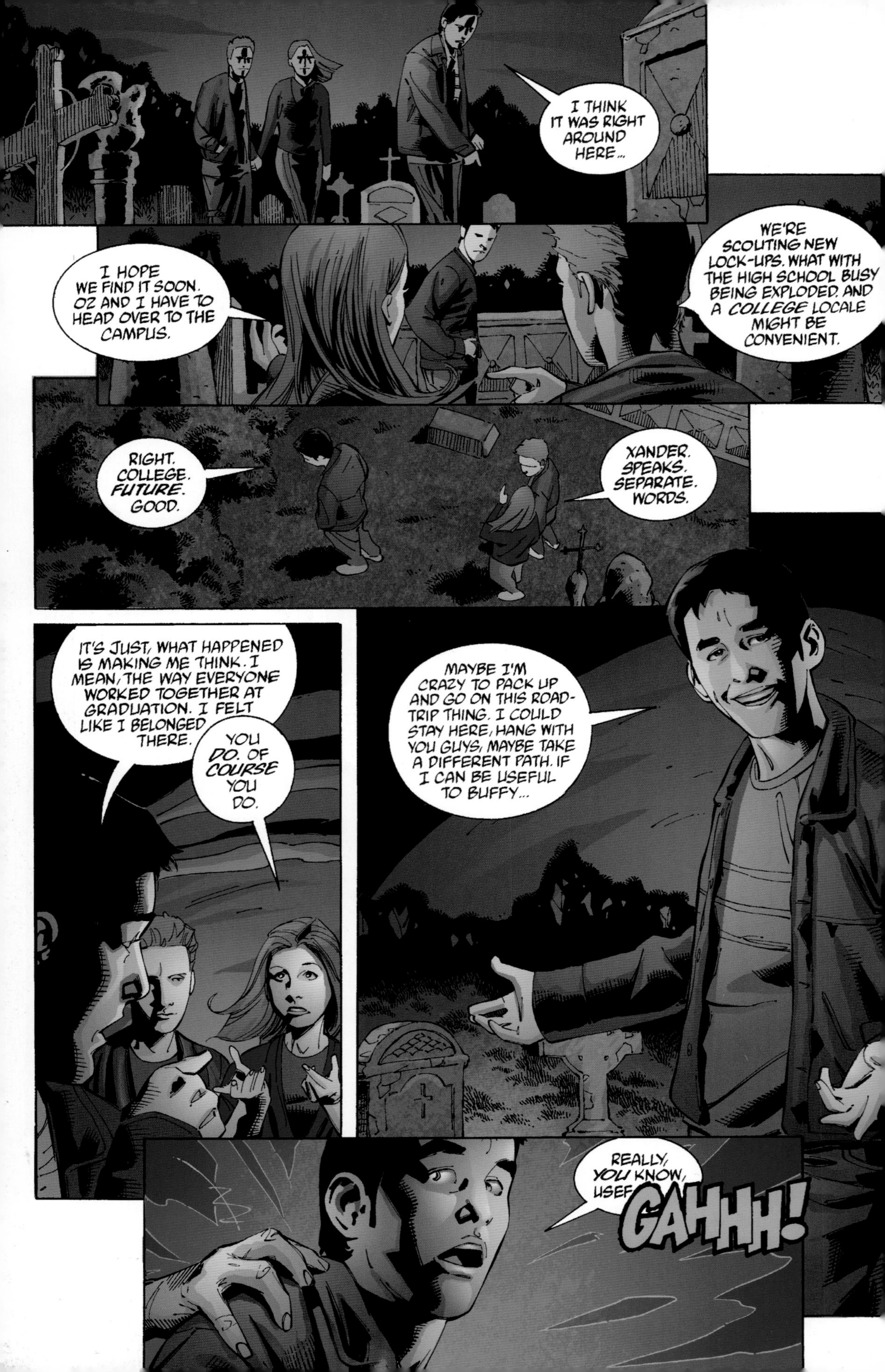
I THINK IT WAS RIGHT AROUND HERE...
I HOPE WE FIND IT SOON. OZ AND I HAVE TO HEAD OVER TO THE CAMPUS.
WE'RE SCOUTING NEW LOCK-UPS. WHAT WITH THE HIGH SCHOOL BUSY BEING EXPLODED. AND A *COLLEGE* LOCALE MIGHT BE CONVENIENT.
RIGHT. COLLEGE. *FUTURE*. GOOD.
XANDER. SPEAKS. SEPARATE. WORDS.
IT'S JUST, WHAT HAPPENED IS MAKING ME THINK. I MEAN, THE WAY EVERYONE WORKED TOGETHER AT GRADUATION. I FELT LIKE I BELONGED THERE.
YOU *DO*. OF *COURSE* YOU DO.
MAYBE I'M CRAZY TO PACK UP AND GO ON THIS ROAD-TRIP THING. I COULD STAY HERE, HANG WITH YOU GUYS, MAYBE TAKE A DIFFERENT PATH. IF I CAN BE USEFUL TO BUFFY...
REALLY, *YOU* KNOW, USEF
GAHHH!

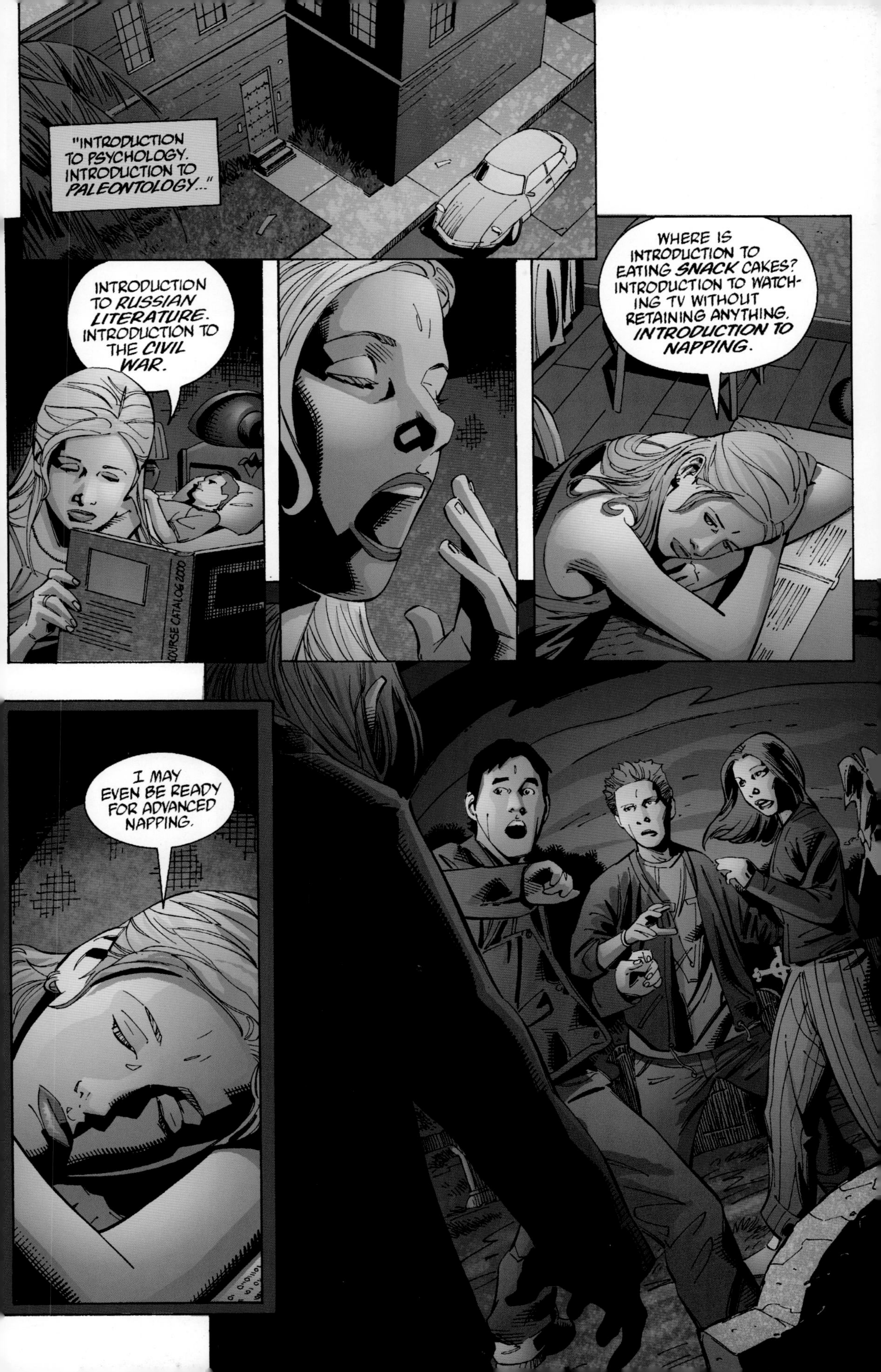
"INTRODUCTION TO PSYCHOLOGY. INTRODUCTION TO PALEONTOLOGY..."
INTRODUCTION TO RUSSIAN LITERATURE. INTRODUCTION TO THE CIVIL WAR.
COURSE CATALOG 2000
WHERE IS INTRODUCTION TO EATING SNACK CAKES? INTRODUCTION TO WATCHING TV WITHOUT RETAINING ANYTHING. INTRODUCTION TO NAPPING.
I MAY EVEN BE READY FOR ADVANCED NAPPING.

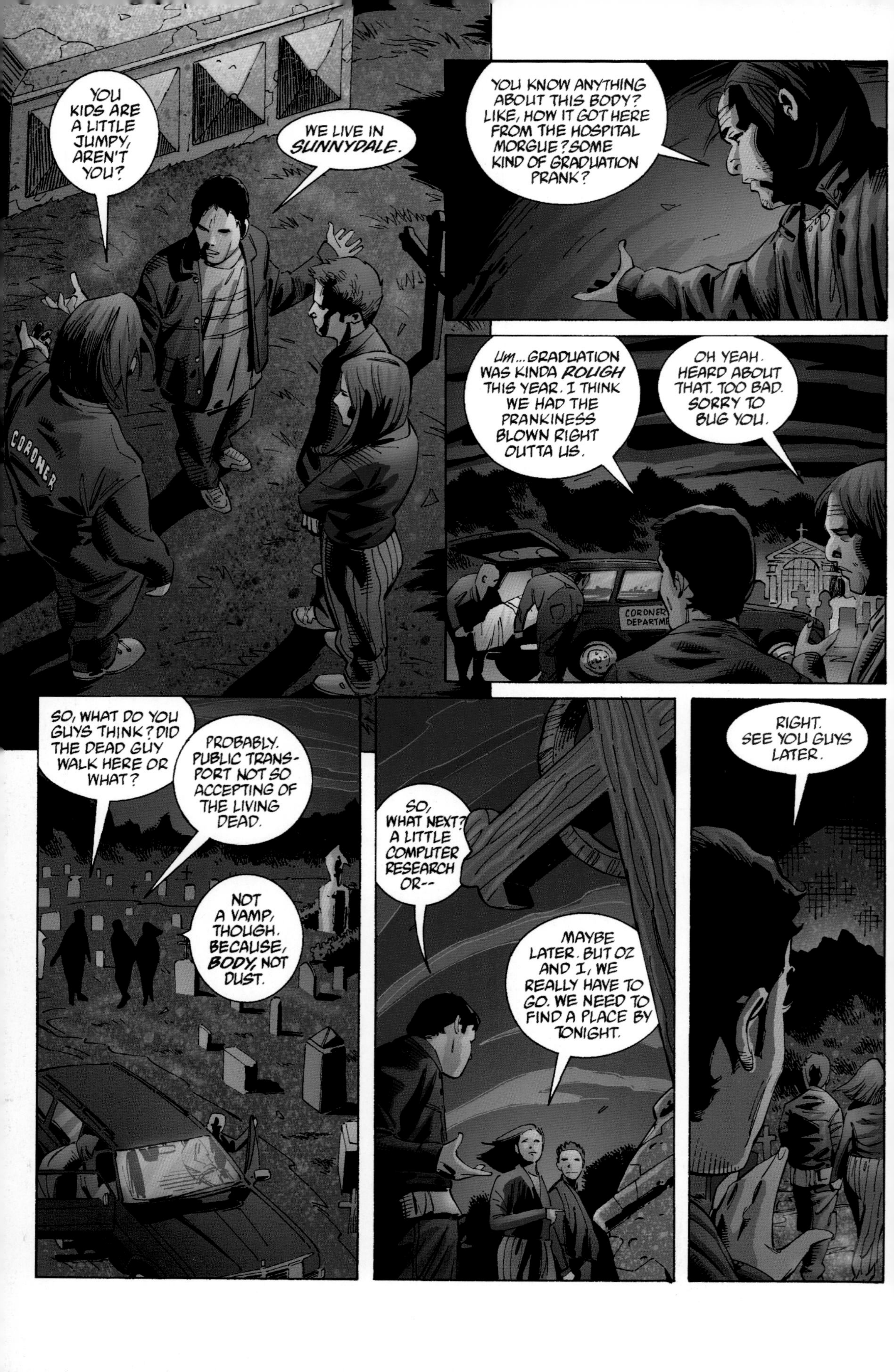
YOU KIDS ARE A LITTLE JUMPY, AREN'T YOU?
WE LIVE IN SUNNYDALE.
YOU KNOW ANYTHING ABOUT THIS BODY? LIKE, HOW IT GOT HERE FROM THE HOSPITAL MORGUE? SOME KIND OF GRADUATION PRANK?
UM... GRADUATION WAS KINDA ROUGH THIS YEAR. I THINK WE HAD THE PRANKINESS BLOWN RIGHT OUTTA US.
OH YEAH. HEARD ABOUT THAT. TOO BAD. SORRY TO BUG YOU.
CORONER DEPARTME
SO, WHAT DO YOU GUYS THINK? DID THE DEAD GUY WALK HERE OR WHAT?
PROBABLY. PUBLIC TRANS-PORT NOT SO ACCEPTING OF THE LIVING DEAD.
NOT A VAMP, THOUGH. BECAUSE, BODY, NOT DUST.
SO, WHAT NEXT? A LITTLE COMPUTER RESEARCH OR--
MAYBE LATER. BUT OZ AND I, WE REALLY HAVE TO GO. WE NEED TO FIND A PLACE BY TONIGHT.
RIGHT. SEE YOU GUYS LATER.

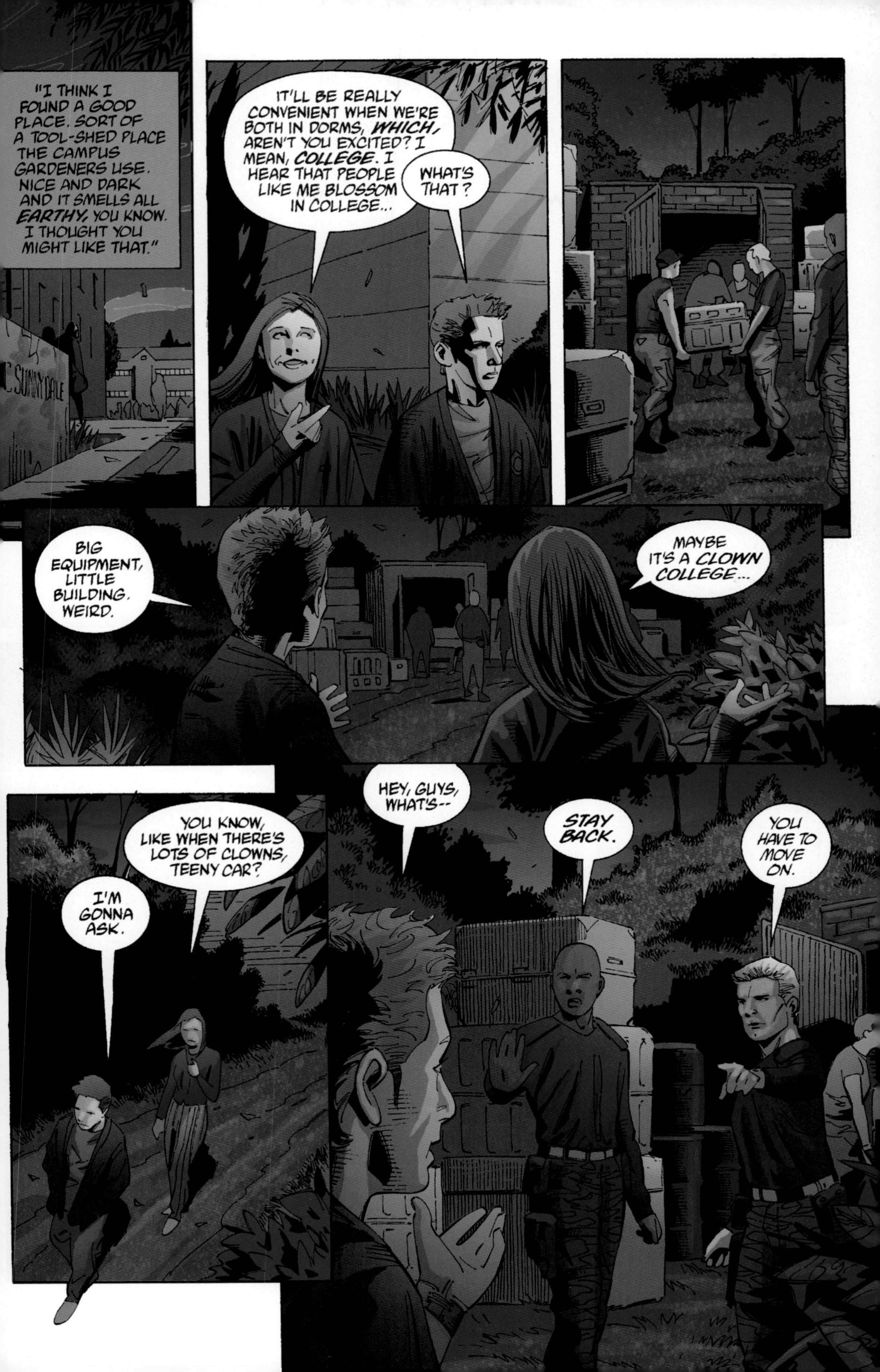
"I THINK I FOUND A GOOD PLACE. SORT OF A TOOL-SHED PLACE THE CAMPUS GARDENERS USE. NICE AND DARK AND IT SMELLS ALL EARTHY, YOU KNOW. I THOUGHT YOU MIGHT LIKE THAT."
IT'LL BE REALLY CONVENIENT WHEN WE'RE BOTH IN DORMS, WHICH, AREN'T YOU EXCITED? I MEAN, COLLEGE. I HEAR THAT PEOPLE LIKE ME BLOSSOM IN COLLEGE...
WHAT'S THAT?
BIG EQUIPMENT, LITTLE BUILDING. WEIRD.
MAYBE IT'S A CLOWN COLLEGE...
YOU KNOW, LIKE WHEN THERE'S LOTS OF CLOWNS, TEENY CAR?
I'M GONNA ASK.
HEY, GUYS, WHAT'S--
STAY BACK.
YOU HAVE TO MOVE ON.

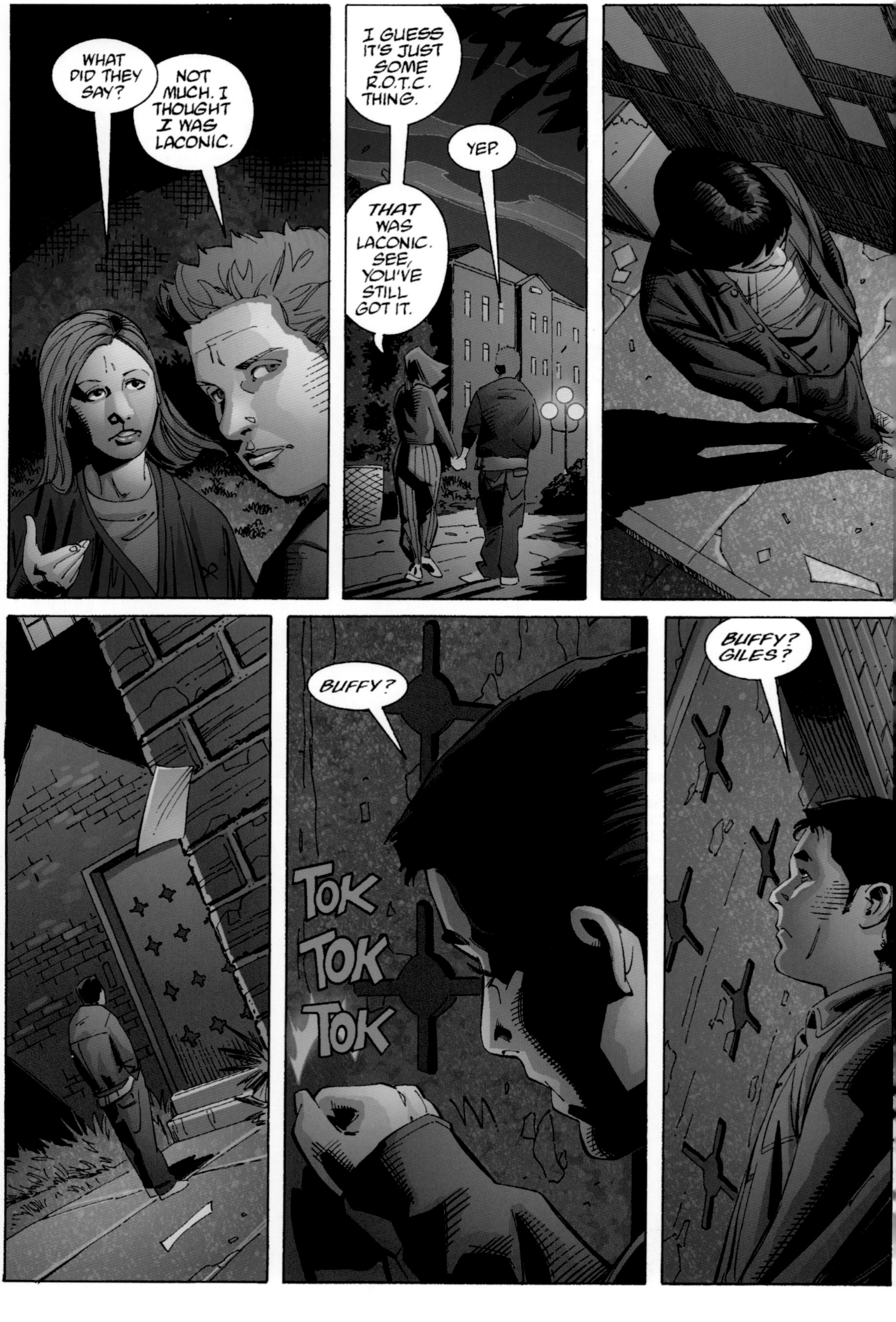
WHAT DID THEY SAY?
NOT MUCH. I THOUGHT I WAS LACONIC.
I GUESS IT'S JUST SOME R.O.T.C. THING.
YEP.
THAT WAS LACONIC. SEE, YOU'VE STILL GOT IT.
BUFFY?
TOK TOK TOK
BUFFY? GILES?

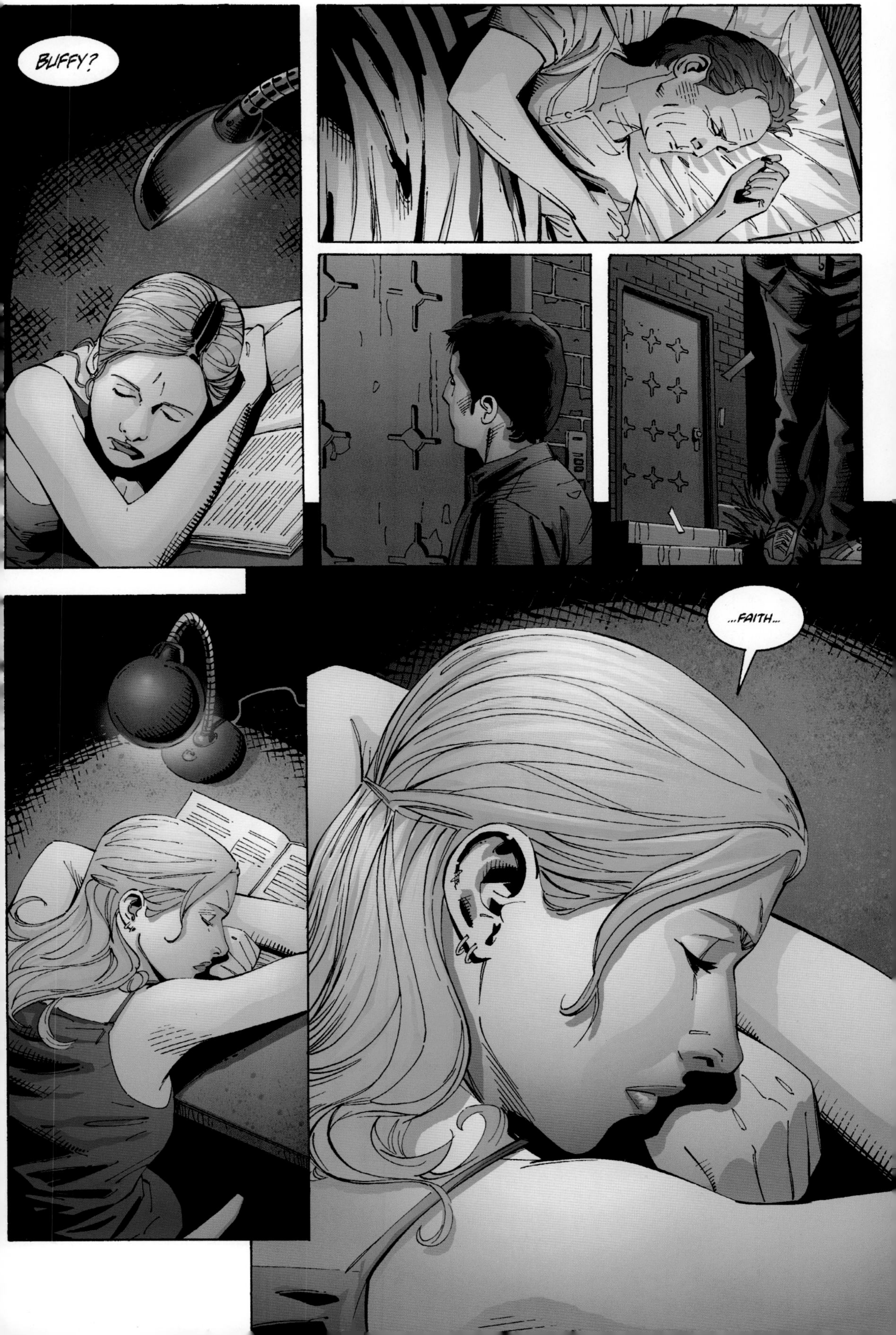
BUFFY?
...FAITH...

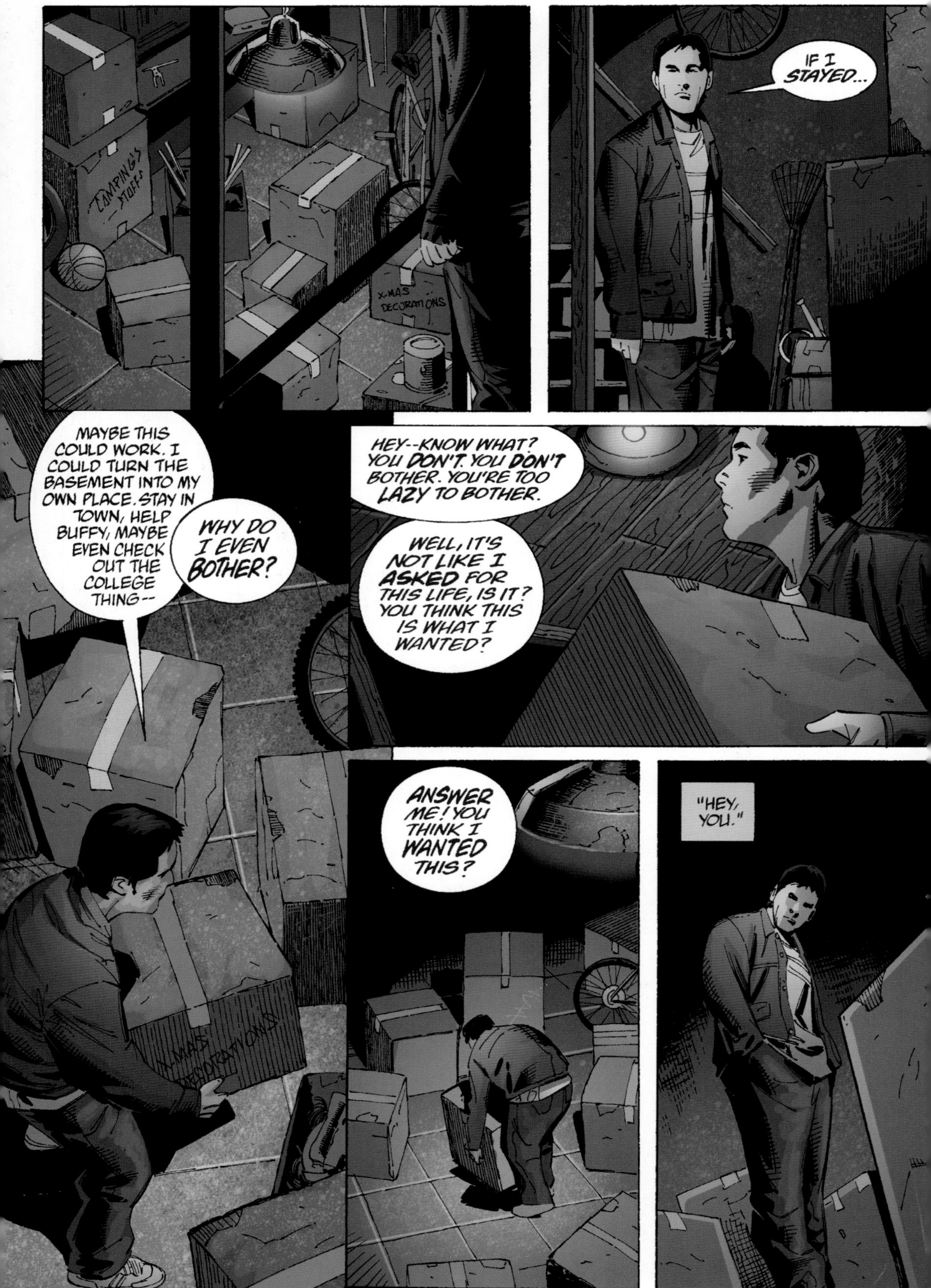
IF I STAYED...
MAYBE THIS COULD WORK. I COULD TURN THE BASEMENT INTO MY OWN PLACE. STAY IN TOWN, HELP BUFFY, MAYBE EVEN CHECK OUT THE COLLEGE THING--
WHY DO I EVEN BOTHER?
HEY--KNOW WHAT? YOU DON'T. YOU DON'T BOTHER. YOU'RE TOO LAZY TO BOTHER.
WELL, IT'S NOT LIKE I ASKED FOR THIS LIFE, IS IT? YOU THINK THIS IS WHAT I WANTED?
ANSWER ME! YOU THINK I WANTED THIS?
"HEY, YOU."

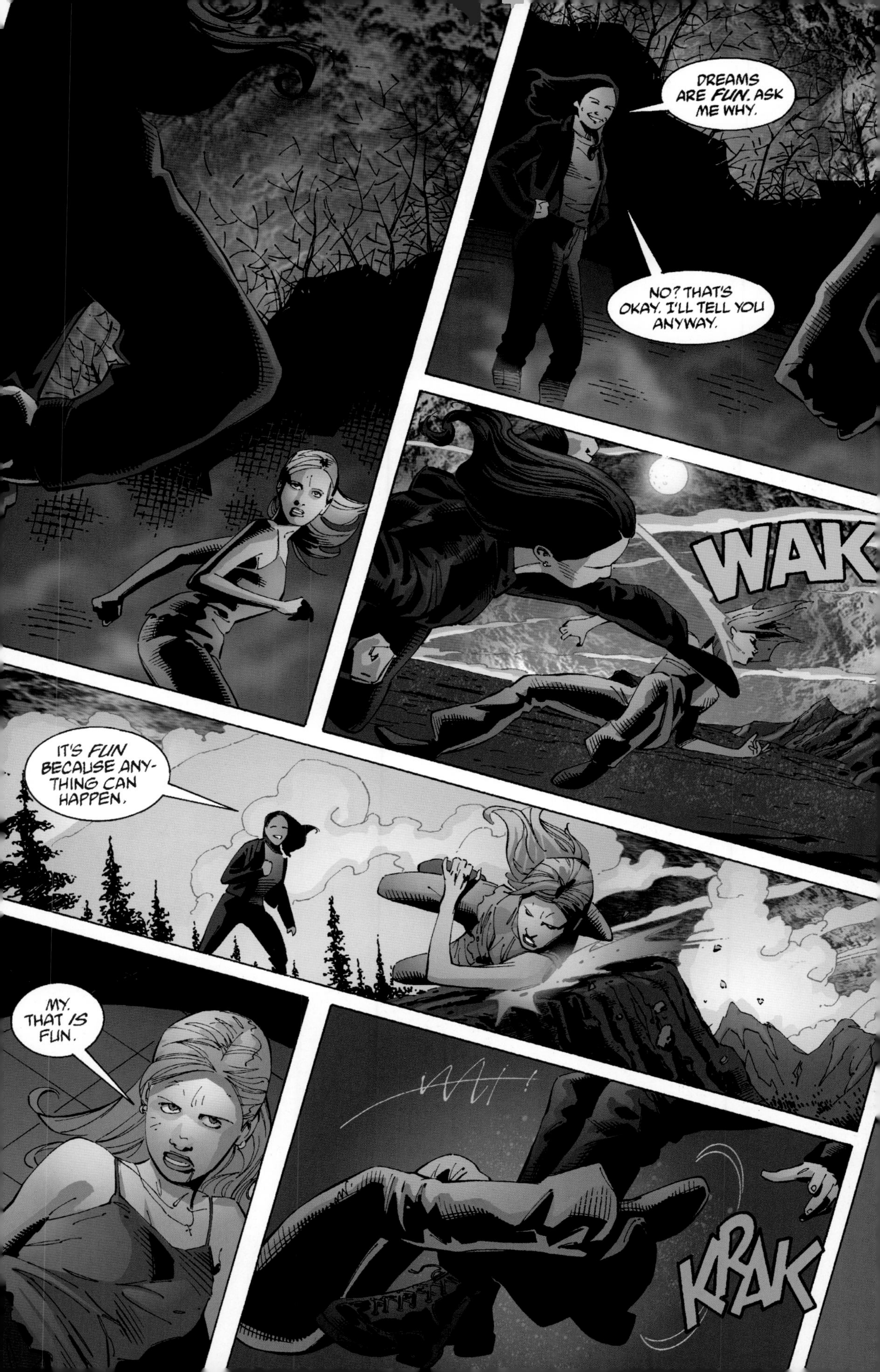
DREAMS ARE FUN. ASK ME WHY.
NO? THAT'S OKAY. I'LL TELL YOU ANYWAY.
WAK
IT'S FUN BECAUSE ANYTHING CAN HAPPEN.
MY. THAT IS FUN.
KRAK

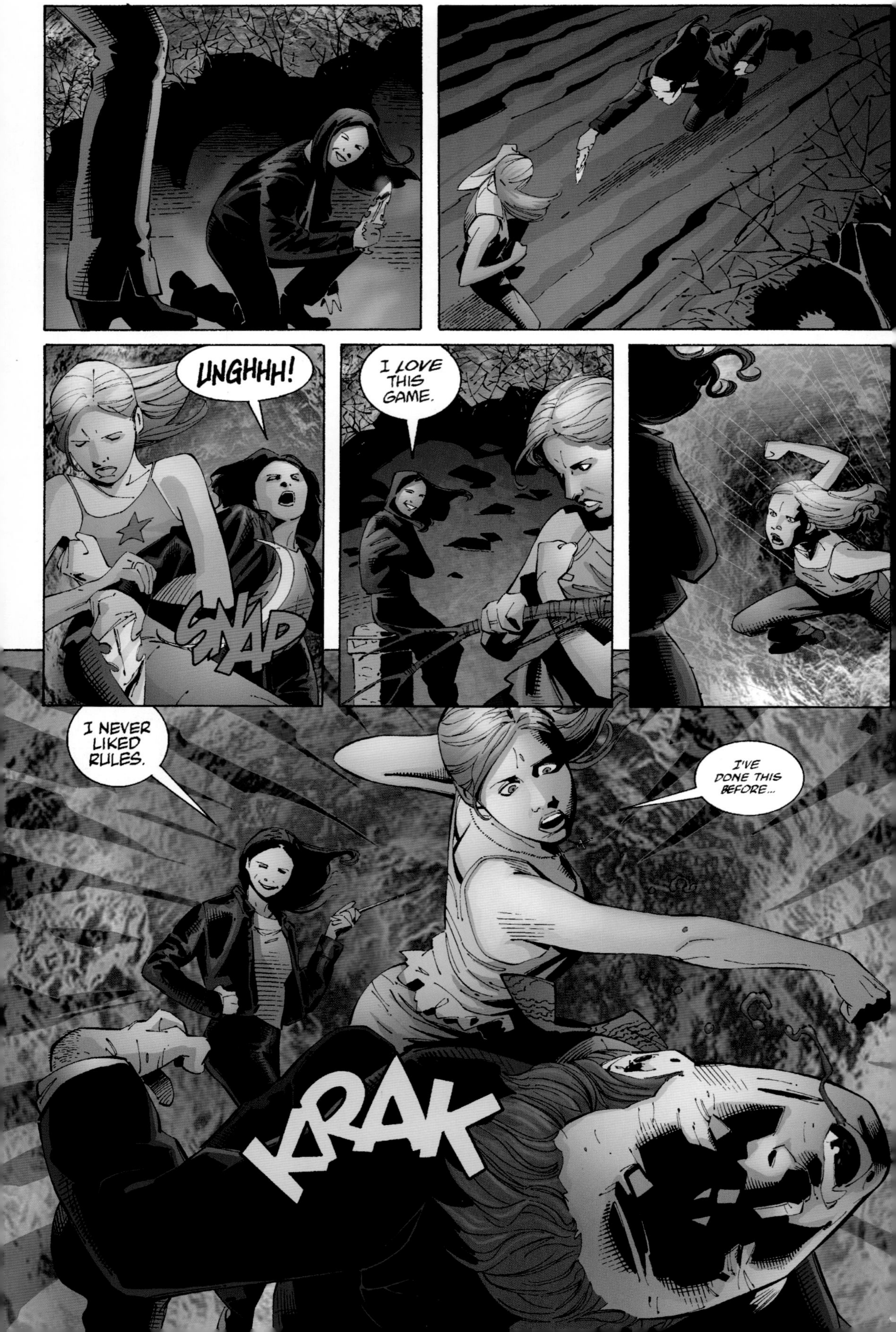
UNGHHH!
SNAP
I LOVE THIS GAME.
I NEVER LIKED RULES.
I'VE DONE THIS BEFORE...
KRAK

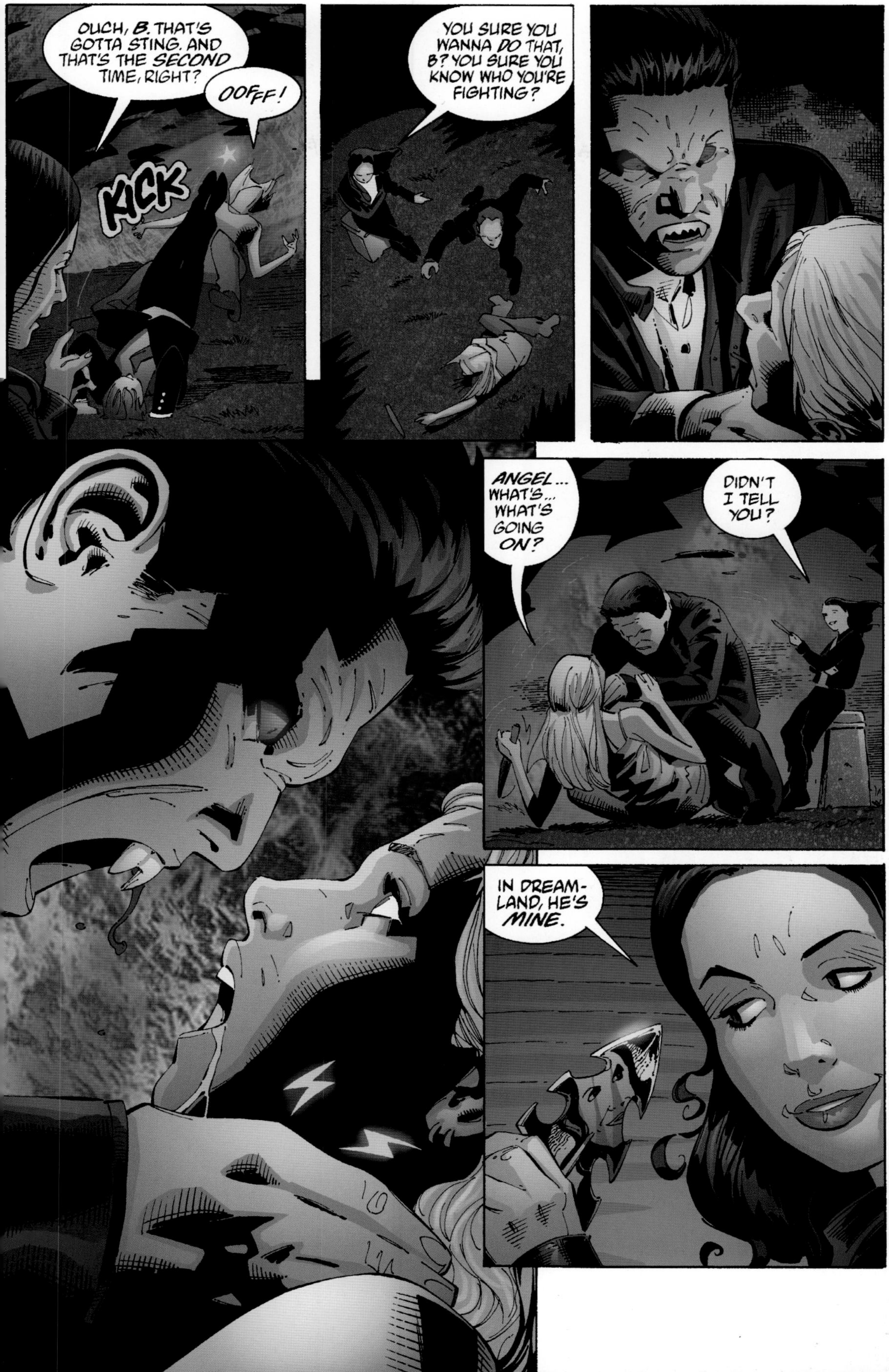

OUCH, B. THAT'S GOTTA STING. AND THAT'S THE SECOND TIME, RIGHT?
OOFFF!
KICK
YOU SURE YOU WANNA DO THAT, B? YOU SURE YOU KNOW WHO YOU'RE FIGHTING?
ANGEL... WHAT'S... WHAT'S GOING ON?
DIDN'T I TELL YOU?
IN DREAM-LAND, HE'S MINE.

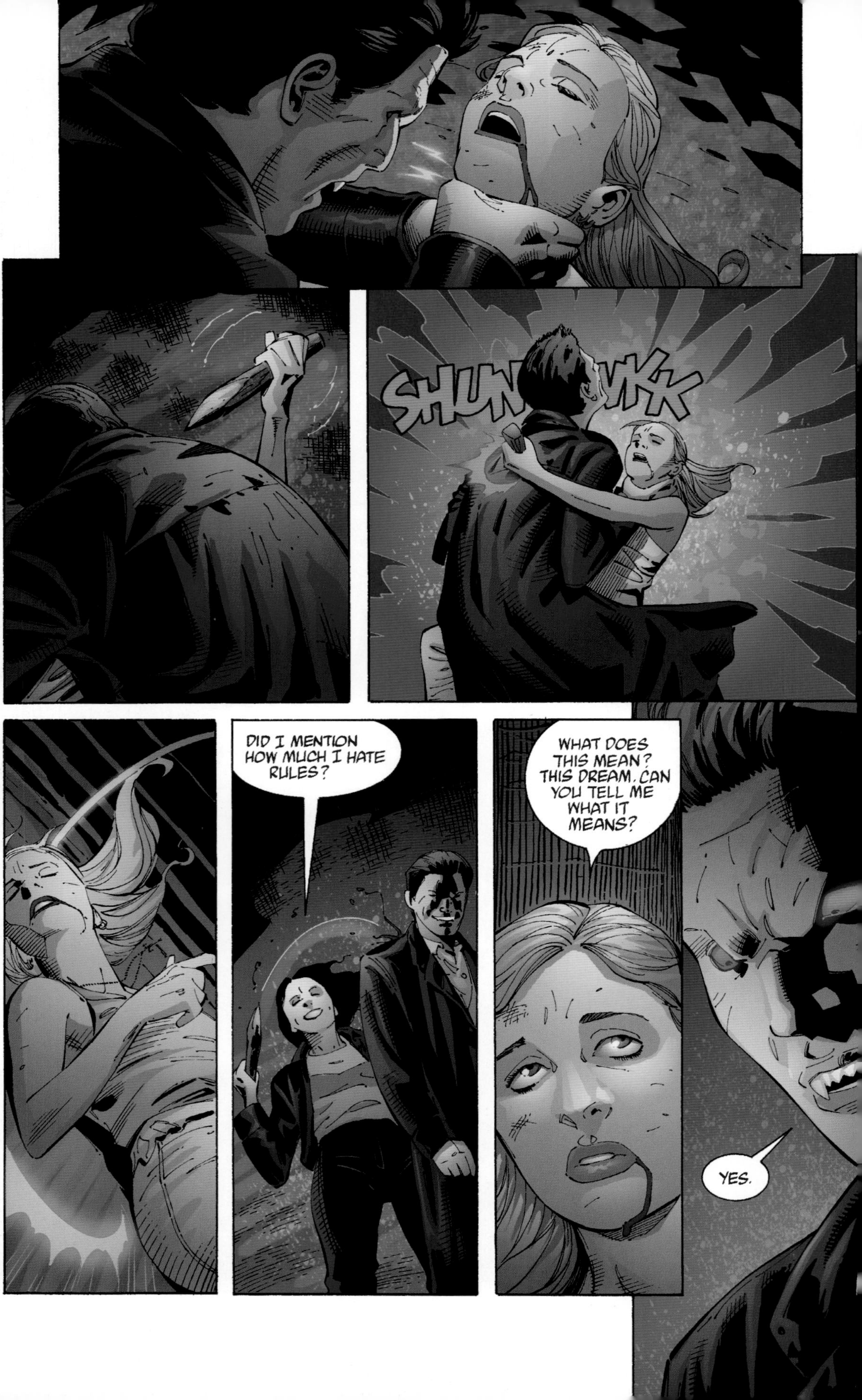
SHUNKKK
DID I MENTION HOW MUCH I HATE RULES?
WHAT DOES THIS MEAN? THIS DREAM. CAN YOU TELL ME WHAT IT MEANS?
YES.

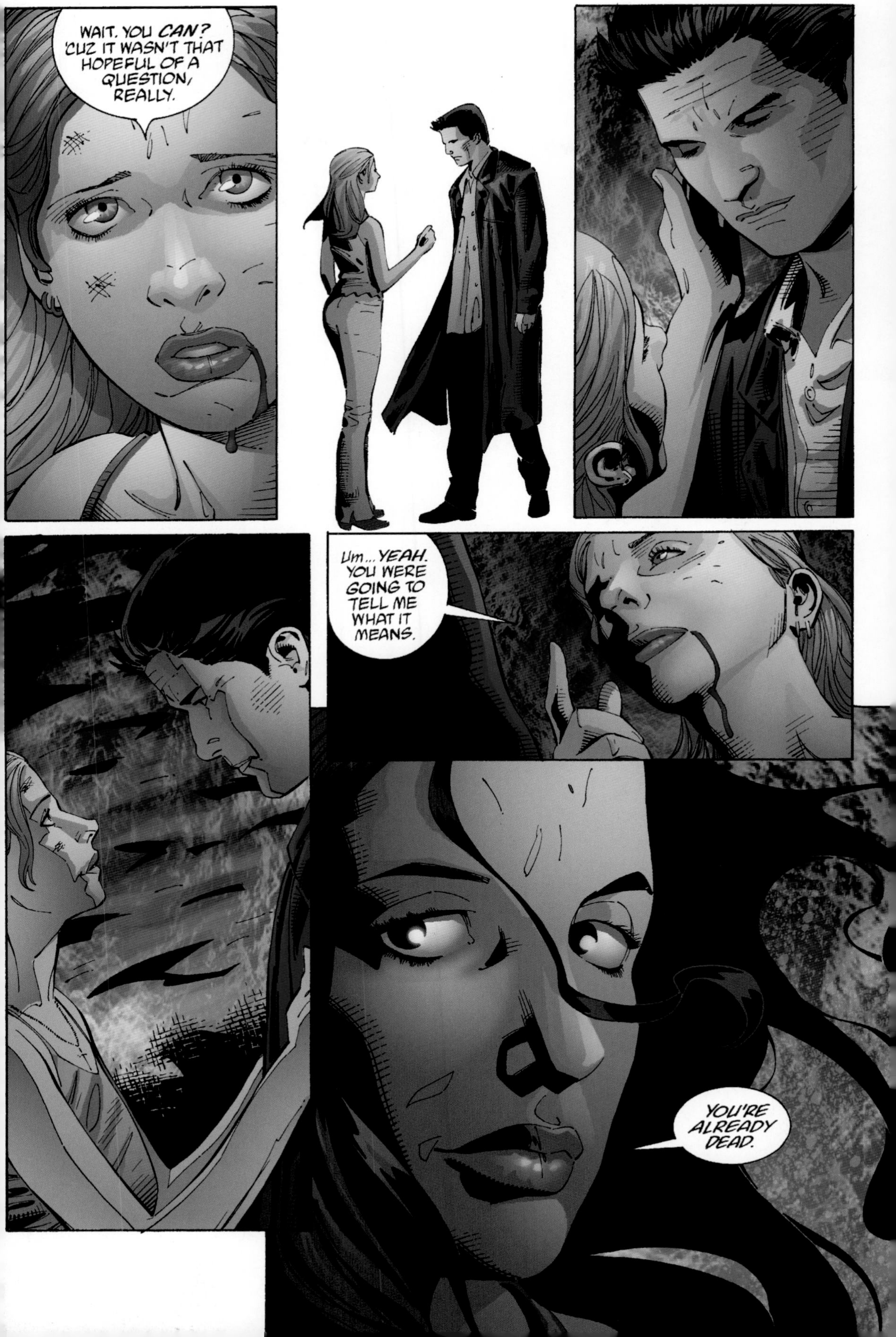
WAIT. YOU CAN? 'CUZ IT WASN'T THAT HOPEFUL OF A QUESTION, REALLY.
Um... YEAH. YOU WERE GOING TO TELL ME WHAT IT MEANS.
YOU'RE ALREADY DEAD.

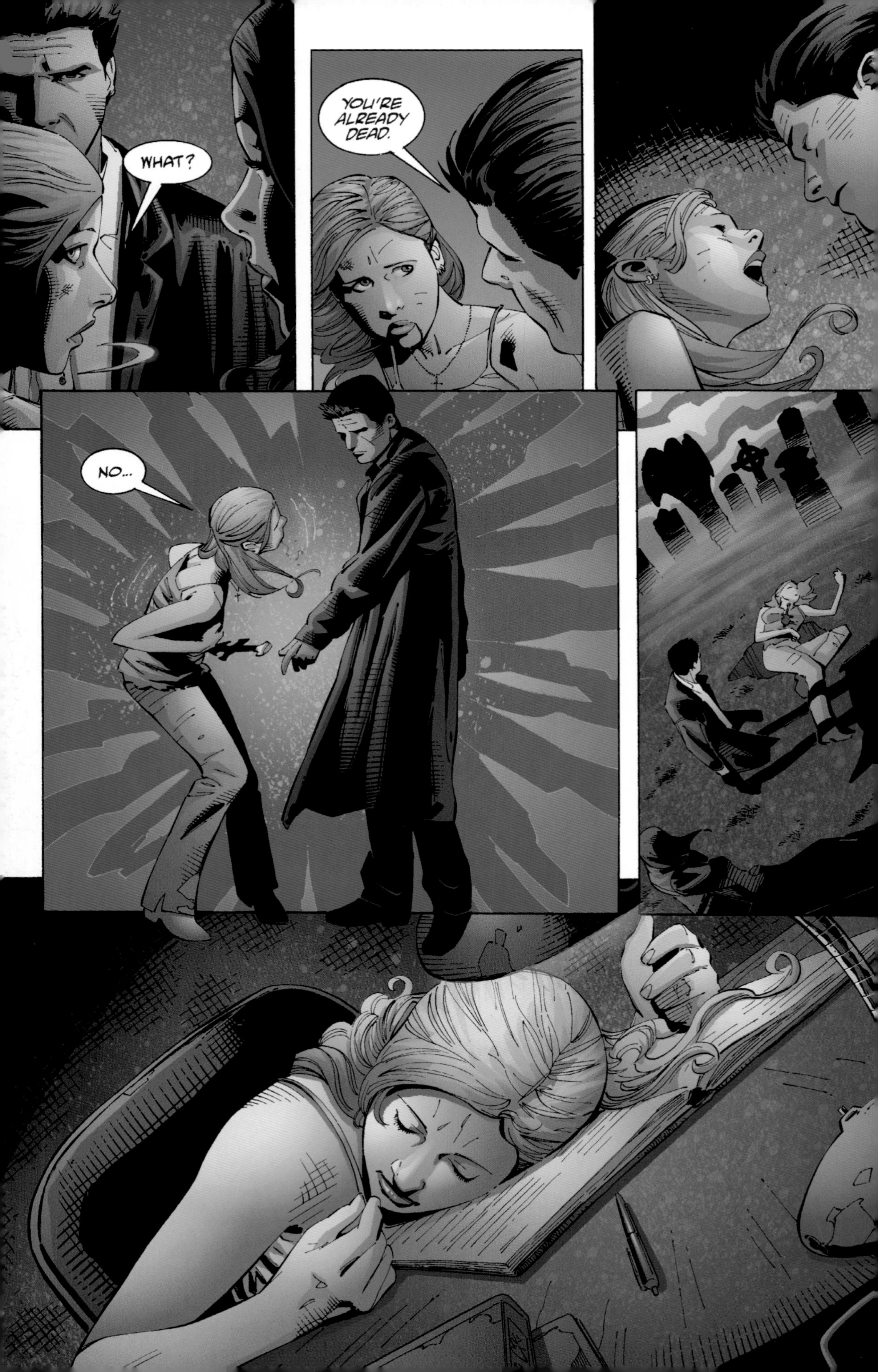
WHAT?
YOU'RE ALREADY DEAD.
NO...

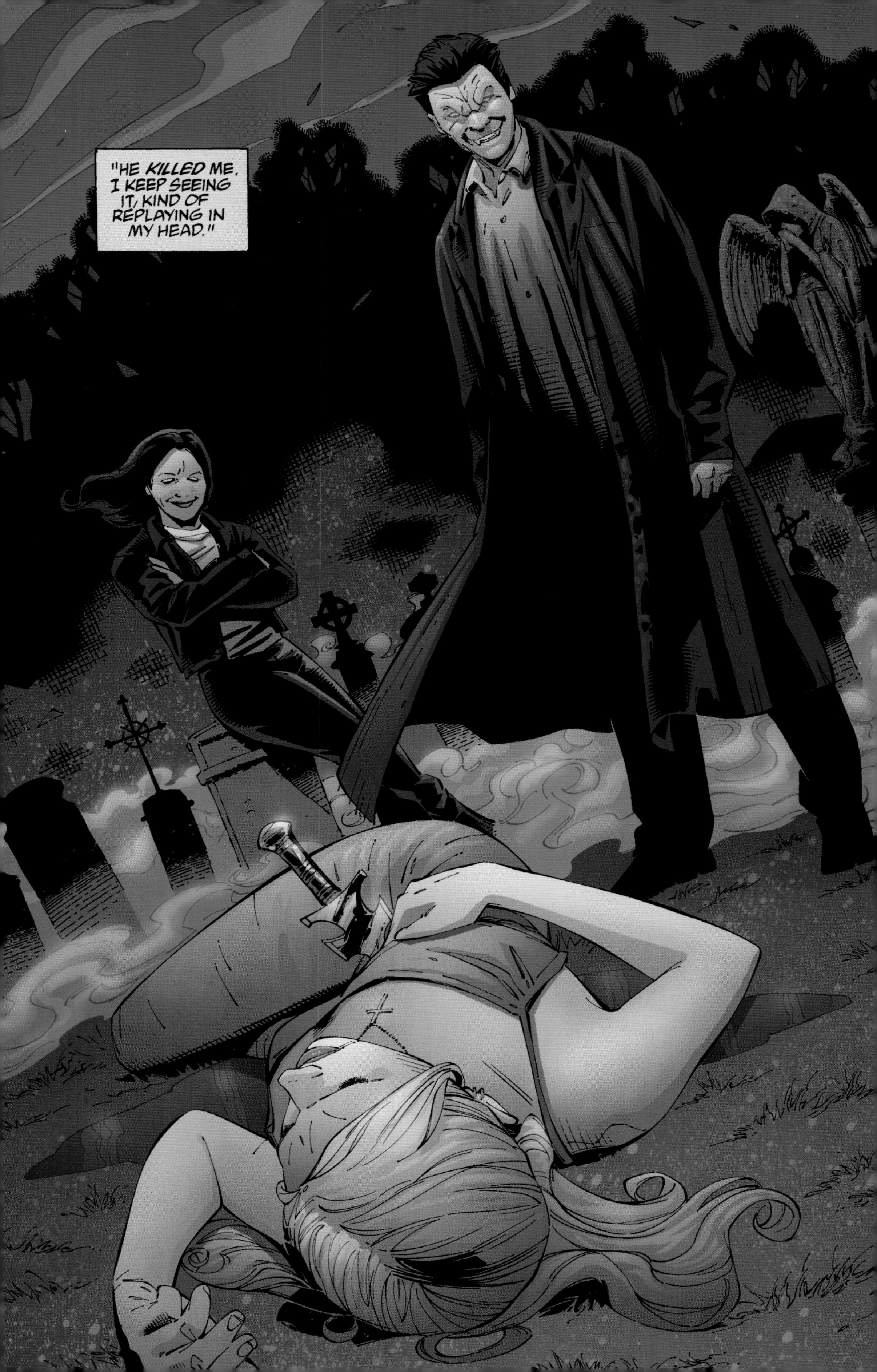
"HE KILLED ME. I KEEP SEEING IT, KIND OF REPLAYING IN MY HEAD."

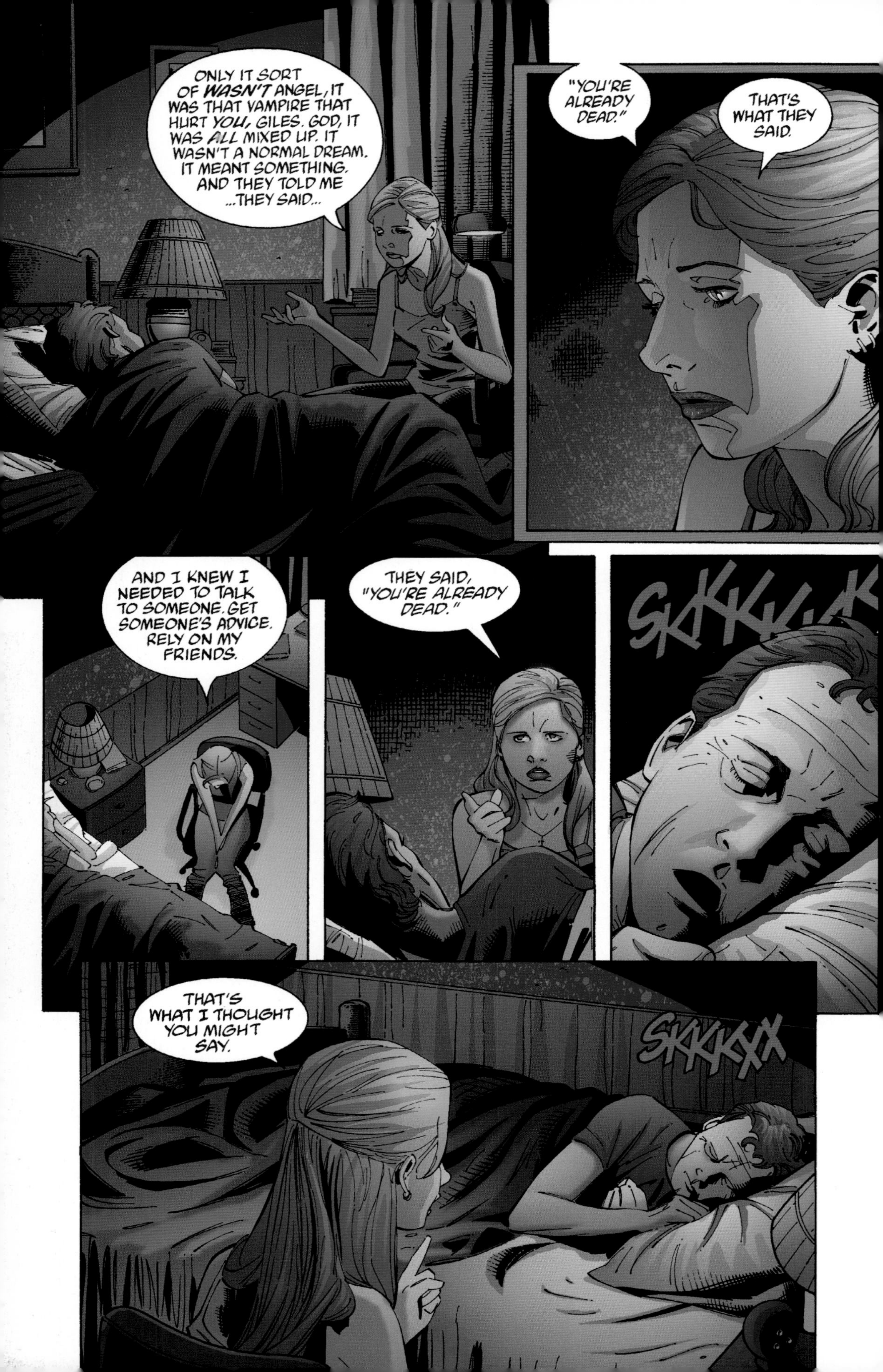
ONLY IT SORT OF WASN'T ANGEL, IT WAS THAT VAMPIRE THAT HURT YOU, GILES. GOD, IT WAS ALL MIXED UP. IT WASN'T A NORMAL DREAM. IT MEANT SOMETHING. AND THEY TOLD ME ...THEY SAID...
"YOU'RE ALREADY DEAD."
THAT'S WHAT THEY SAID.
AND I KNEW I NEEDED TO TALK TO SOMEONE. GET SOMEONE'S ADVICE. RELY ON MY FRIENDS.
THEY SAID, "YOU'RE ALREADY DEAD."
SKKKKK
THAT'S WHAT I THOUGHT YOU MIGHT SAY.
SKKKXX

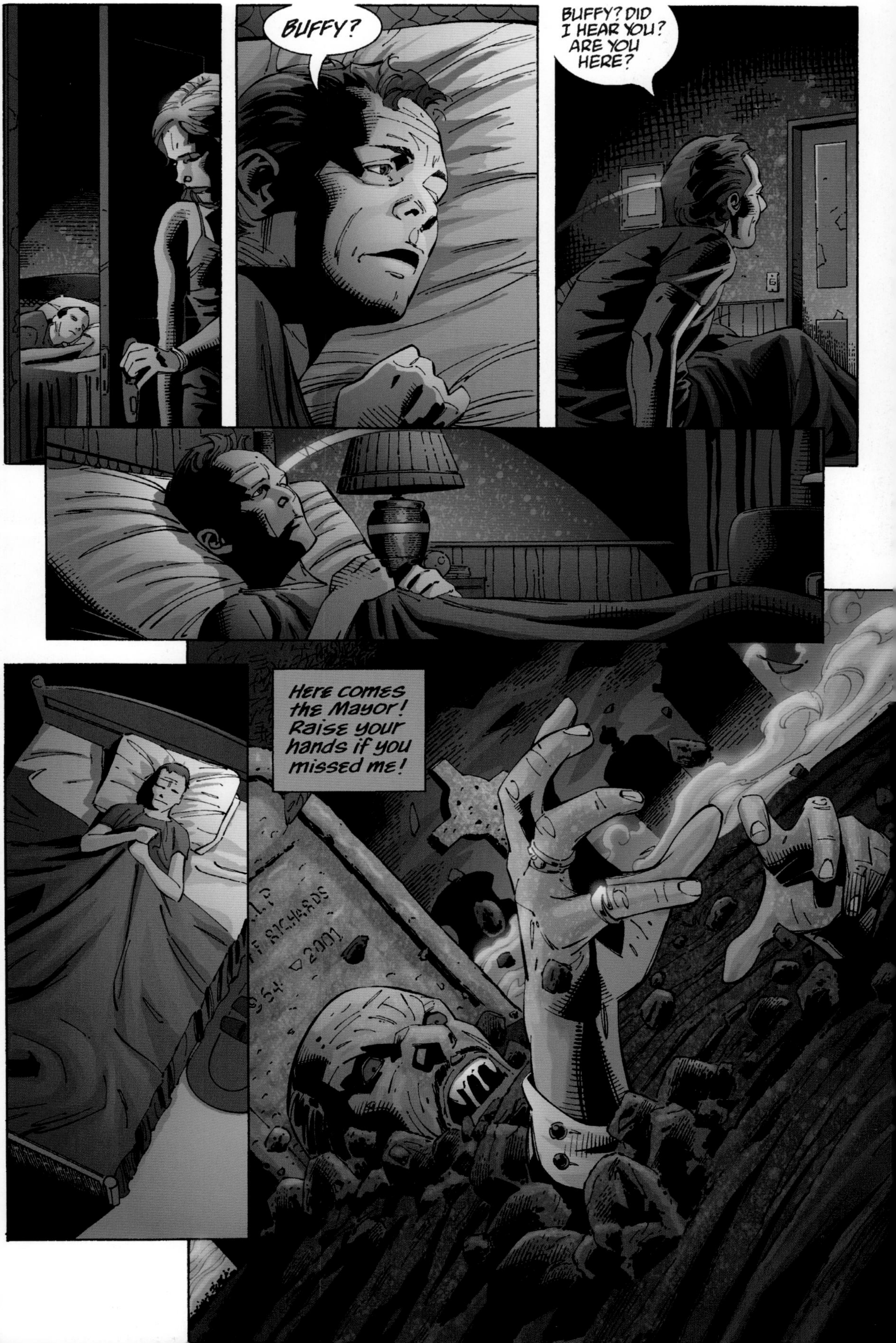
BUFFY?
BUFFY? DID I HEAR YOU? ARE YOU HERE?
Here comes the Mayor! Raise your hands if you missed me!

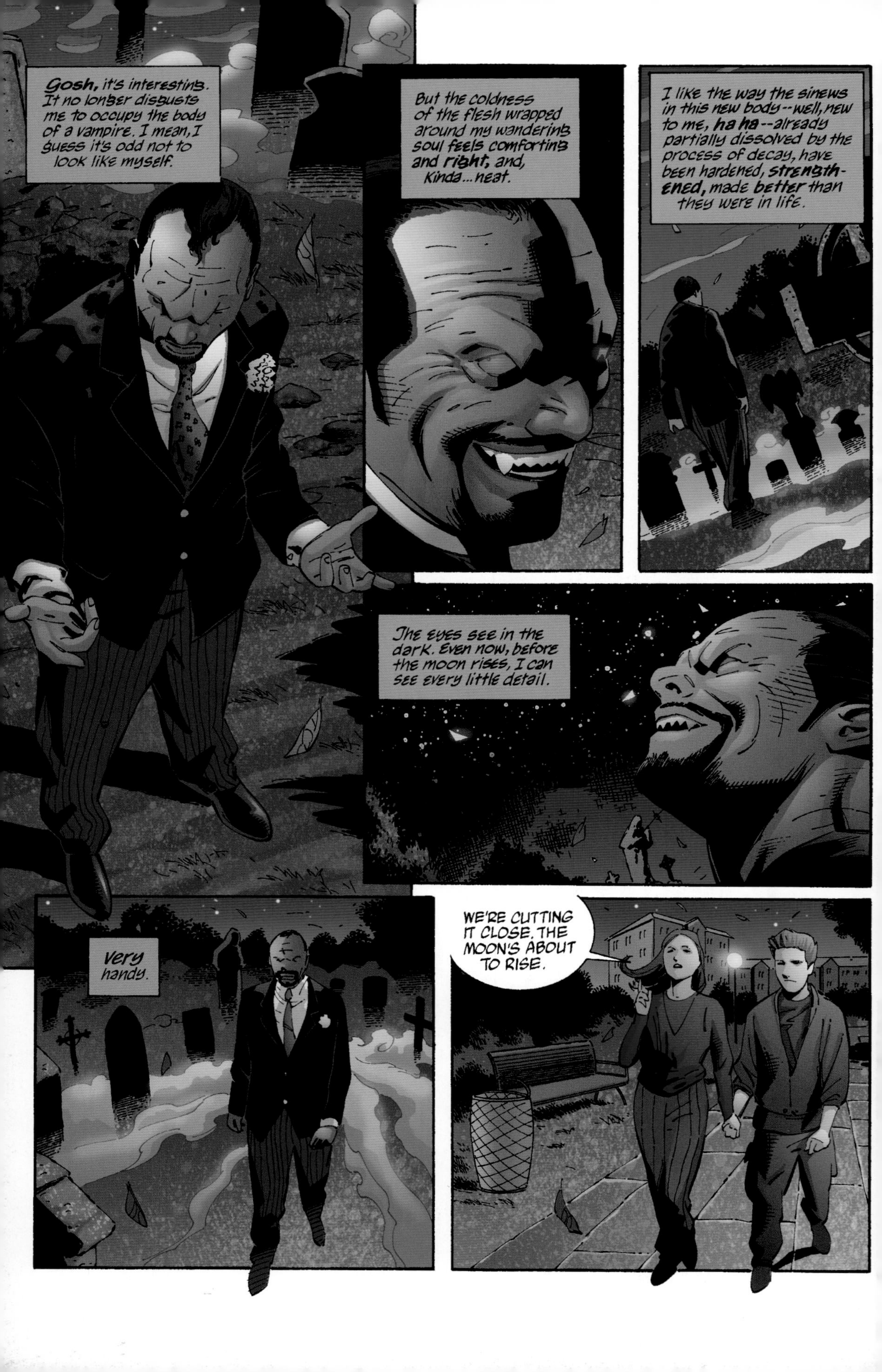
Gosh, it's interesting. It no longer disgusts me to occupy the body of a vampire. I mean, I guess it's odd not to look like myself.
But the coldness of the flesh wrapped around my wandering soul feels comforting and right, and, kinda... neat.
I like the way the sinews in this new body--well, new to me, ha ha--already partially dissolved by the process of decay, have been hardened, strength-ened, made better than they were in life.
The eyes see in the dark. Even now, before the moon rises, I can see every little detail.
Very handy.
WE'RE CUTTING IT CLOSE. THE MOON'S ABOUT TO RISE.

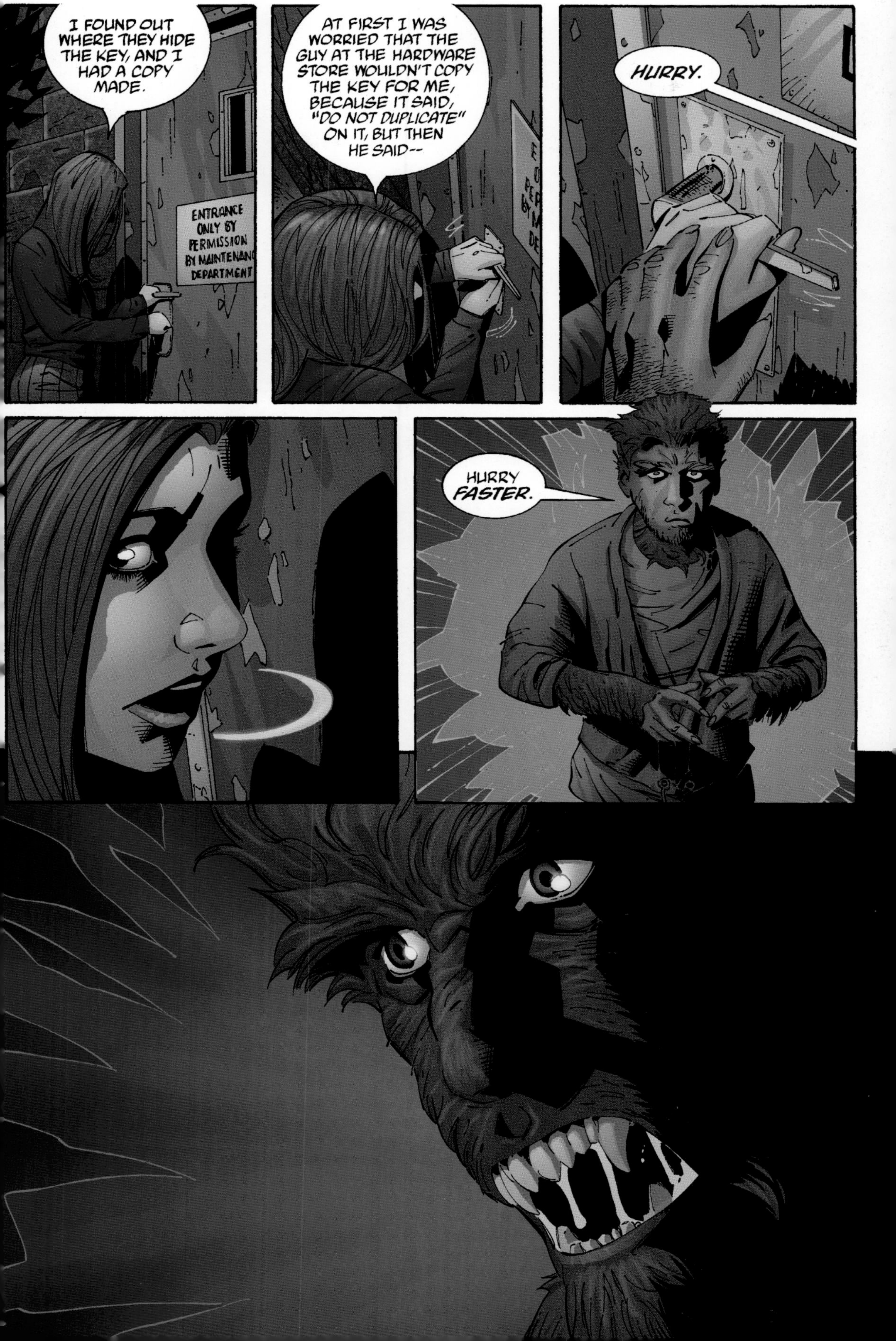
I FOUND OUT WHERE THEY HIDE THE KEY, AND I HAD A COPY MADE.
ENTRANCE ONLY BY PERMISSION BY MAINTENANCE DEPARTMENT
AT FIRST I WAS WORRIED THAT THE GUY AT THE HARDWARE STORE WOULDN'T COPY THE KEY FOR ME, BECAUSE IT SAID, "DO NOT DUPLICATE" ON IT, BUT THEN HE SAID--
HURRY.
HURRY FASTER.

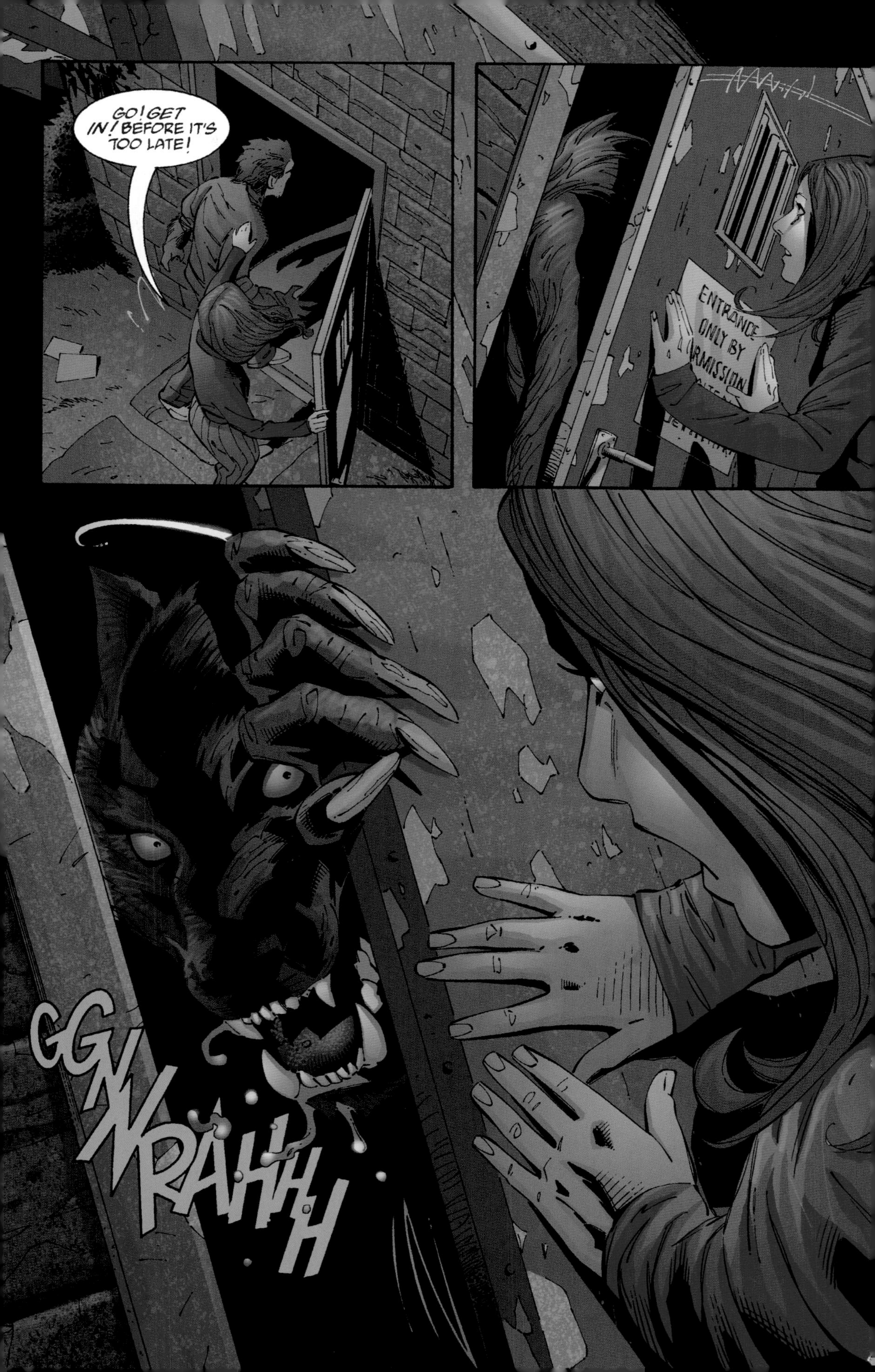
GO! GET IN! BEFORE IT'S TOO LATE!
ENTRANCE ONLY BY [P]ERMISSION
GGNNRAHHHH

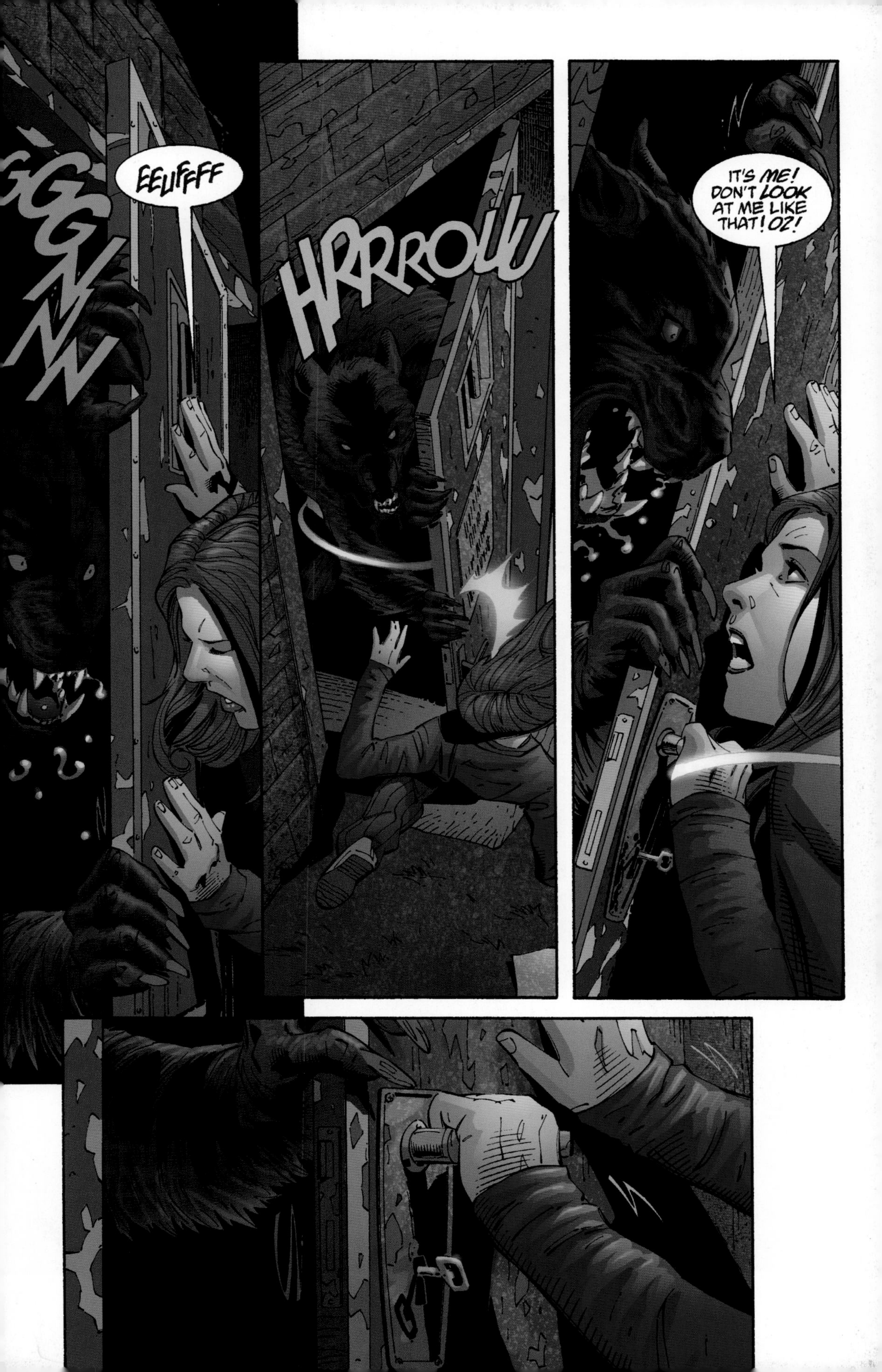

GGGNNN
EEUFFFF
HRRROUU
IT'S ME! DON'T LOOK AT ME LIKE THAT! OZ!

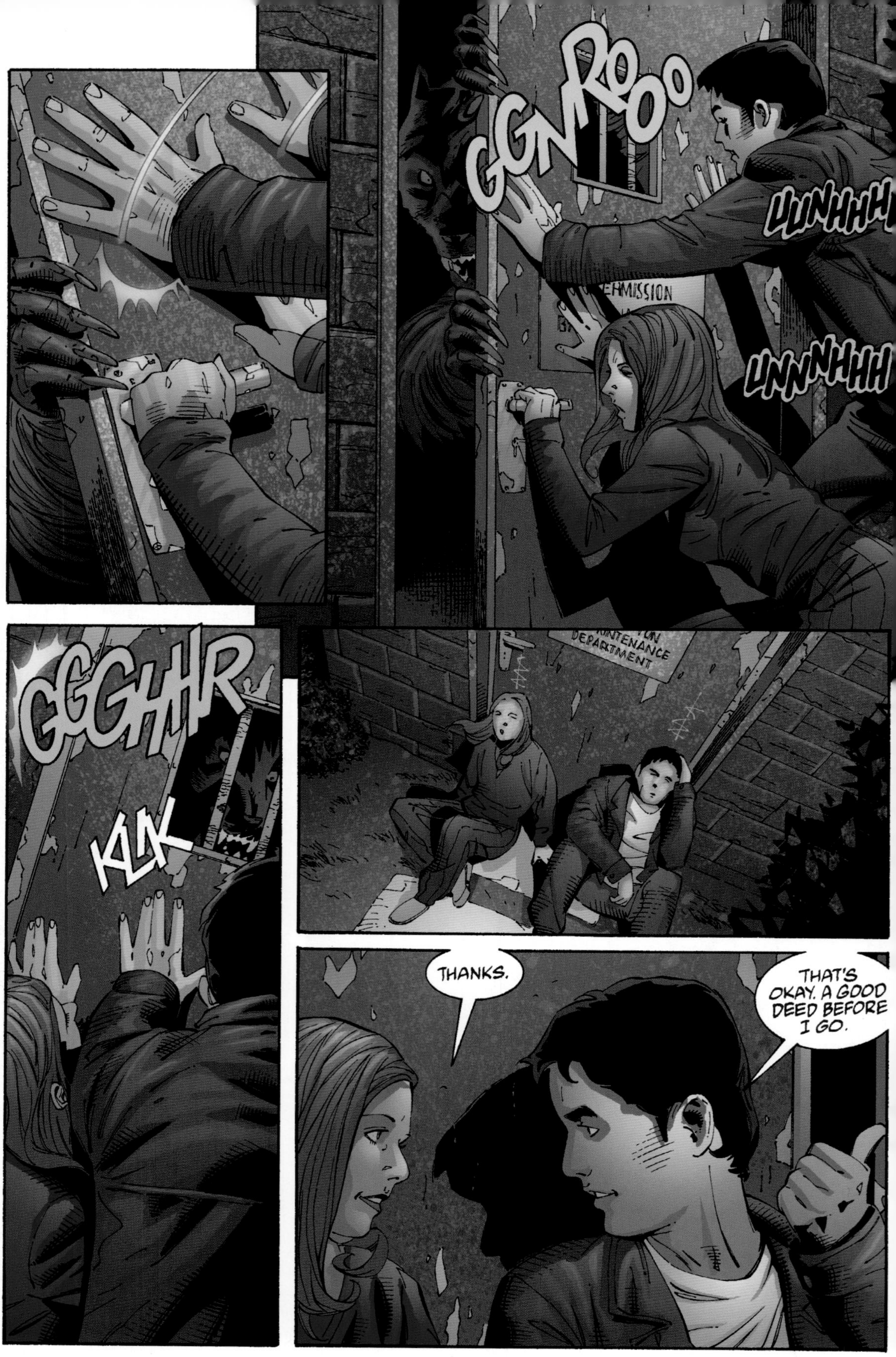
GGNROOO
UUNHHH
UNNHHH
GGGHR
KLIK
THANKS.
THAT'S OKAY. A GOOD DEED BEFORE I GO.

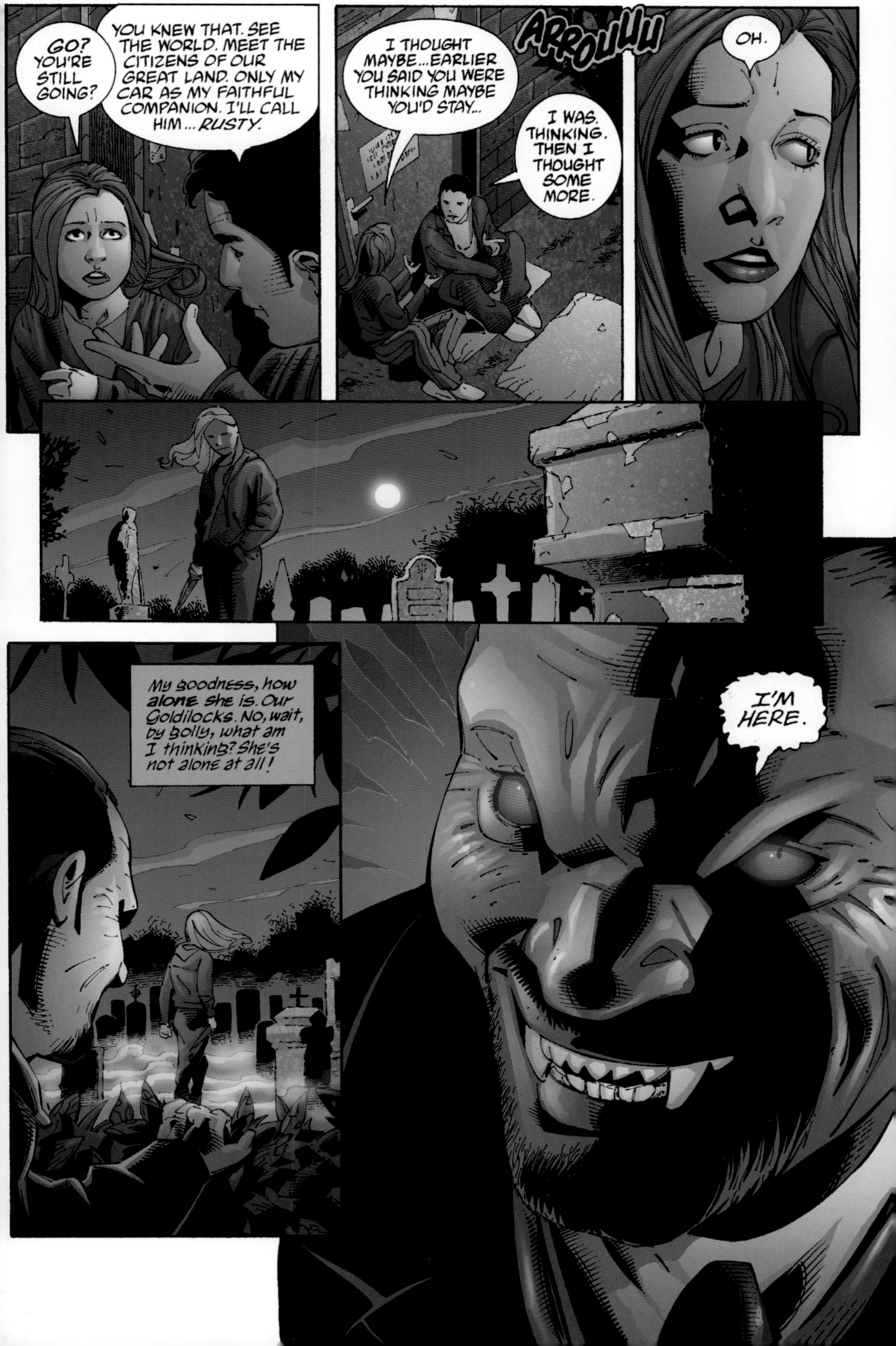
GO? YOU'RE STILL GOING?
YOU KNEW THAT. SEE THE WORLD. MEET THE CITIZENS OF OUR GREAT LAND. ONLY MY CAR AS MY FAITHFUL COMPANION. I'LL CALL HIM... RUSTY.
I THOUGHT MAYBE... EARLIER YOU SAID YOU WERE THINKING MAYBE YOU'D STAY...
I WAS. THINKING. THEN I THOUGHT SOME MORE.
ARROUUUU
OH.
My goodness, how alone she is. Our Goldilocks. No, wait, by golly, what am I thinking? She's not alone at all!
I'M HERE.

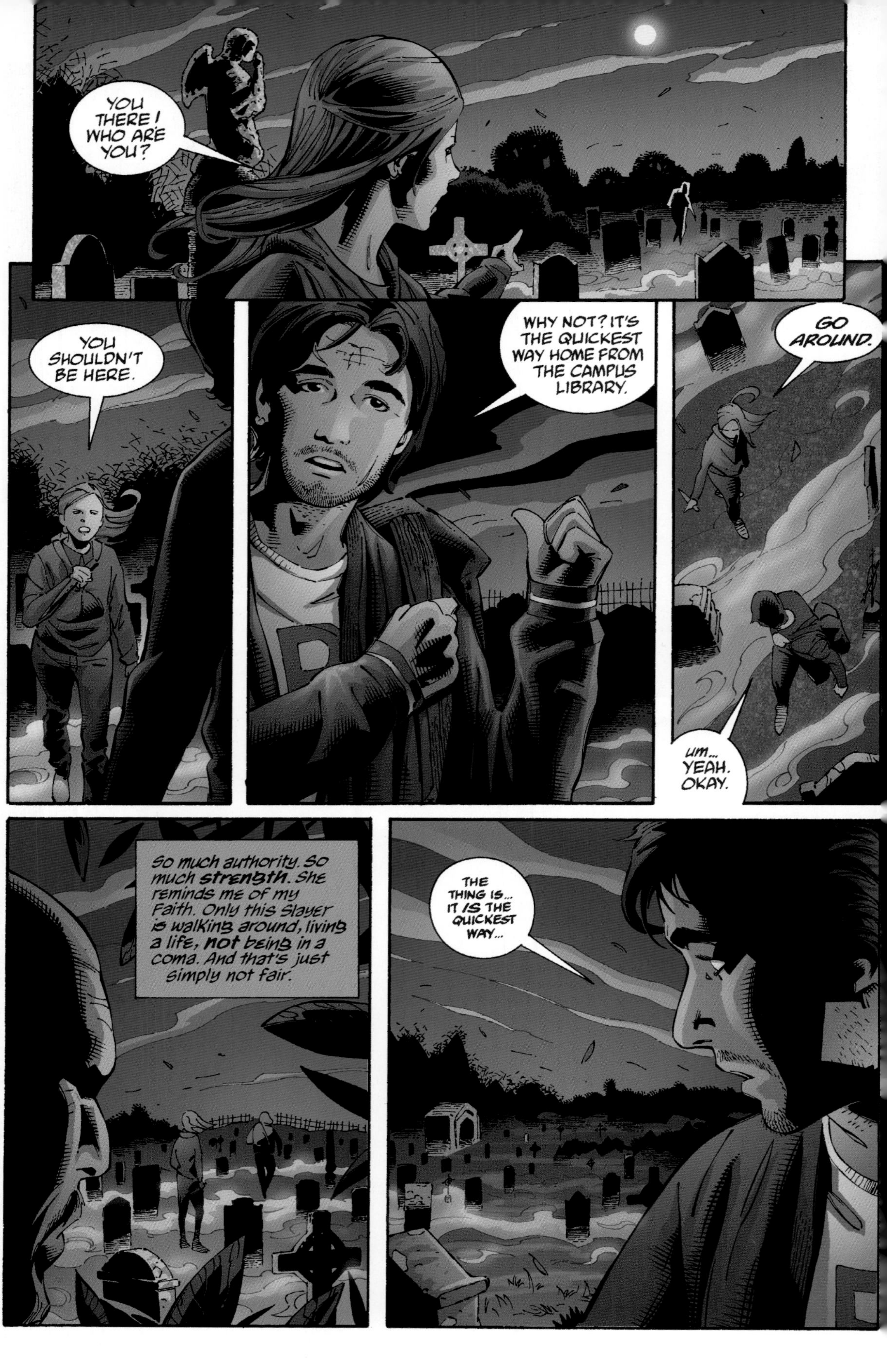

YOU THERE! WHO ARE YOU?
YOU SHOULDN'T BE HERE.
WHY NOT? IT'S THE QUICKEST WAY HOME FROM THE CAMPUS LIBRARY.
GO AROUND.
UM... YEAH. OKAY.
So much authority. So much strength. She reminds me of my Faith. Only this Slayer is walking around, living a life, not being in a coma. And that's just simply not fair.
THE THING IS... IT IS THE QUICKEST WAY...

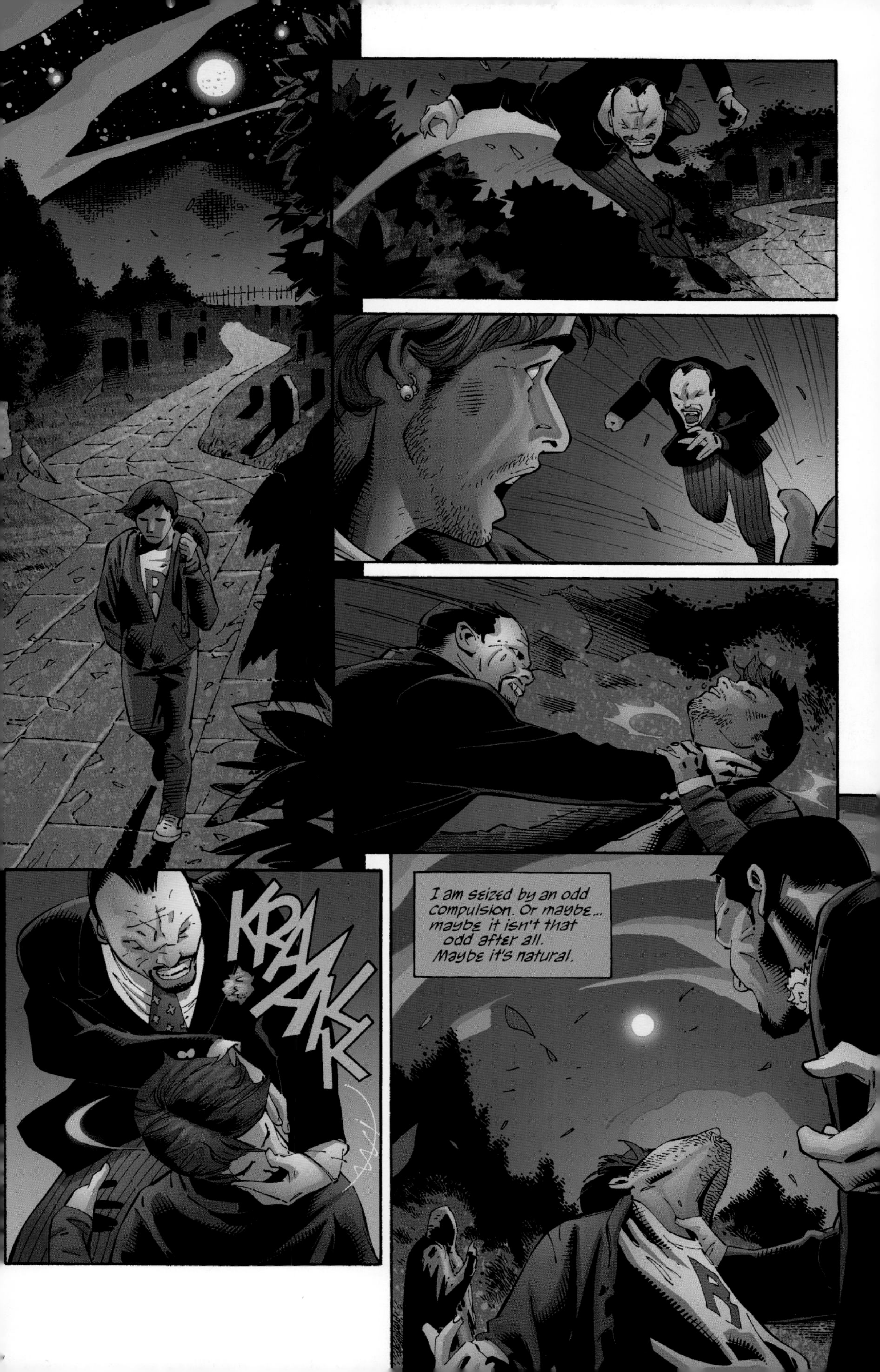
KRAKAKK
I am seized by an odd compulsion. Or maybe... maybe it isn't that odd after all. Maybe it's natural.

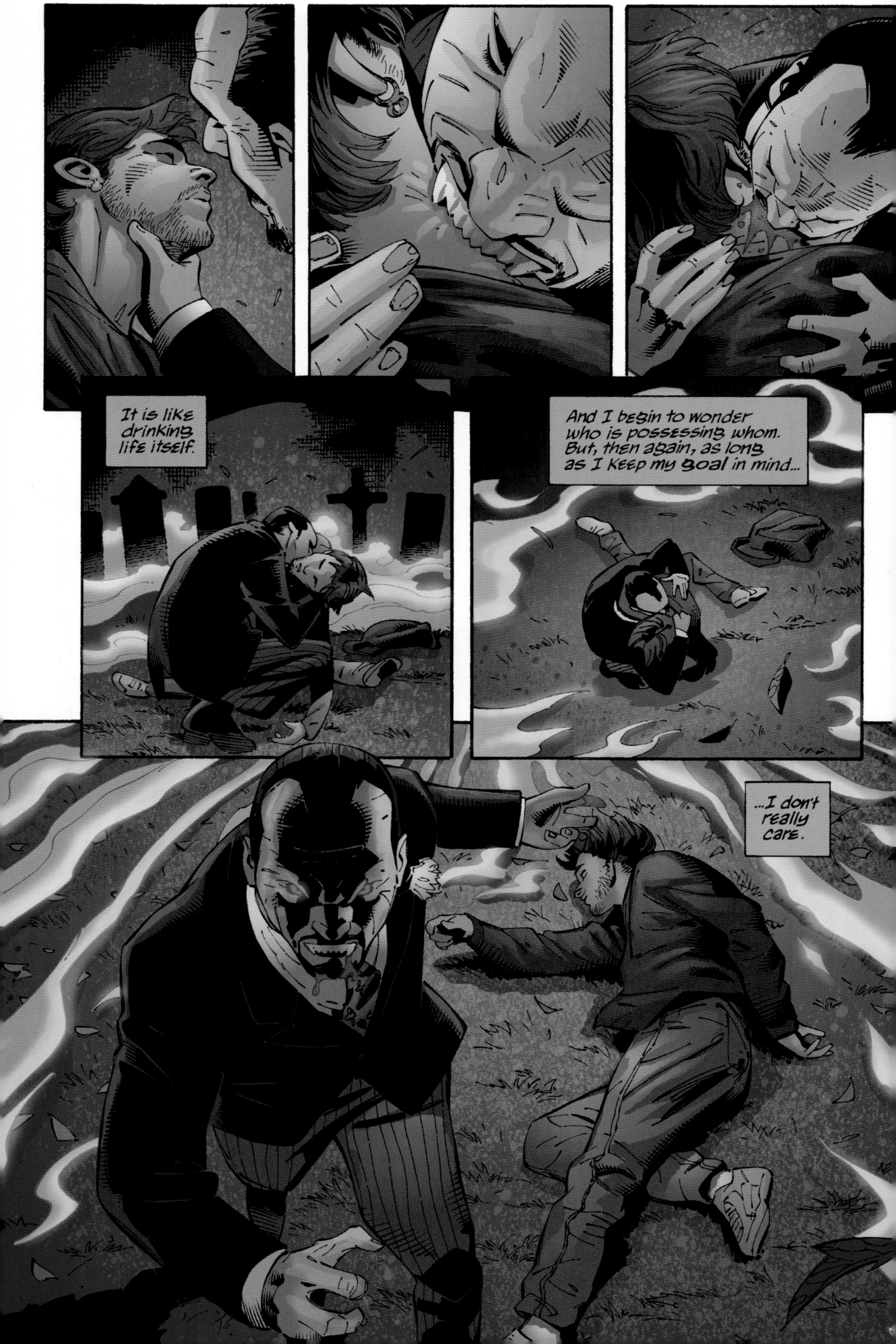
It is like drinking life itself.
And I begin to wonder who is possessing whom. But, then again, as long as I keep my goal in mind...
...I don't really care.

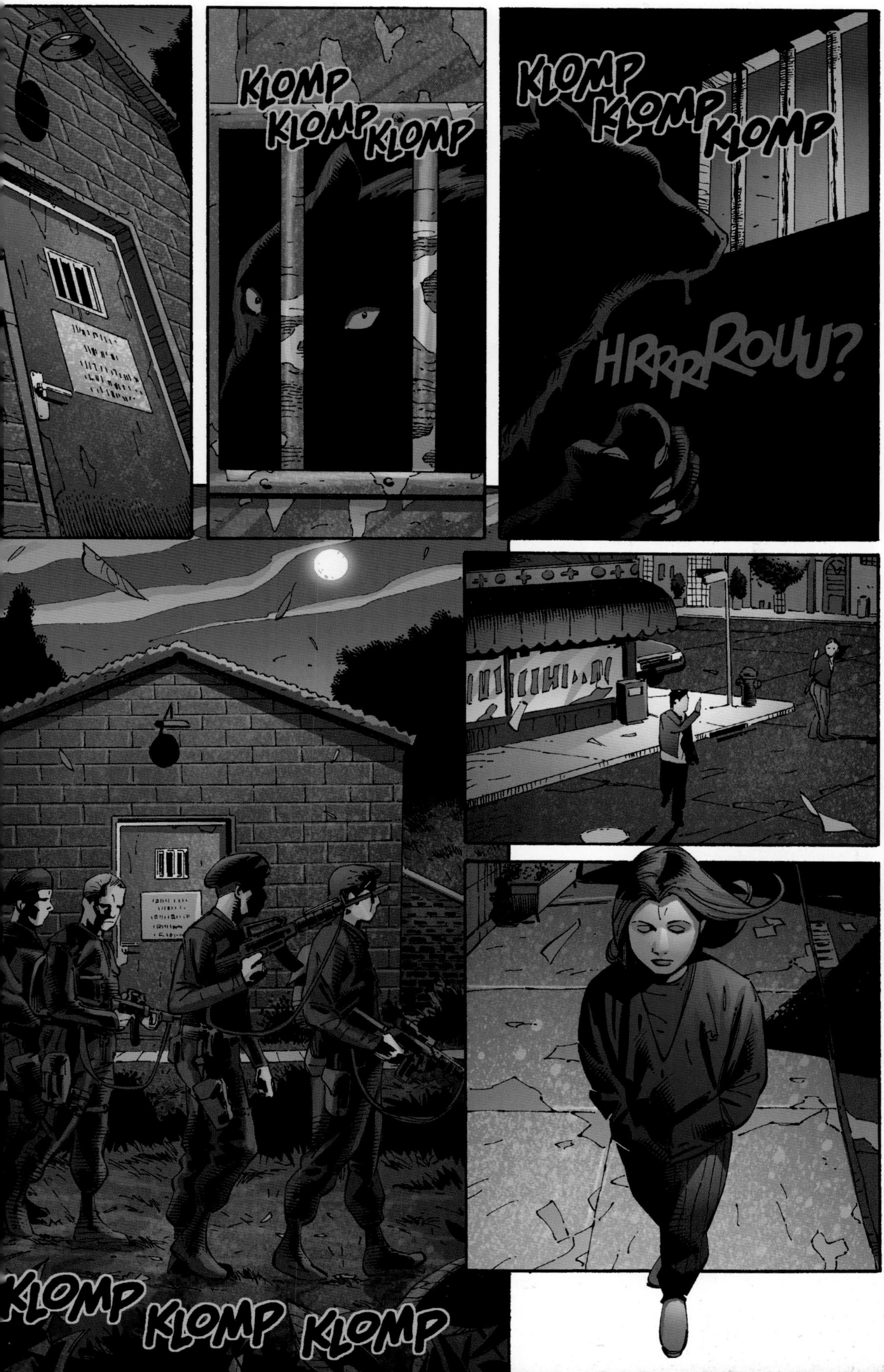
KLOMP
KLOMP KLOMP
KLOMP
KLOMP KLOMP
KLOMP
HRRRROUU?
KLOMP KLOMP KLOMP

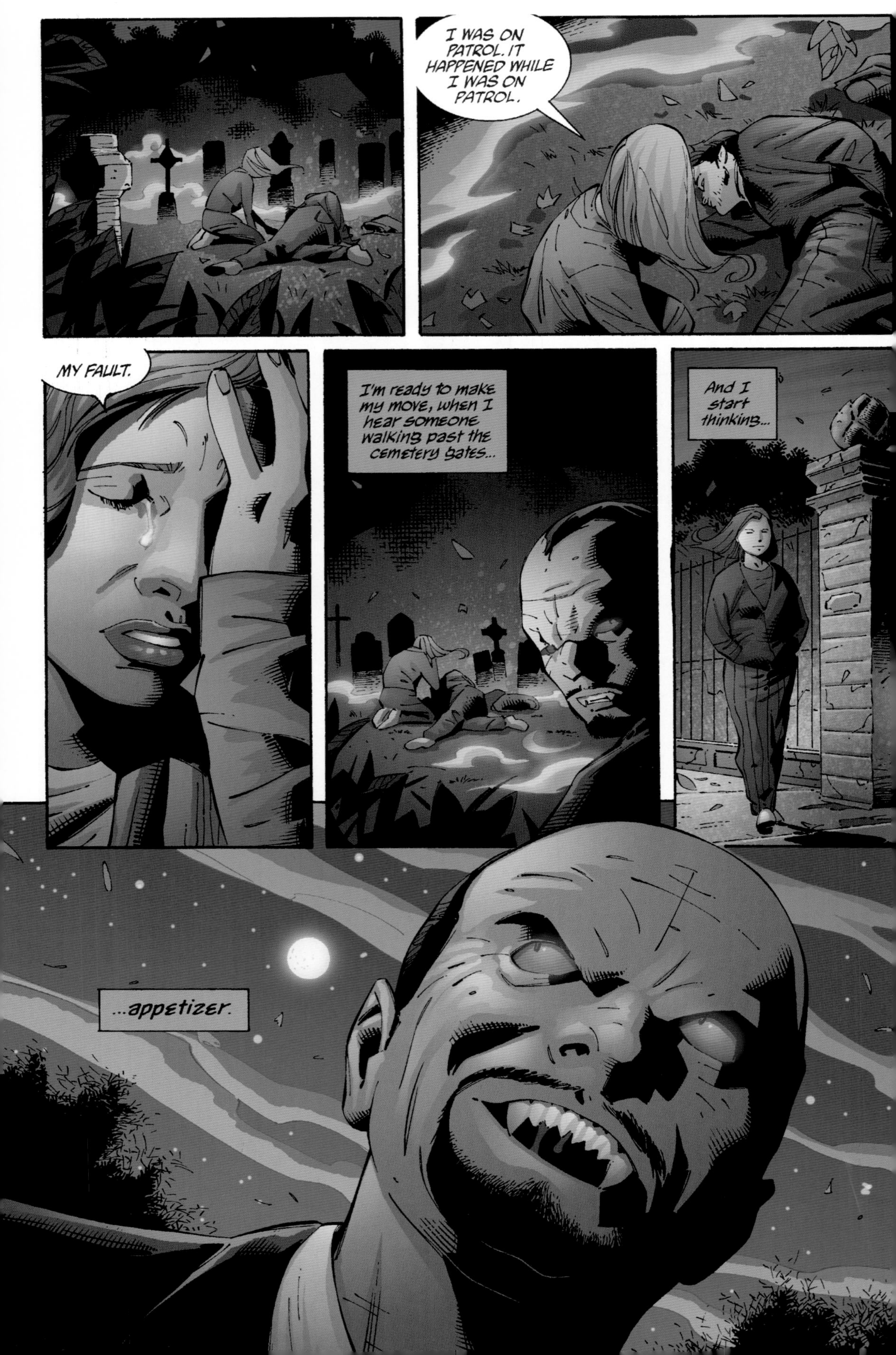

I WAS ON PATROL. IT HAPPENED WHILE I WAS ON PATROL.
MY FAULT.
I'm ready to make my move, when I hear someone walking past the cemetery gates...
And I start thinking...
...appetizer.

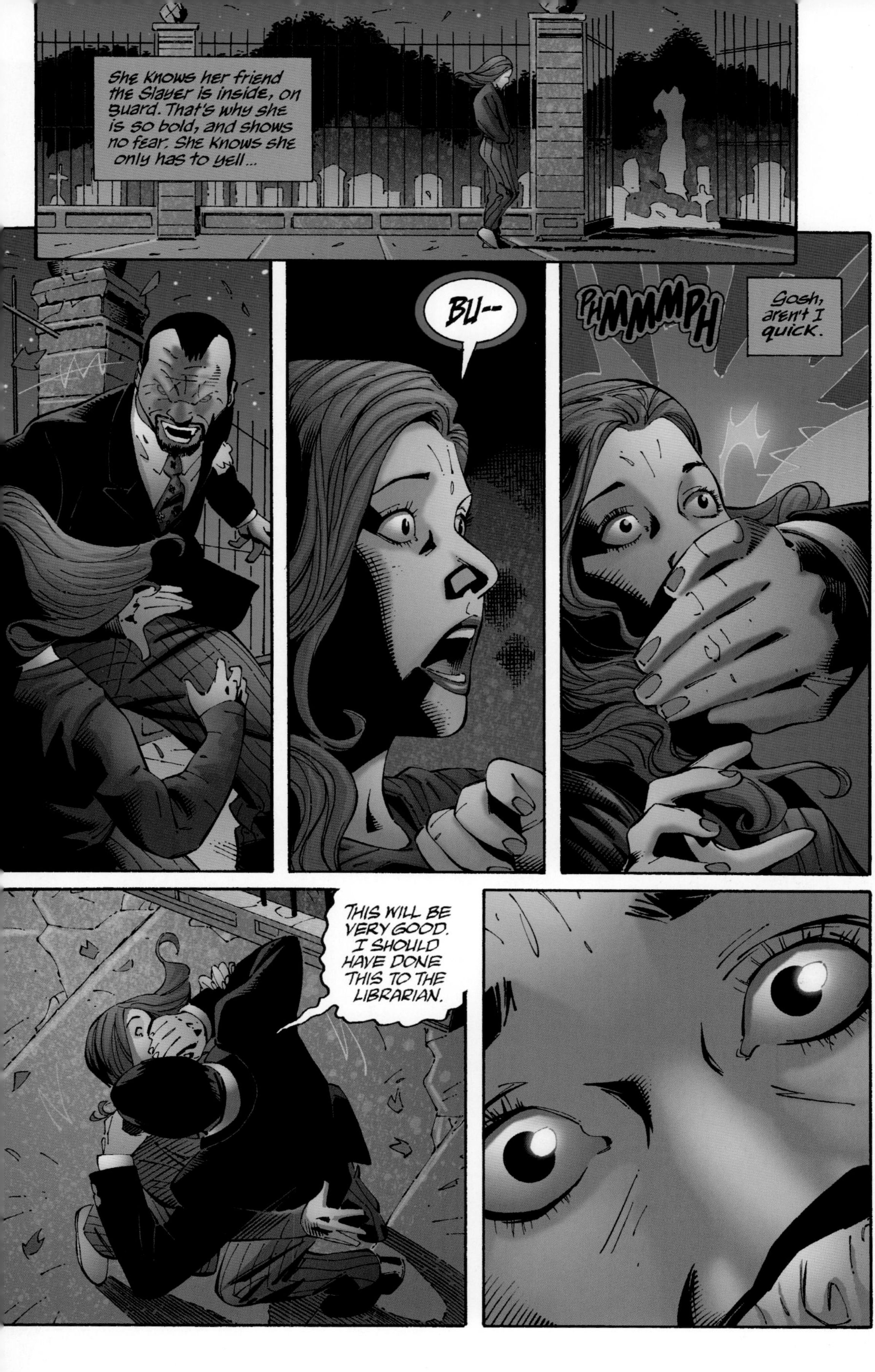
She knows her friend the Slayer is inside, on guard. That's why she is so bold, and shows no fear. She knows she only has to yell...
BU--
PHMMMPH
Gosh, aren't I quick.
THIS WILL BE VERY GOOD. I SHOULD HAVE DONE THIS TO THE LIBRARIAN.

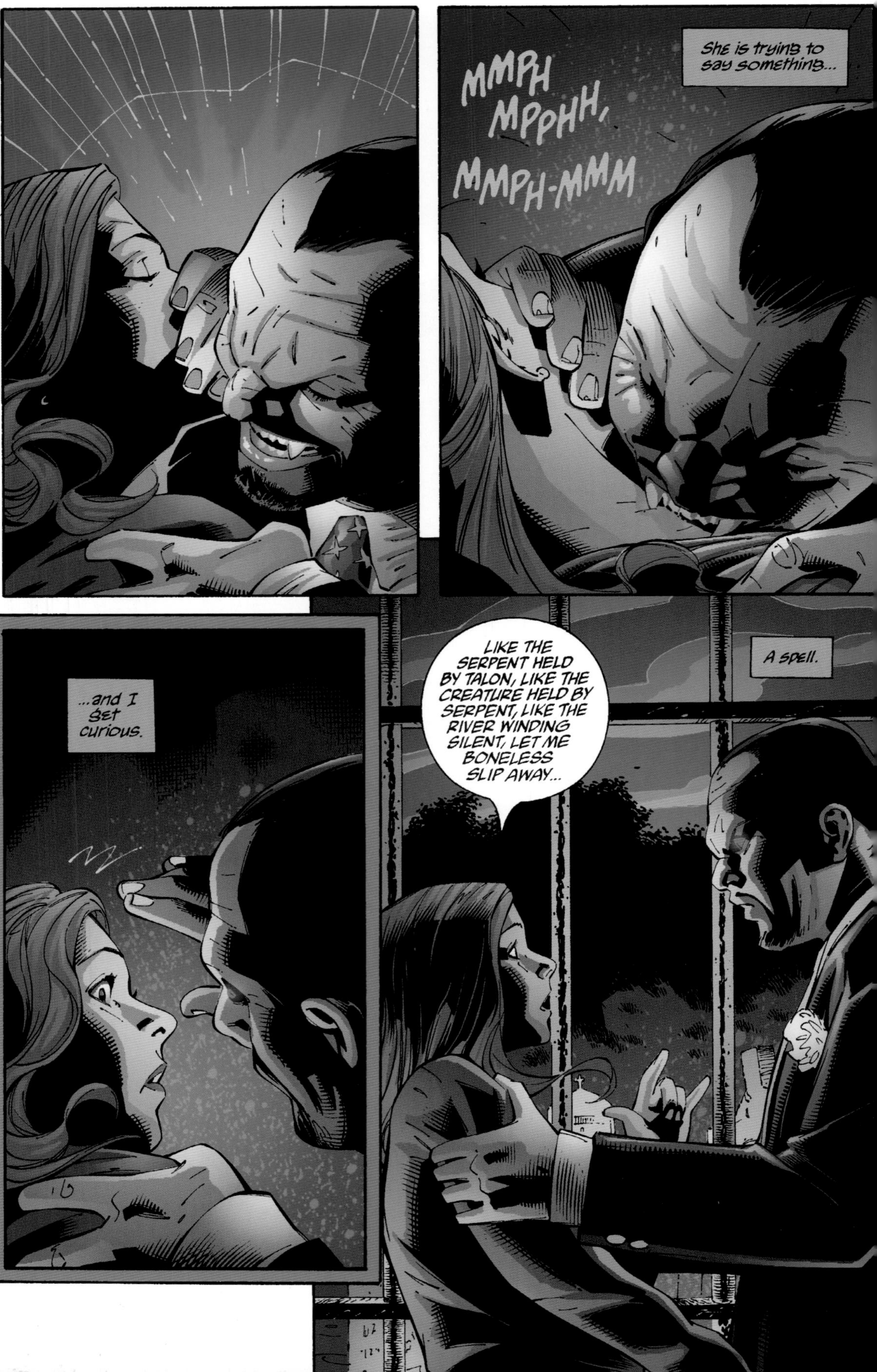
She is trying to say something...
MMPH MPPHH, MMPH-MMM
...and I get curious.
A spell.
LIKE THE SERPENT HELD BY TALON, LIKE THE CREATURE HELD BY SERPENT, LIKE THE RIVER WINDING SILENT, LET ME BONELESS SLIP AWAY...

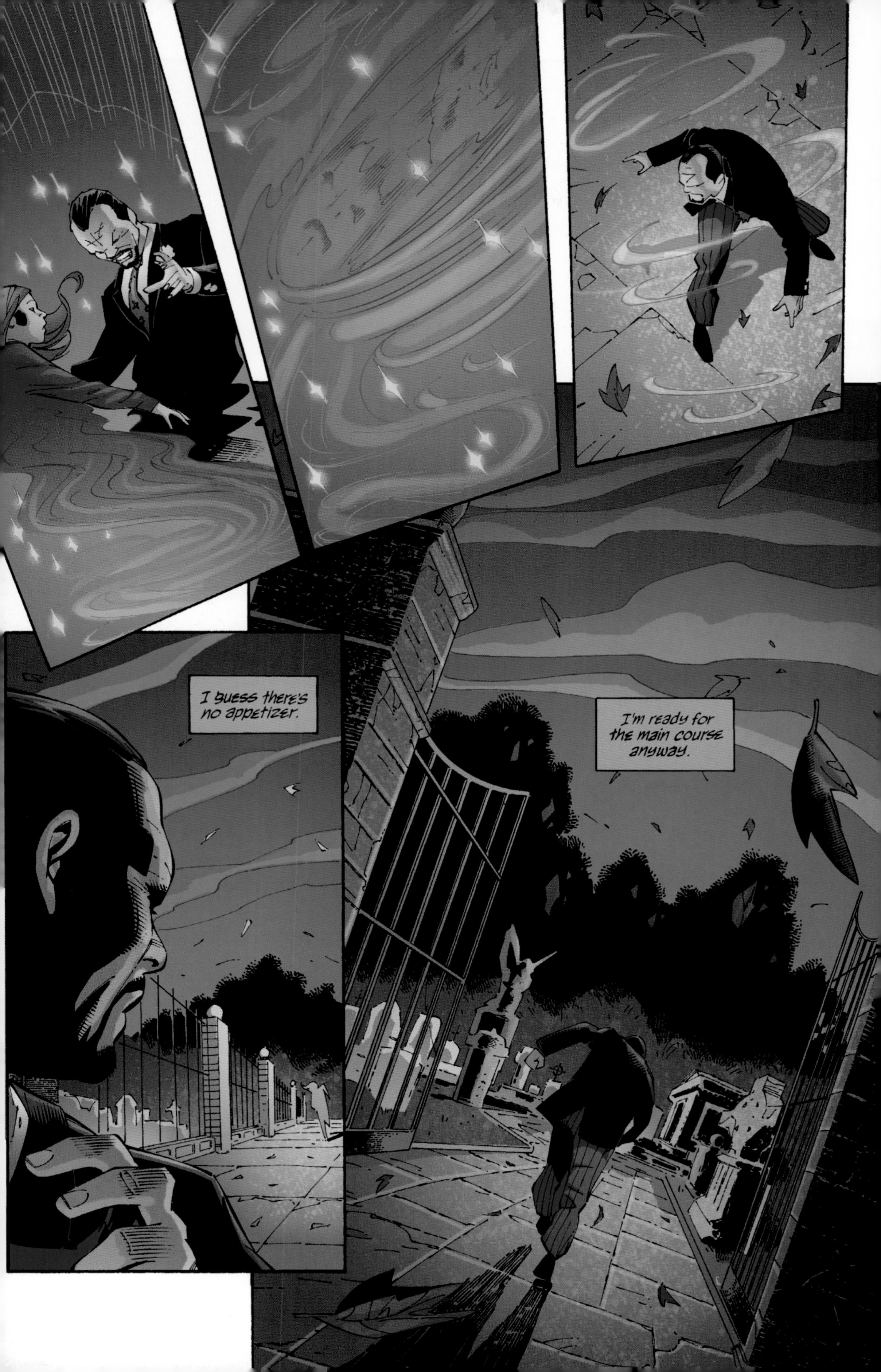
I guess there's no appetizer.
I'm ready for the main course anyway.

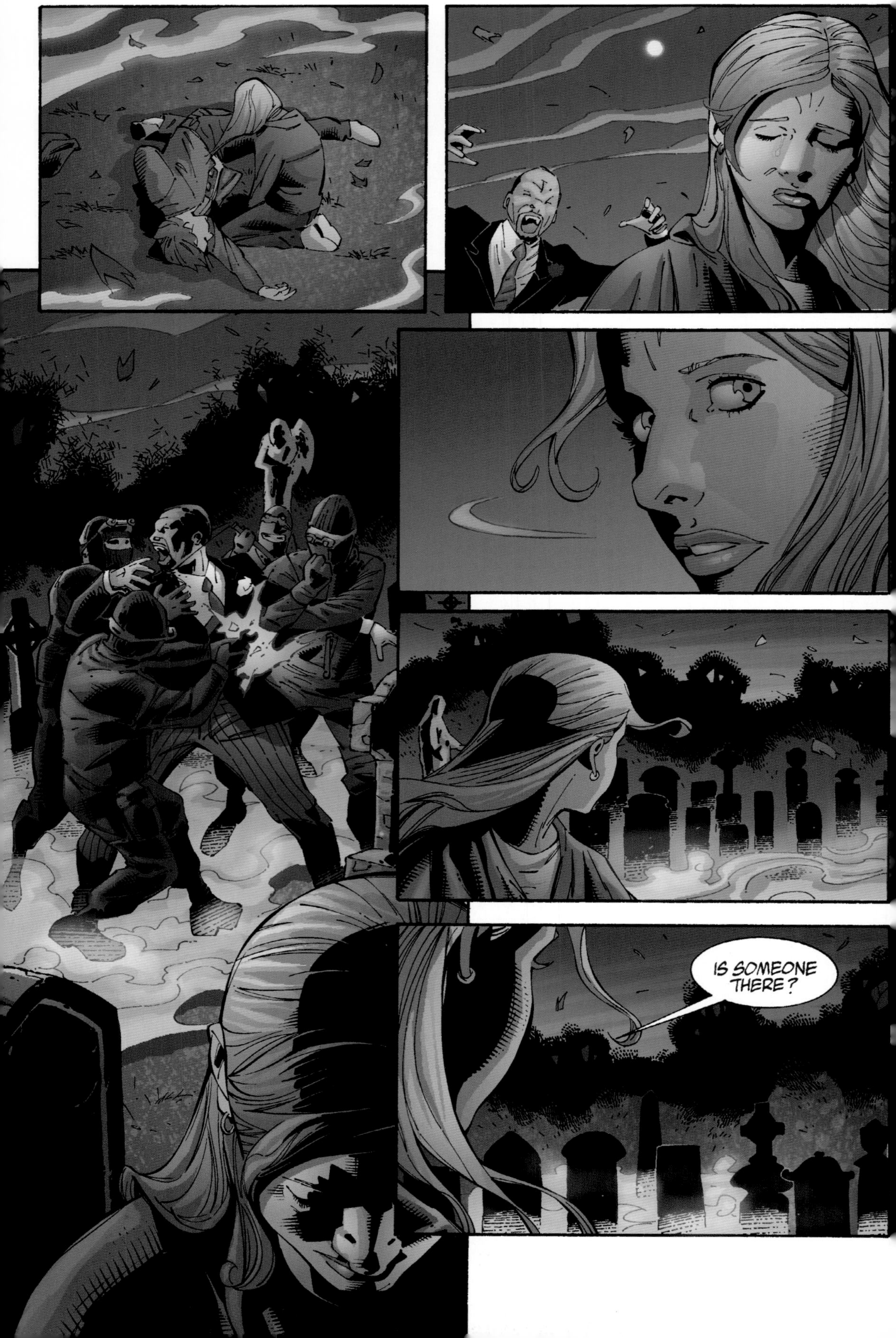
IS SOMEONE THERE?

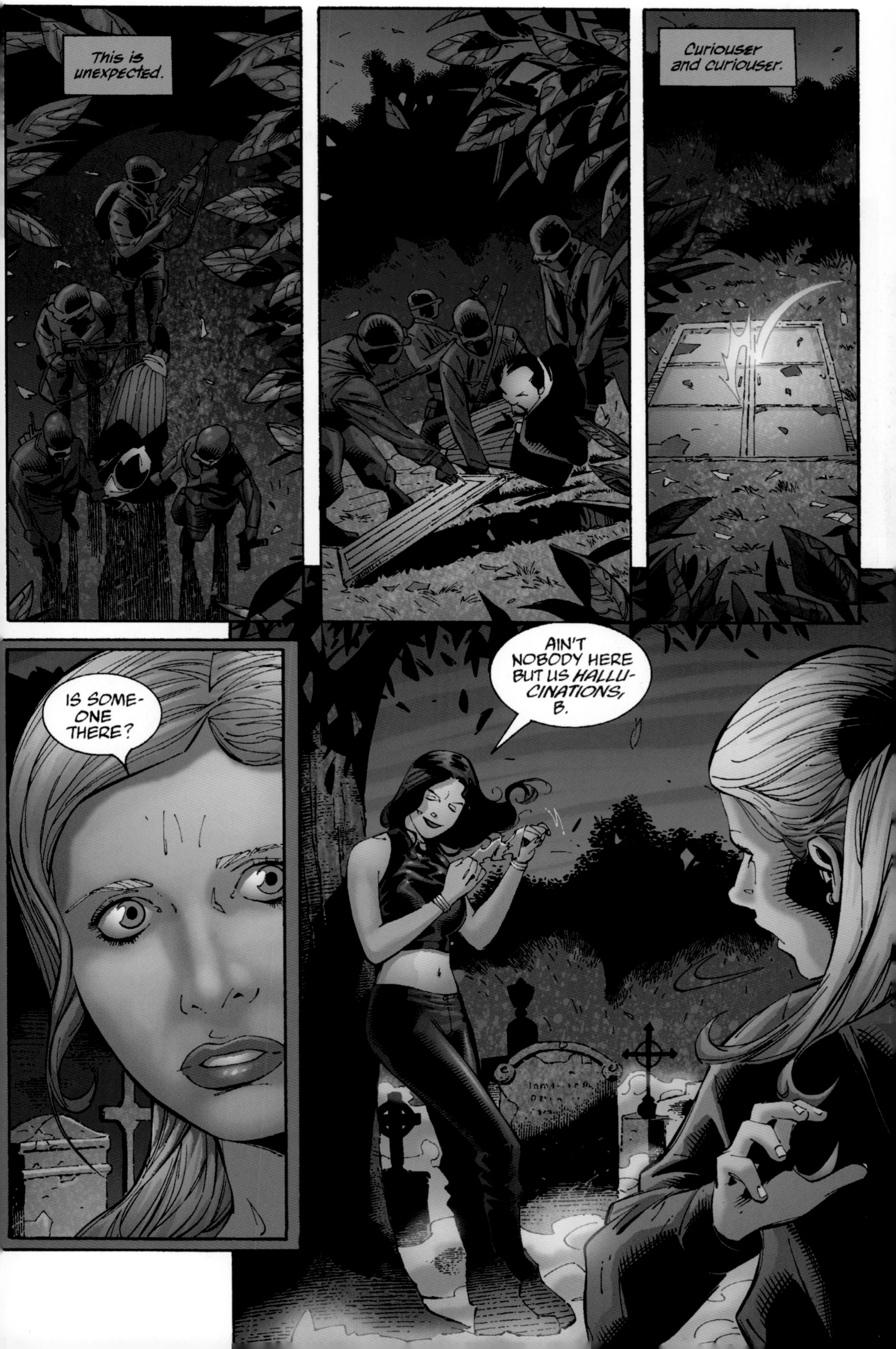
This is unexpected.
Curiouser and curiouser.
IS SOME-ONE THERE?
AIN'T NOBODY HERE BUT US HALLU-CINATIONS, B.

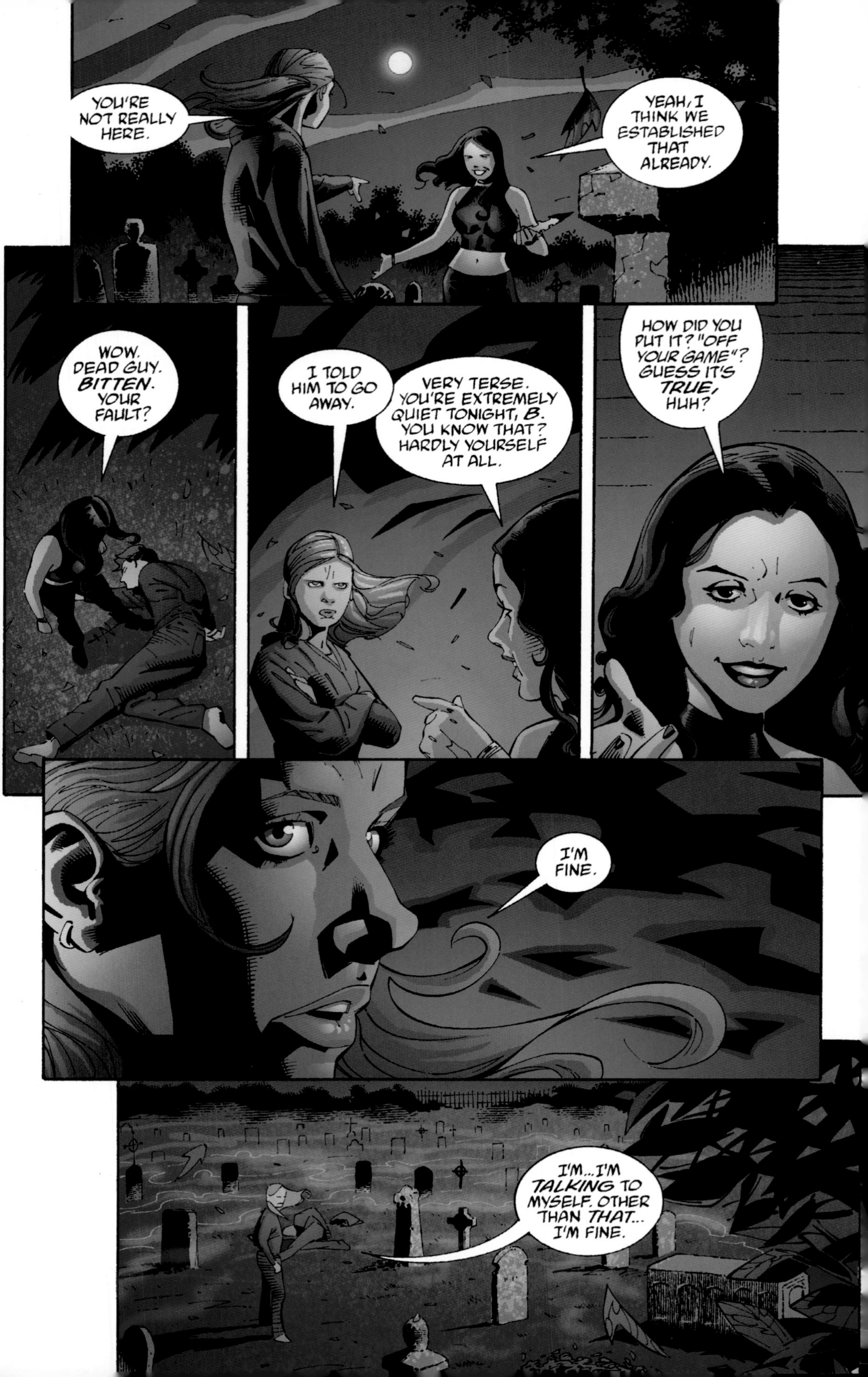
YOU'RE NOT REALLY HERE.
YEAH, I THINK WE ESTABLISHED THAT ALREADY.
WOW. DEAD GUY. BITTEN. YOUR FAULT?
I TOLD HIM TO GO AWAY.
VERY TERSE. YOU'RE EXTREMELY QUIET TONIGHT, B. YOU KNOW THAT? HARDLY YOURSELF AT ALL.
HOW DID YOU PUT IT? "OFF YOUR GAME"? GUESS IT'S TRUE, HUH?
I'M FINE.
I'M...I'M TALKING TO MYSELF. OTHER THAN THAT... I'M FINE.

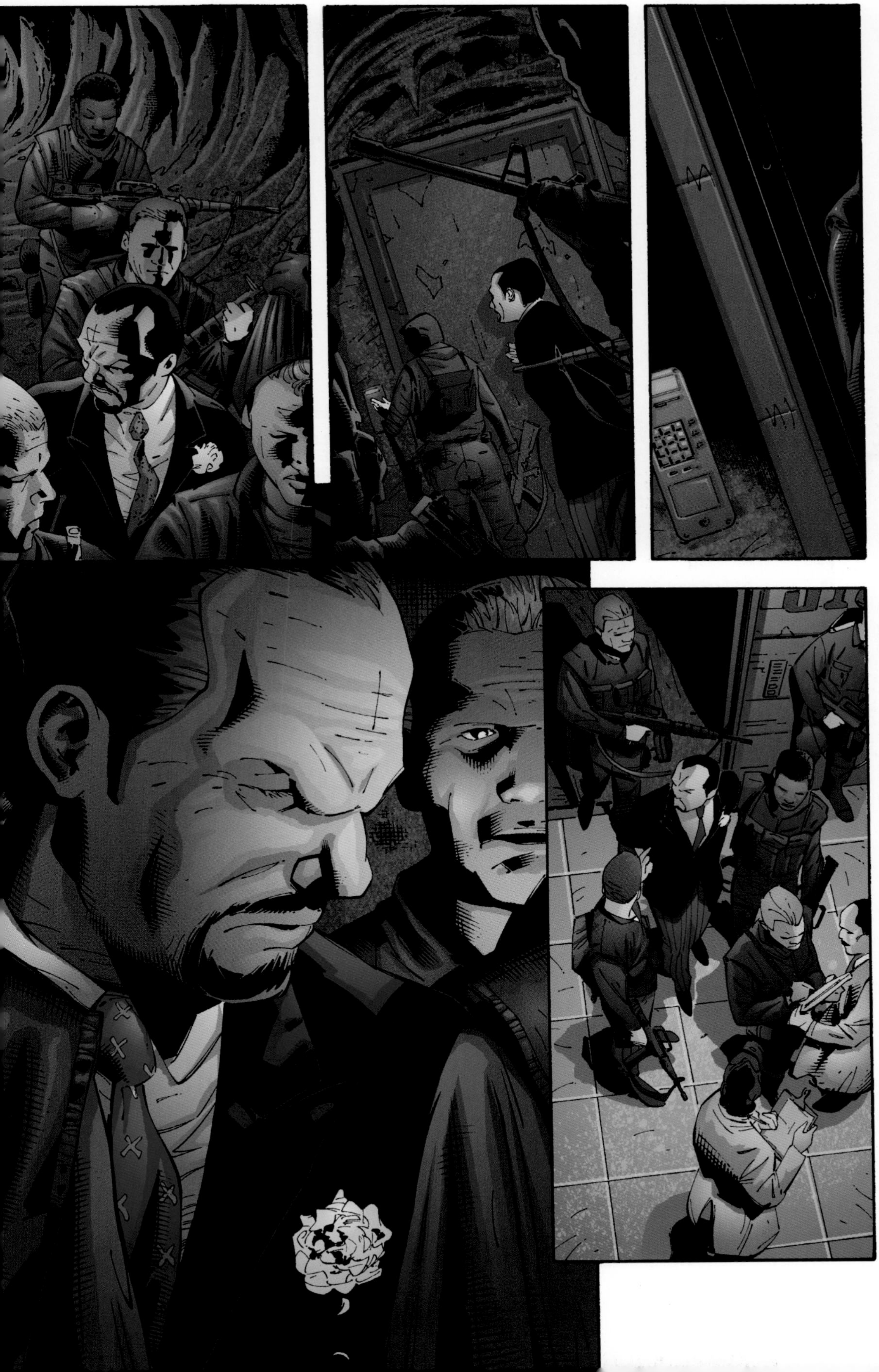

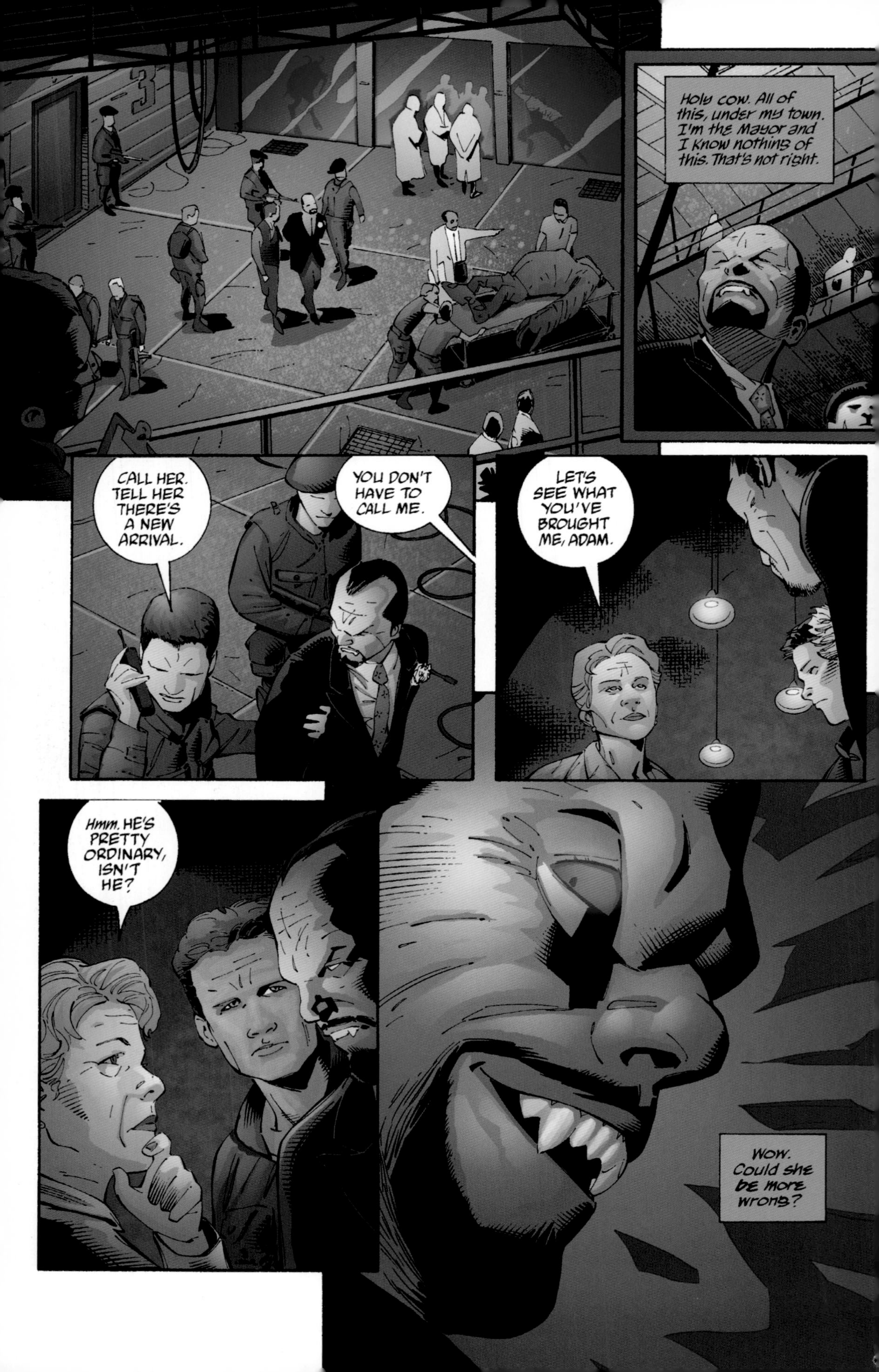
Holy cow. All of this, under my town. I'm the Mayor and I know nothing of this. That's not right.
CALL HER. TELL HER THERE'S A NEW ARRIVAL.
YOU DON'T HAVE TO CALL ME.
LET'S SEE WHAT YOU'VE BROUGHT ME, ADAM.
Hmm. HE'S PRETTY ORDINARY, ISN'T HE?
Wow. Could she be more wrong?

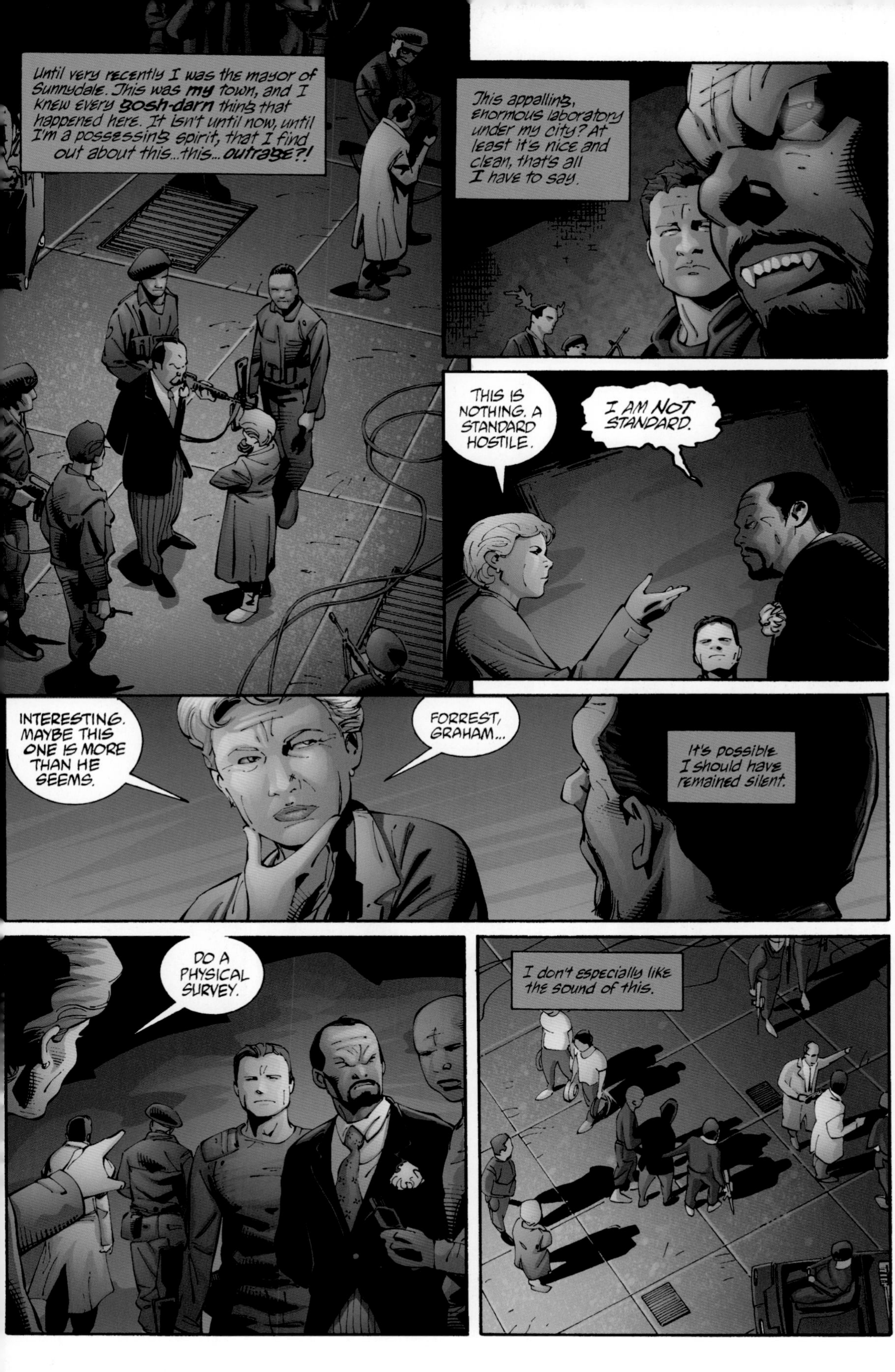
Until very recently I was the mayor of Sunnydale. This was **my** town, and I knew every **gosh-darn** thing that happened here. It isn't until now, until I'm a possessing spirit, that I find out about this...this... ***outrage?!***
This appalling, enormous laboratory under my city? At least it's nice and clean, that's all I have to say.
THIS IS NOTHING. A STANDARD HOSTILE.
I AM *NOT* STANDARD.
INTERESTING. MAYBE THIS ONE IS MORE THAN HE SEEMS.
FORREST, GRAHAM...
It's possible I should have remained silent.
DO A PHYSICAL SURVEY.
I don't especially like the sound of this.

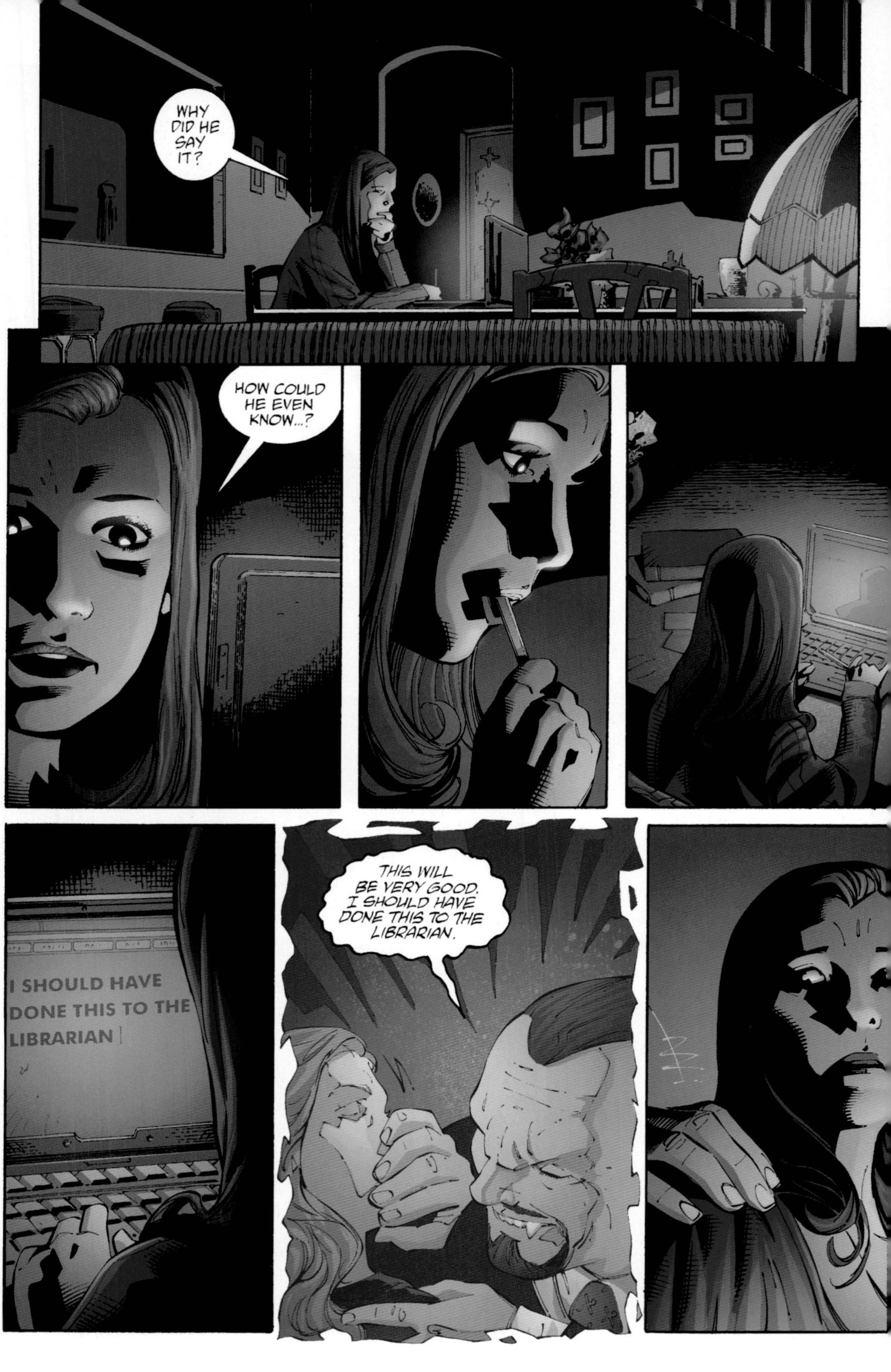
WHY DID HE SAY IT?
HOW COULD HE EVEN KNOW...?
I SHOULD HAVE DONE THIS TO THE LIBRARIAN
THIS WILL BE VERY GOOD. I SHOULD HAVE DONE THIS TO THE LIBRARIAN.

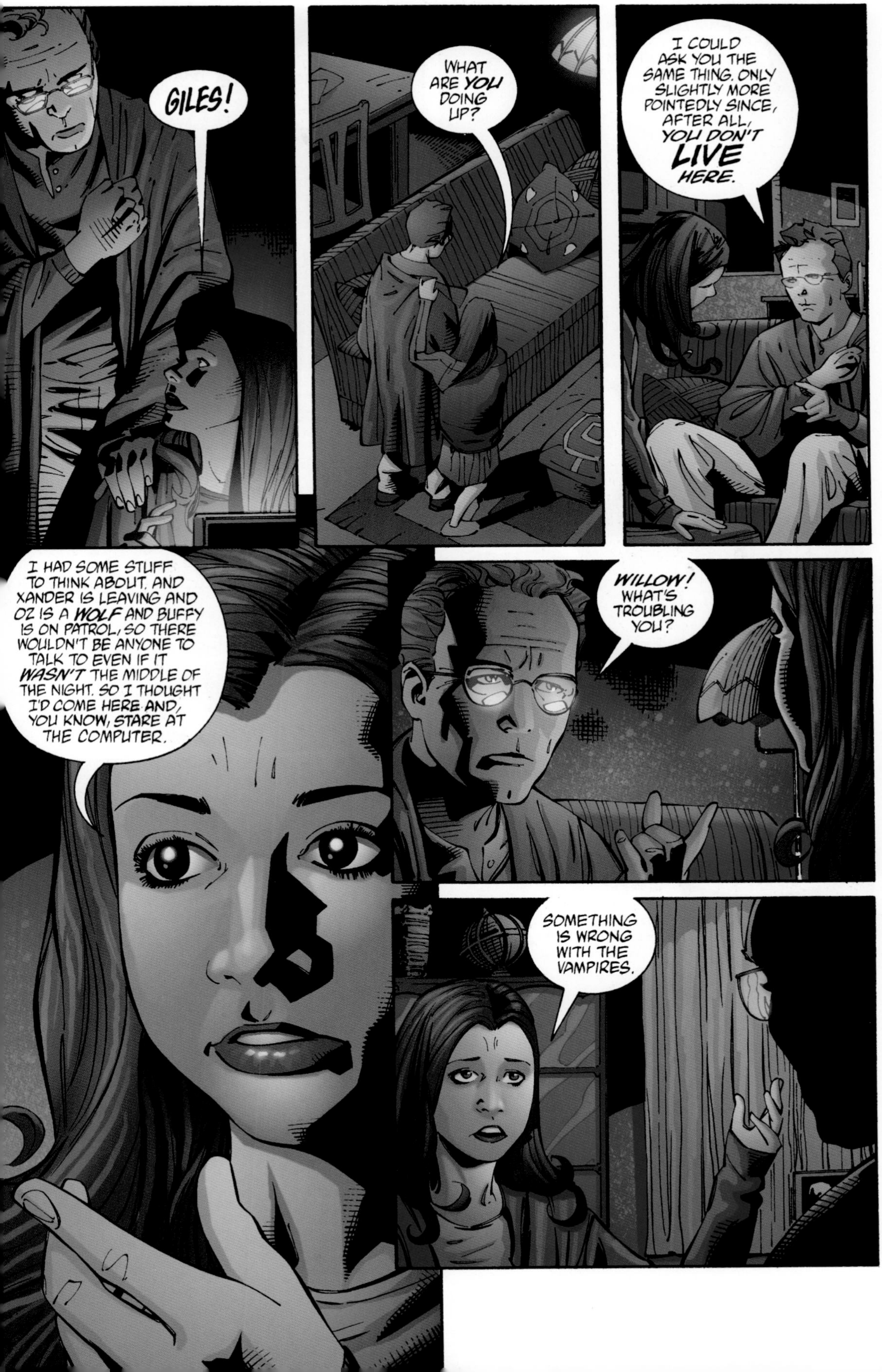
GILES!
WHAT ARE YOU DOING UP?
I COULD ASK YOU THE SAME THING. ONLY SLIGHTLY MORE POINTEDLY SINCE, AFTER ALL, YOU DON'T LIVE HERE.
I HAD SOME STUFF TO THINK ABOUT, AND XANDER IS LEAVING AND OZ IS A WOLF AND BUFFY IS ON PATROL, SO THERE WOULDN'T BE ANYONE TO TALK TO EVEN IF IT WASN'T THE MIDDLE OF THE NIGHT. SO I THOUGHT I'D COME HERE AND, YOU KNOW, STARE AT THE COMPUTER.
WILLOW! WHAT'S TROUBLING YOU?
SOMETHING IS WRONG WITH THE VAMPIRES.

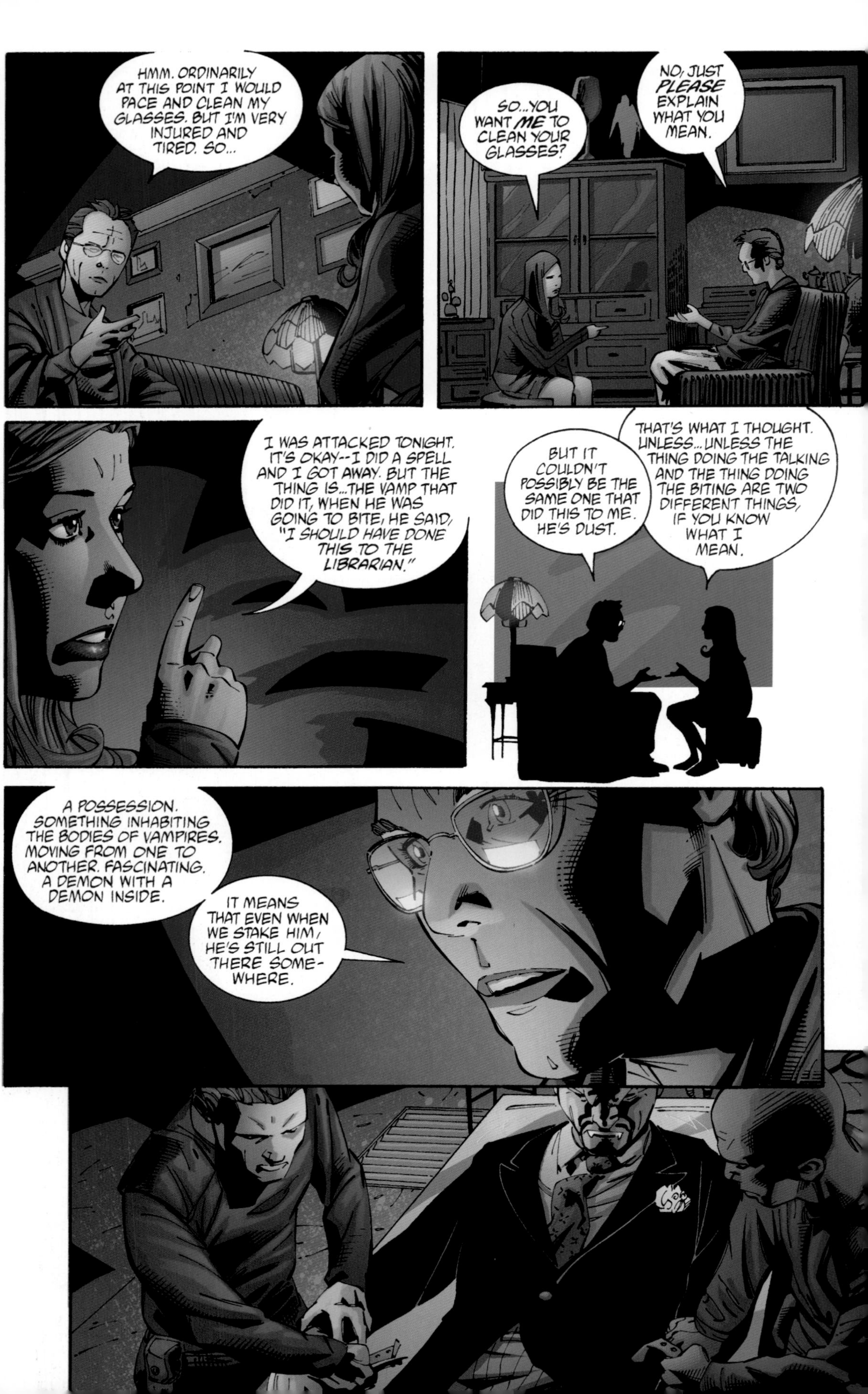
HMM. ORDINARILY AT THIS POINT I WOULD PACE AND CLEAN MY GLASSES. BUT I'M VERY INJURED AND TIRED. SO...
SO...YOU WANT ME TO CLEAN YOUR GLASSES?
NO, JUST PLEASE EXPLAIN WHAT YOU MEAN.
I WAS ATTACKED TONIGHT. IT'S OKAY--I DID A SPELL AND I GOT AWAY. BUT THE THING IS...THE VAMP THAT DID IT, WHEN HE WAS GOING TO BITE, HE SAID, "I SHOULD HAVE DONE THIS TO THE LIBRARIAN."
BUT IT COULDN'T POSSIBLY BE THE SAME ONE THAT DID THIS TO ME. HE'S DUST.
THAT'S WHAT I THOUGHT. UNLESS...UNLESS THE THING DOING THE TALKING AND THE THING DOING THE BITING ARE TWO DIFFERENT THINGS, IF YOU KNOW WHAT I MEAN.
A POSSESSION. SOMETHING INHABITING THE BODIES OF VAMPIRES. MOVING FROM ONE TO ANOTHER. FASCINATING. A DEMON WITH A DEMON INSIDE.
IT MEANS THAT EVEN WHEN WE STAKE HIM, HE'S STILL OUT THERE SOME-WHERE.

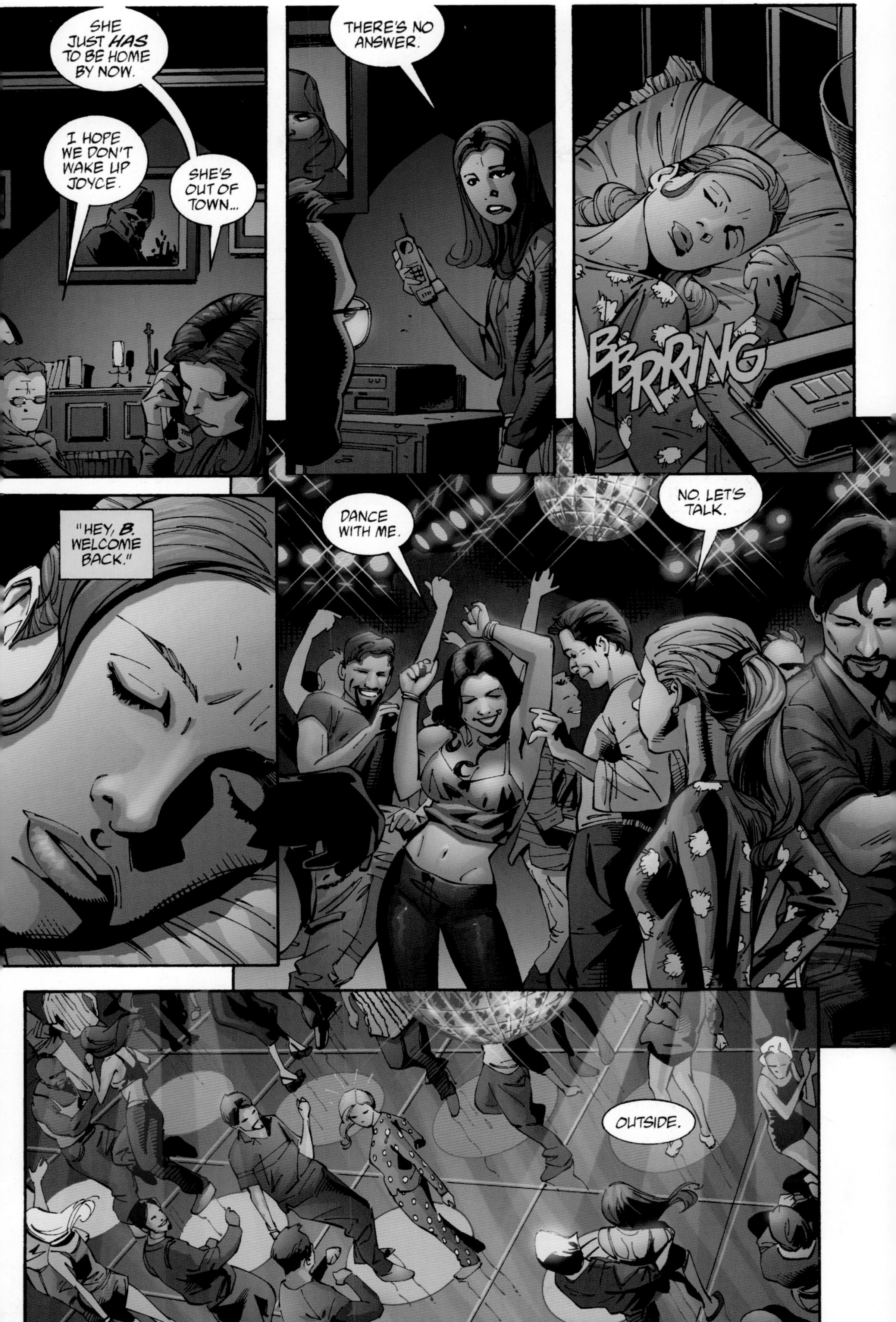
SHE JUST HAS TO BE HOME BY NOW.
I HOPE WE DON'T WAKE UP JOYCE.
SHE'S OUT OF TOWN...
THERE'S NO ANSWER.
BBRRRING
"HEY, B. WELCOME BACK."
DANCE WITH ME.
NO. LET'S TALK.
OUTSIDE.

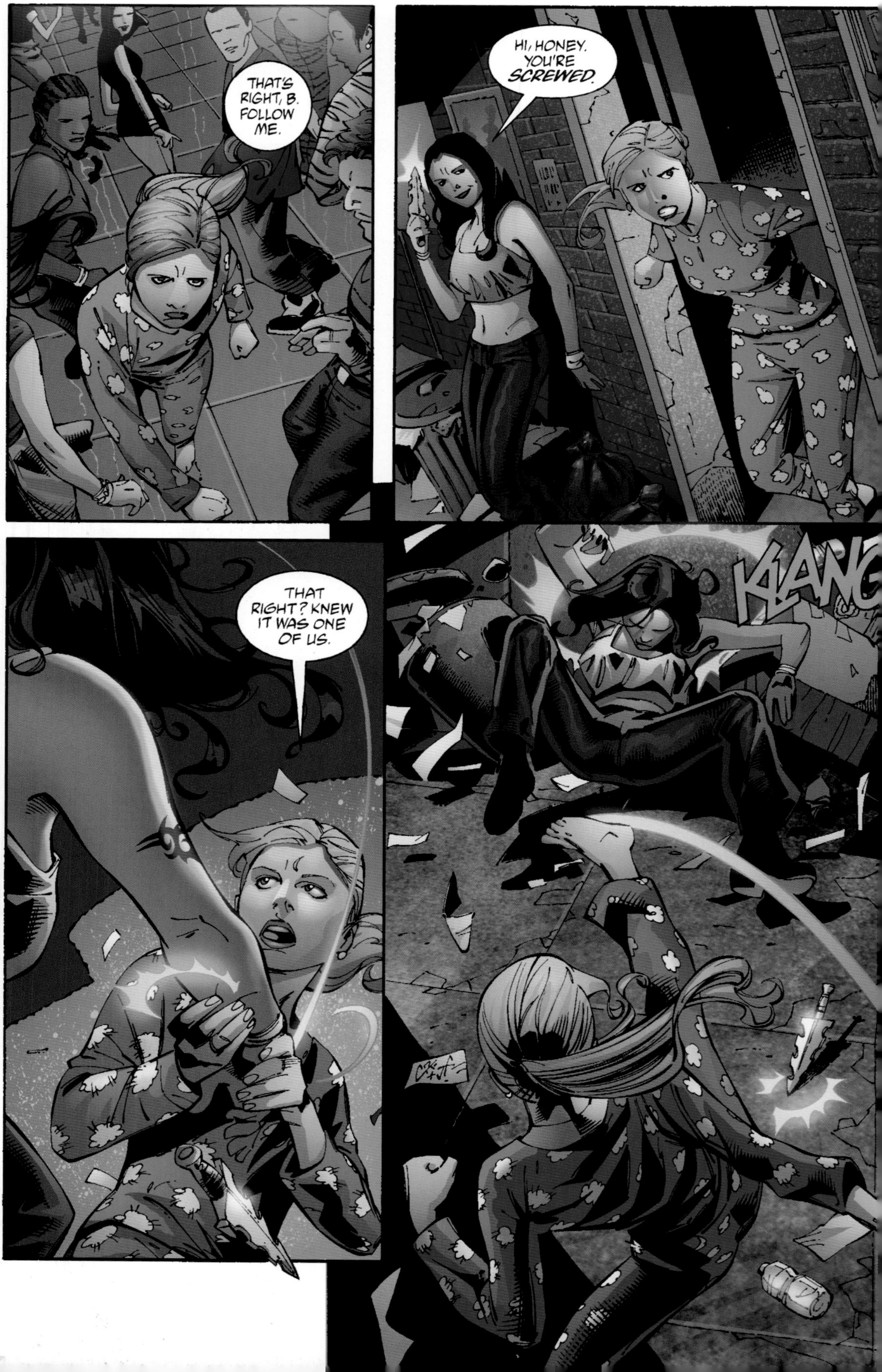
THAT'S RIGHT, B. FOLLOW ME.
HI, HONEY. YOU'RE SCREWED.
THAT RIGHT? KNEW IT WAS ONE OF US.
KLANG

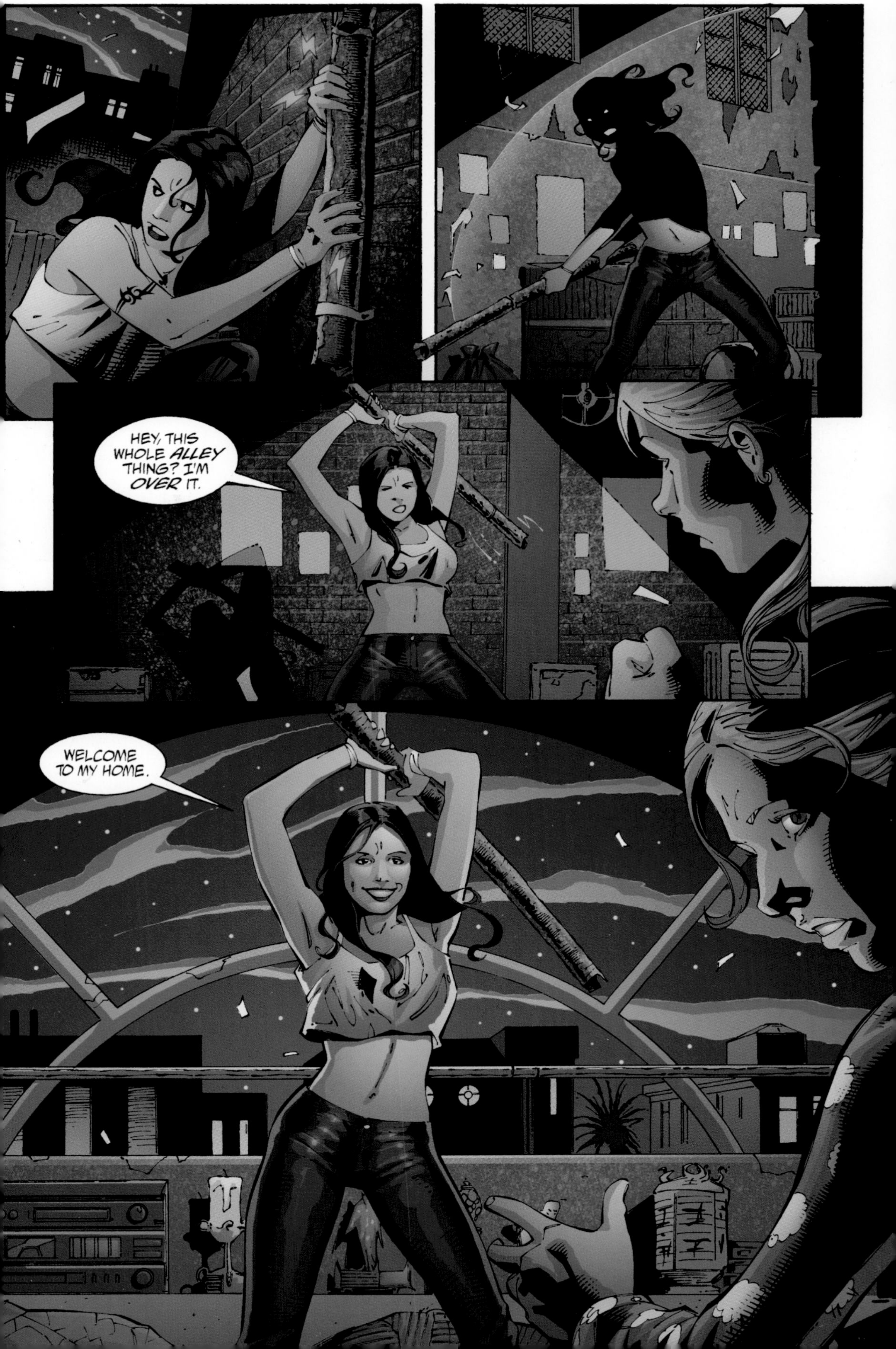
HEY, THIS WHOLE ALLEY THING? I'M OVER IT.
WELCOME TO MY HOME.

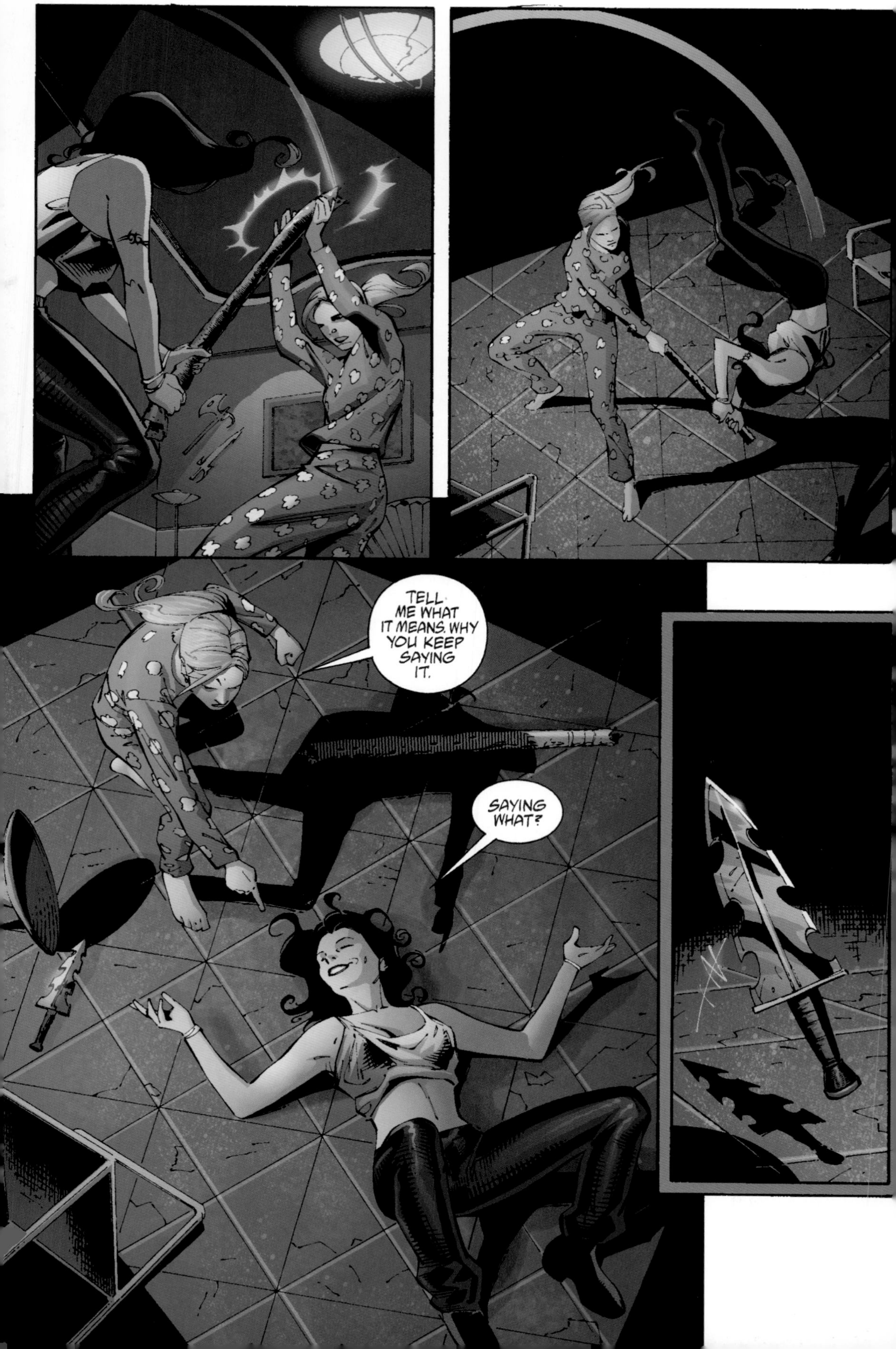
TELL ME WHAT IT MEANS. WHY YOU KEEP SAYING IT.
SAYING WHAT?

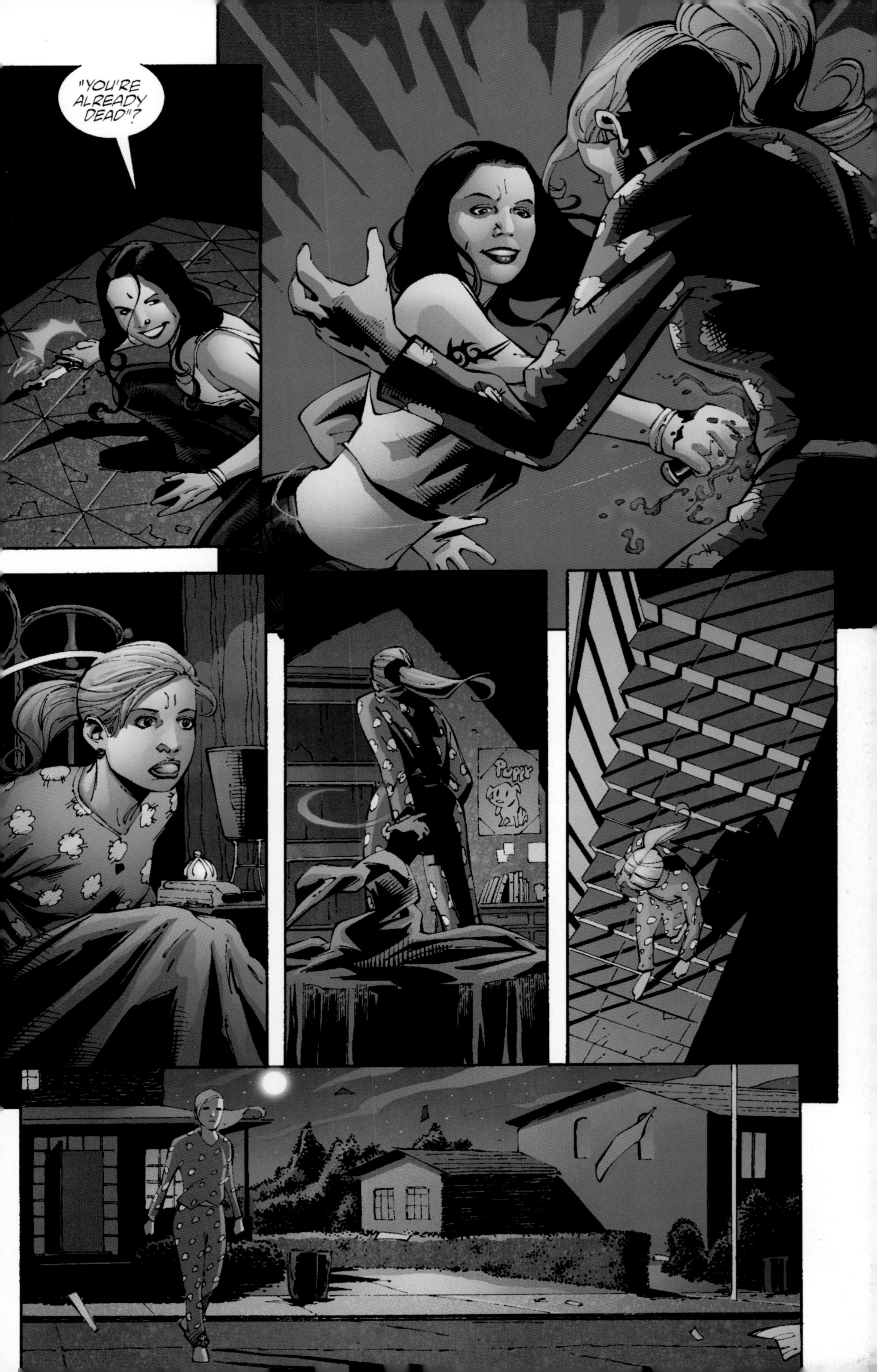
"YOU'RE ALREADY DEAD"?
PUPPY

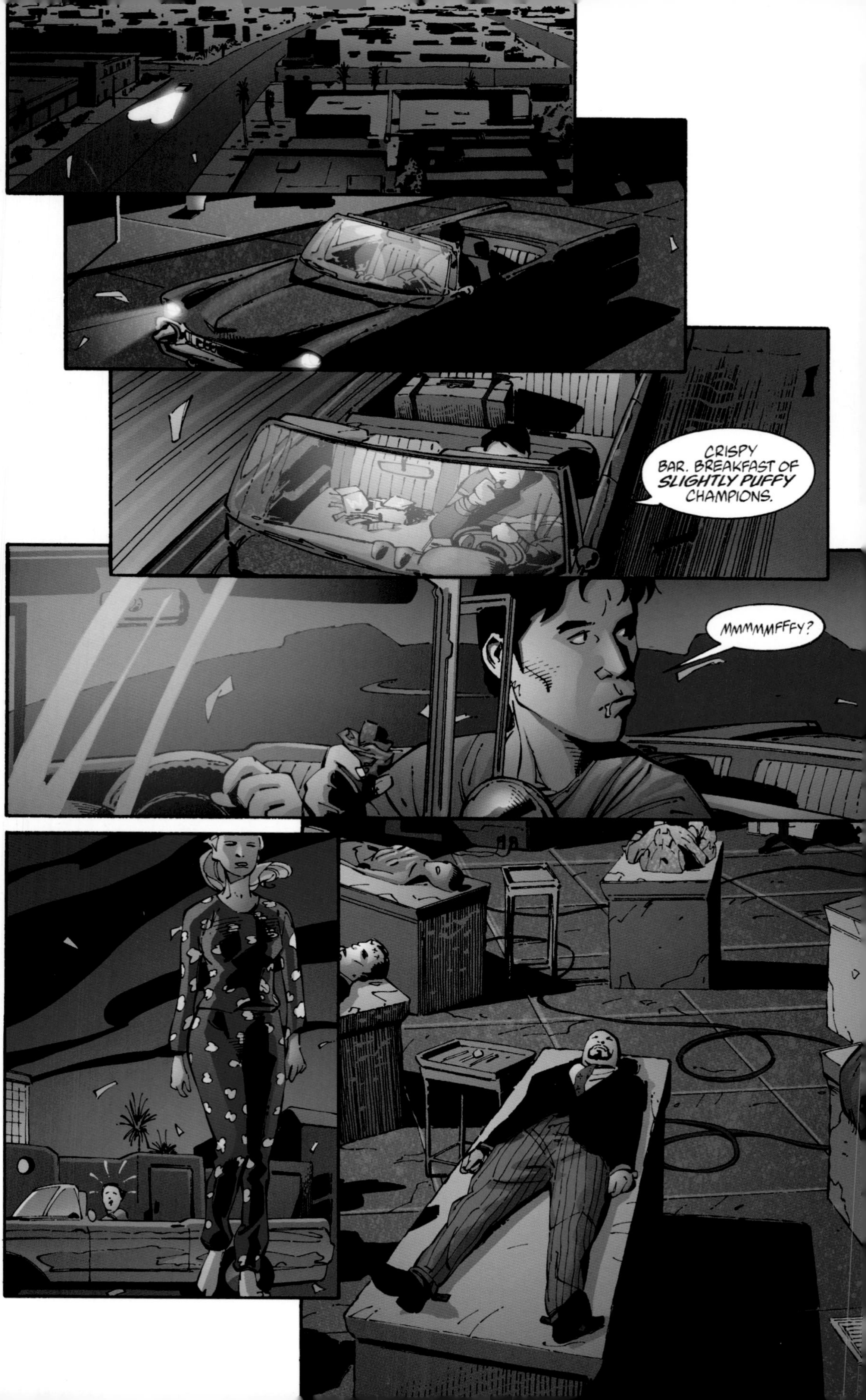
CRISPY BAR. BREAKFAST OF SLIGHTLY PUFFY CHAMPIONS.
MMMMMFFFY?

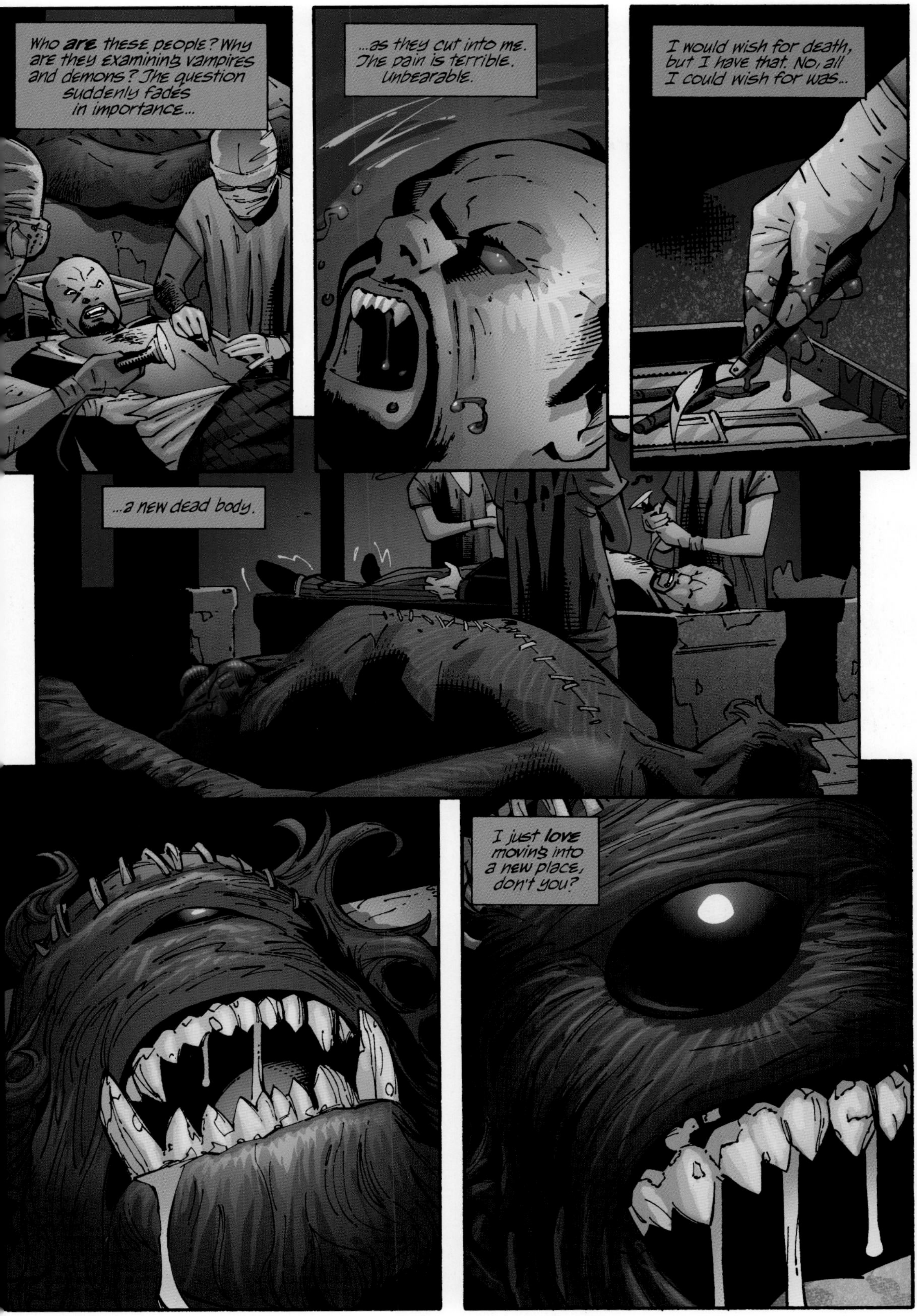
Who **are** these people? Why are they examining vampires and demons? The question suddenly fades in importance...
...as they cut into me. The pain is terrible. Unbearable.
I would wish for death, but I have that. No, all I could wish for was...
...a new dead body.
I just **love** moving into a new place, don't you?

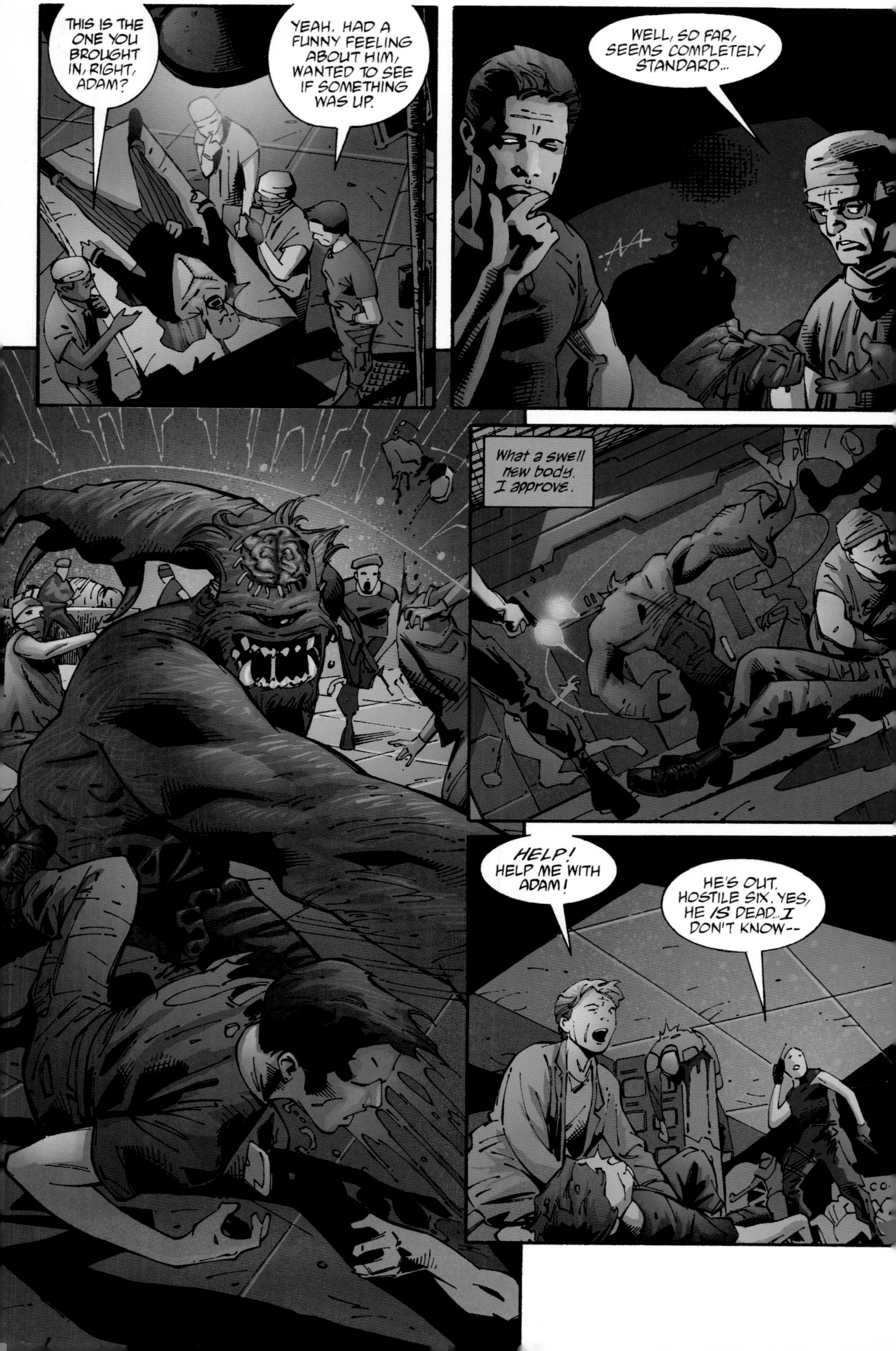

THIS IS THE ONE YOU BROUGHT IN, RIGHT, ADAM?
YEAH. HAD A FUNNY FEELING ABOUT HIM, WANTED TO SEE IF SOMETHING WAS UP.
WELL, SO FAR, SEEMS COMPLETELY STANDARD...
What a swell new body. I approve.
HELP! HELP ME WITH ADAM!
HE'S OUT. HOSTILE SIX. YES, HE IS DEAD... I DON'T KNOW--

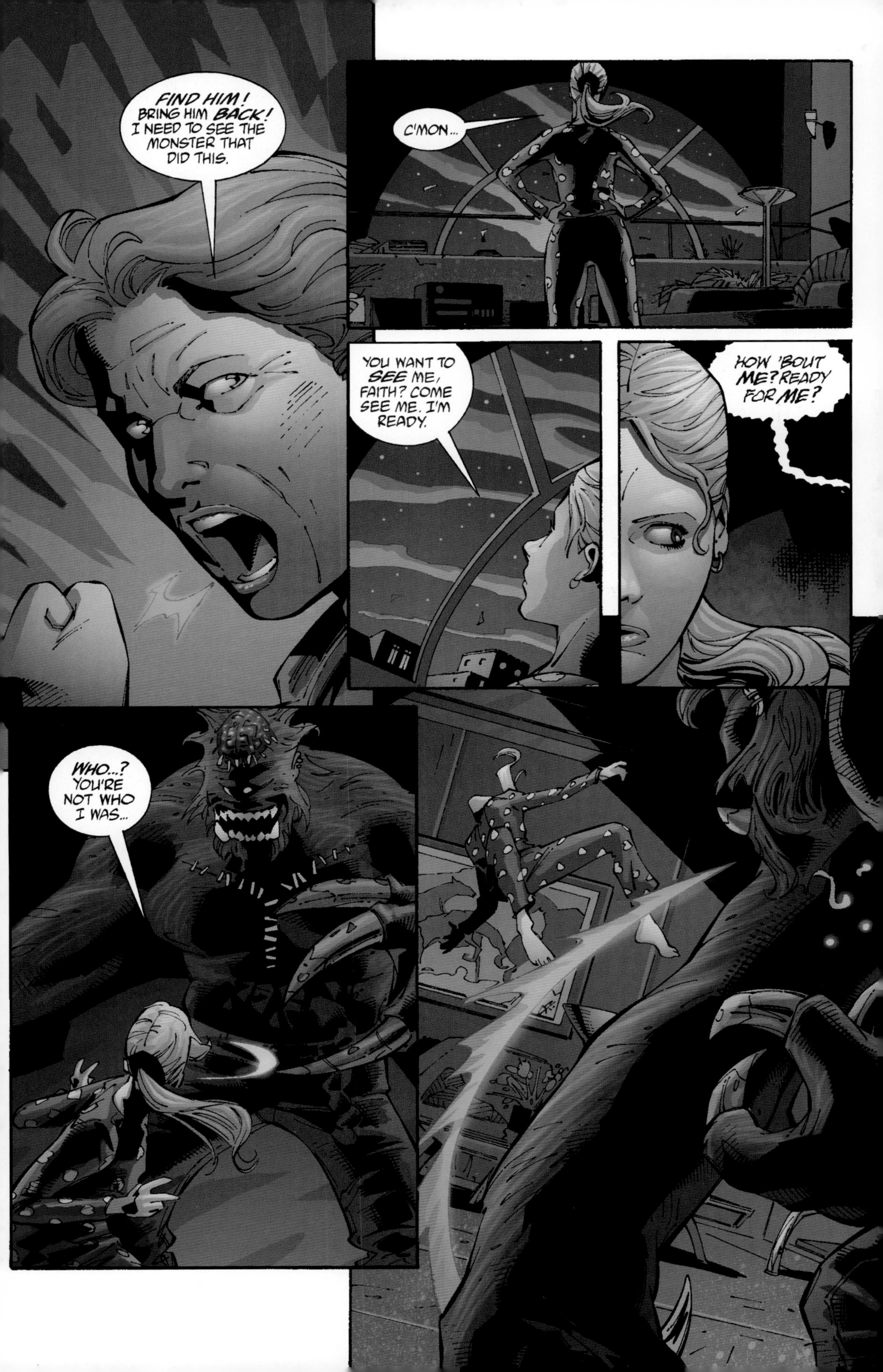
FIND HIM! BRING HIM BACK! I NEED TO SEE THE MONSTER THAT DID THIS.
C'MON...
YOU WANT TO SEE ME, FAITH? COME SEE ME. I'M READY.
HOW 'BOUT ME? READY FOR ME?
WHO...? YOU'RE NOT WHO I WAS...

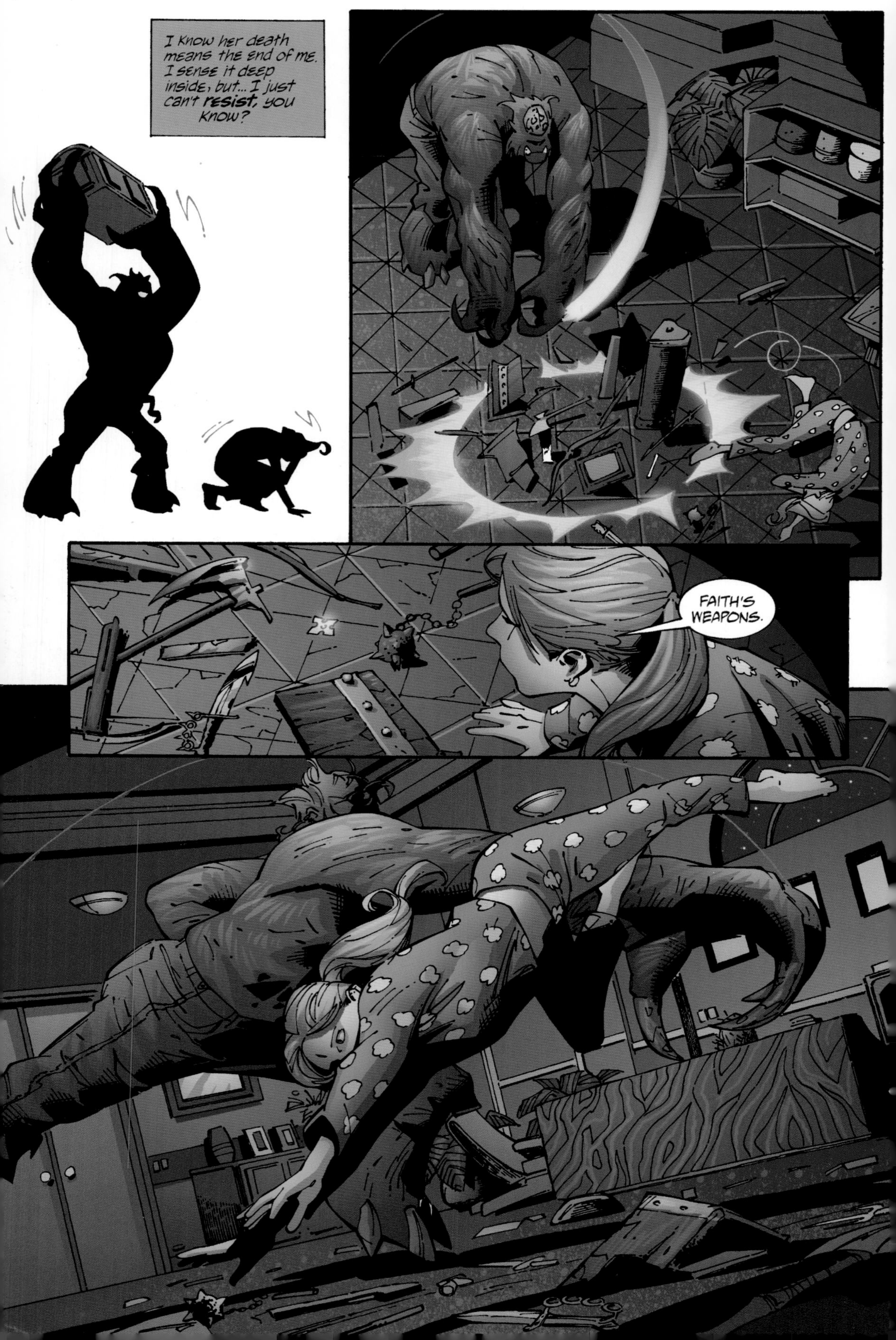
I know her death means the end of me. I sense it deep inside, but... I just can't **resist,** you know?
FAITH'S WEAPONS.

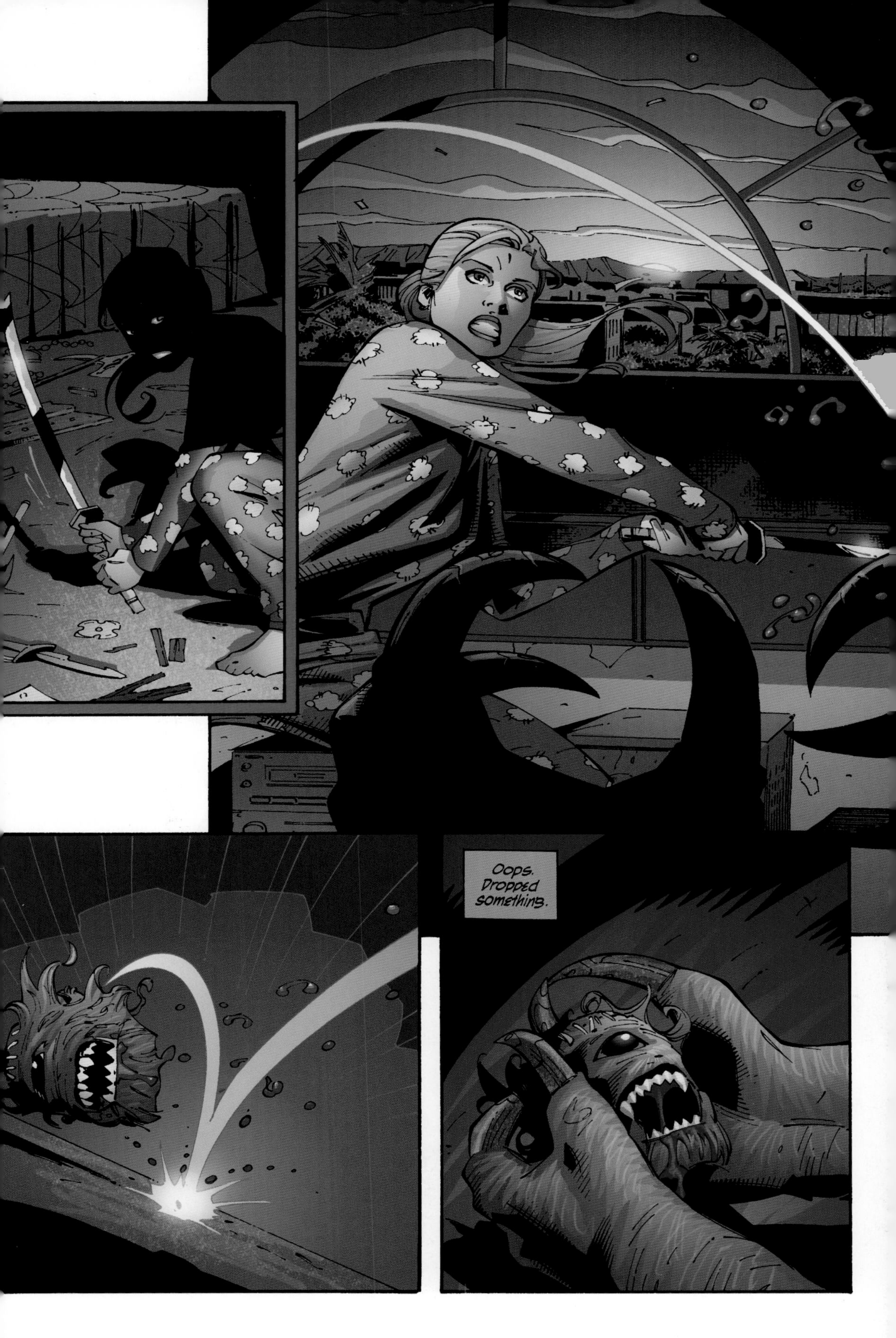
Oops. Dropped something.

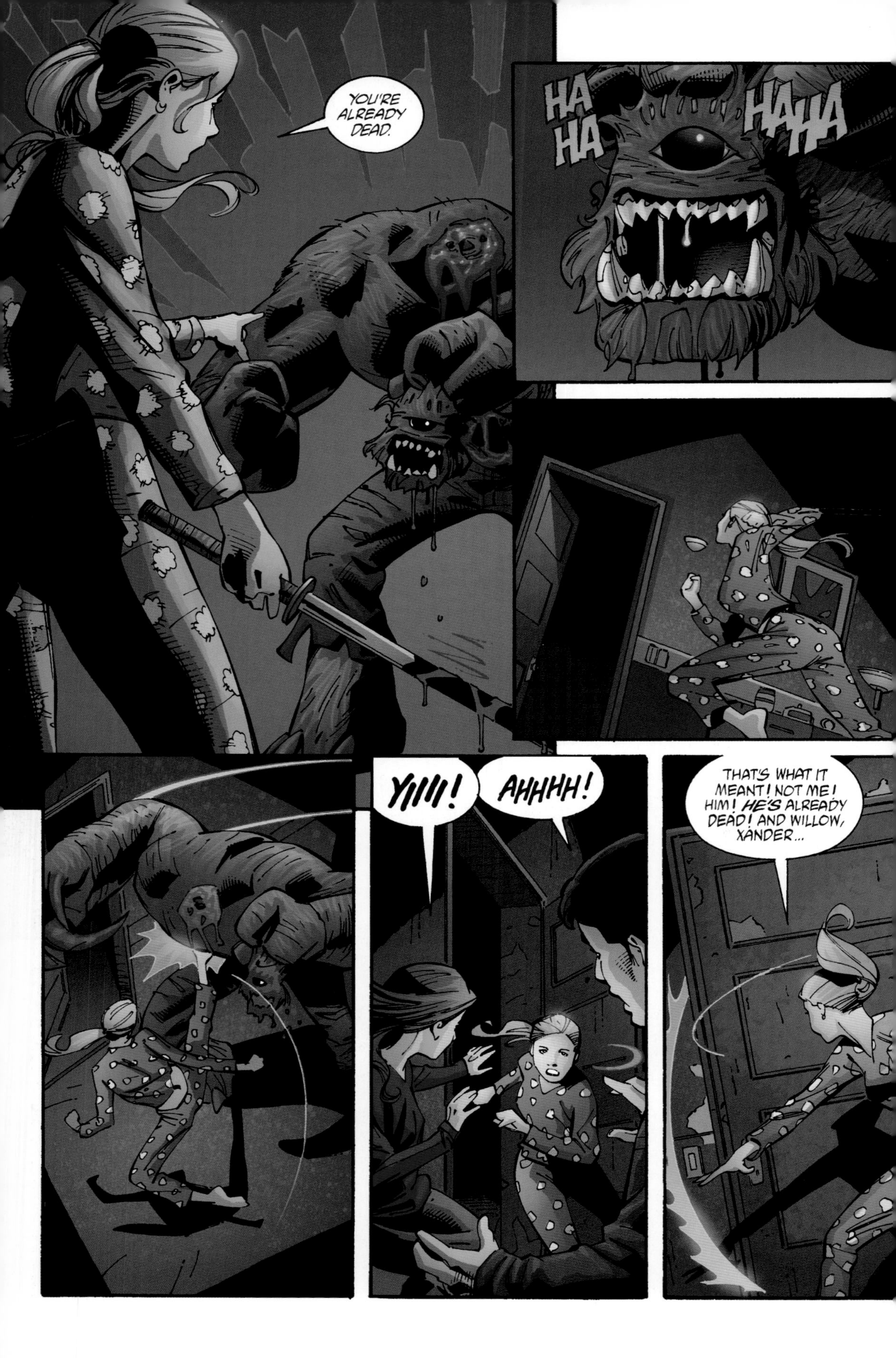
YOU'RE ALREADY DEAD.
HA HA
HAHA
YIII!
AHHHH!
THAT'S WHAT IT MEANT! NOT ME! HIM! HE'S ALREADY DEAD! AND WILLOW, XANDER...

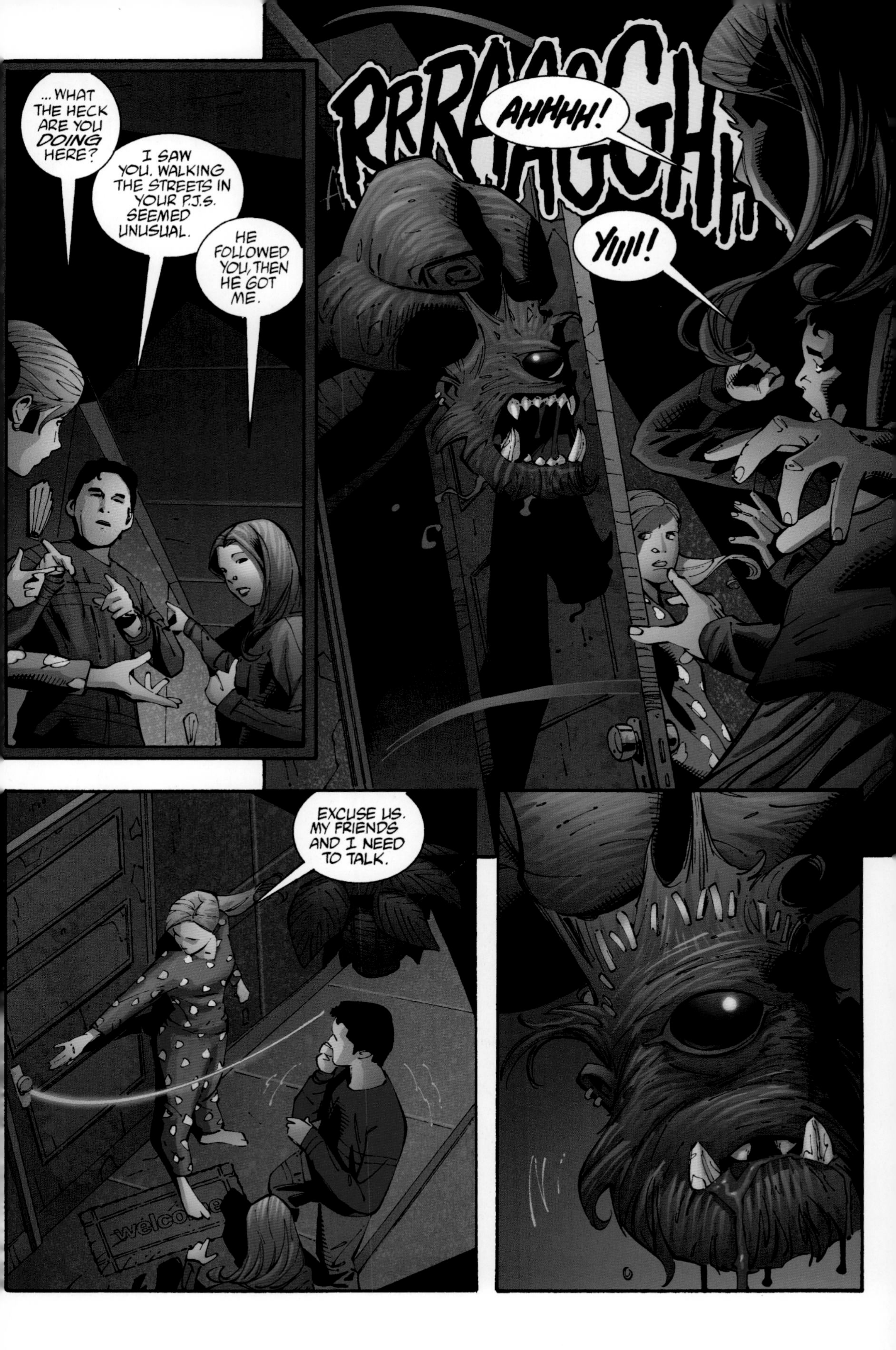
...WHAT THE HECK ARE YOU DOING HERE?
I SAW YOU. WALKING THE STREETS IN YOUR P.J.S. SEEMED UNUSUAL.
HE FOLLOWED YOU, THEN HE GOT ME.
RRRAAGGH
AHHHH!
YIII!
EXCUSE US. MY FRIENDS AND I NEED TO TALK.
welcome

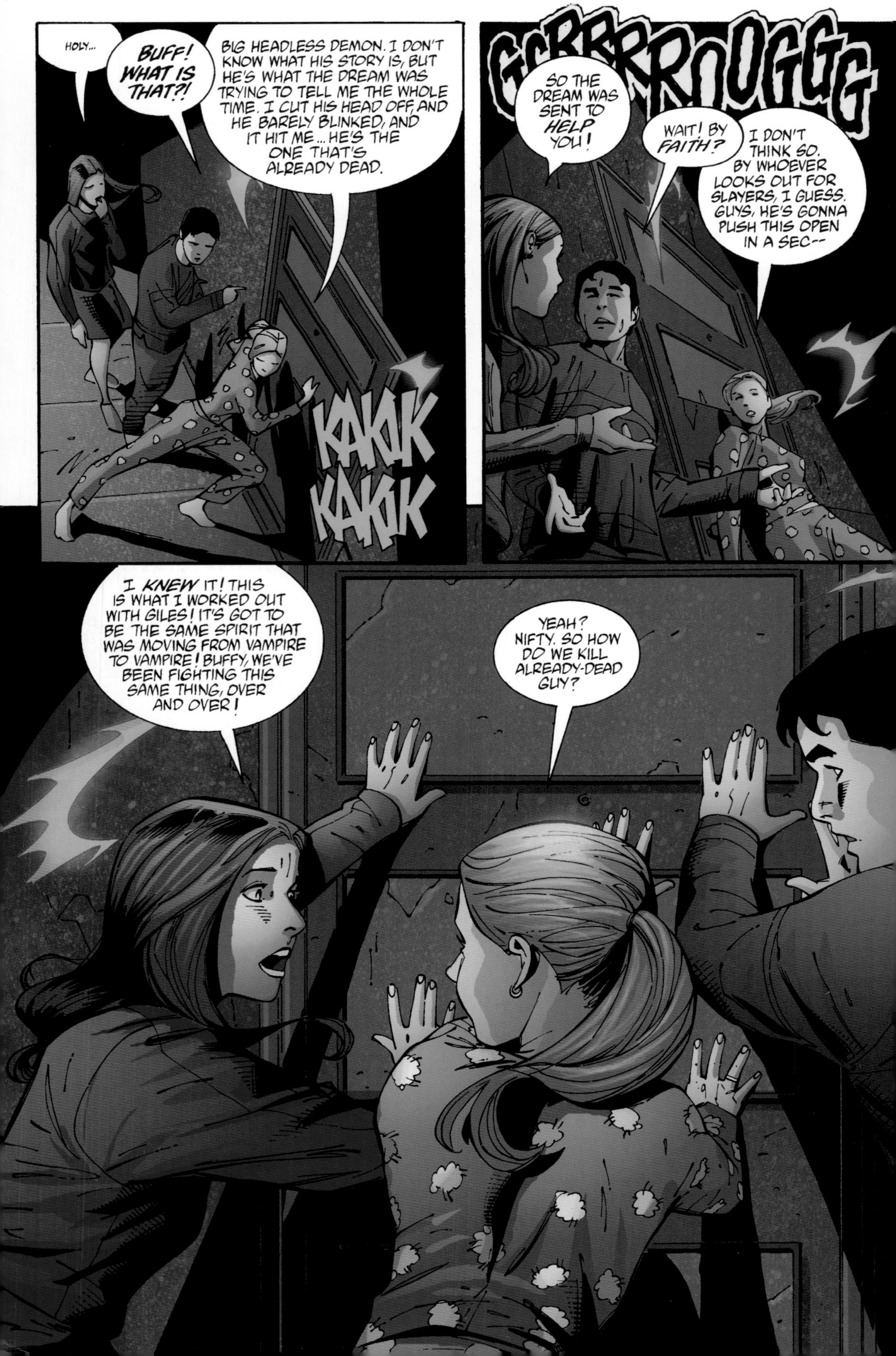
HOLY...
BUFF! WHAT IS THAT?!
BIG HEADLESS DEMON. I DON'T KNOW WHAT HIS STORY IS, BUT HE'S WHAT THE DREAM WAS TRYING TO TELL ME THE WHOLE TIME. I CUT HIS HEAD OFF, AND HE BARELY BLINKED, AND IT HIT ME... HE'S THE ONE THAT'S ALREADY DEAD.
KAKOK KAKOK
GCRRRRROOGGG
SO THE DREAM WAS SENT TO HELP YOU!
WAIT! BY FAITH?
I DON'T THINK SO. BY WHOEVER LOOKS OUT FOR SLAYERS, I GUESS. GUYS, HE'S GONNA PUSH THIS OPEN IN A SEC--
I KNEW IT! THIS IS WHAT I WORKED OUT WITH GILES! IT'S GOT TO BE THE SAME SPIRIT THAT WAS MOVING FROM VAMPIRE TO VAMPIRE! BUFFY, WE'VE BEEN FIGHTING THIS SAME THING, OVER AND OVER!
YEAH? NIFTY. SO HOW DO WE KILL ALREADY-DEAD GUY?

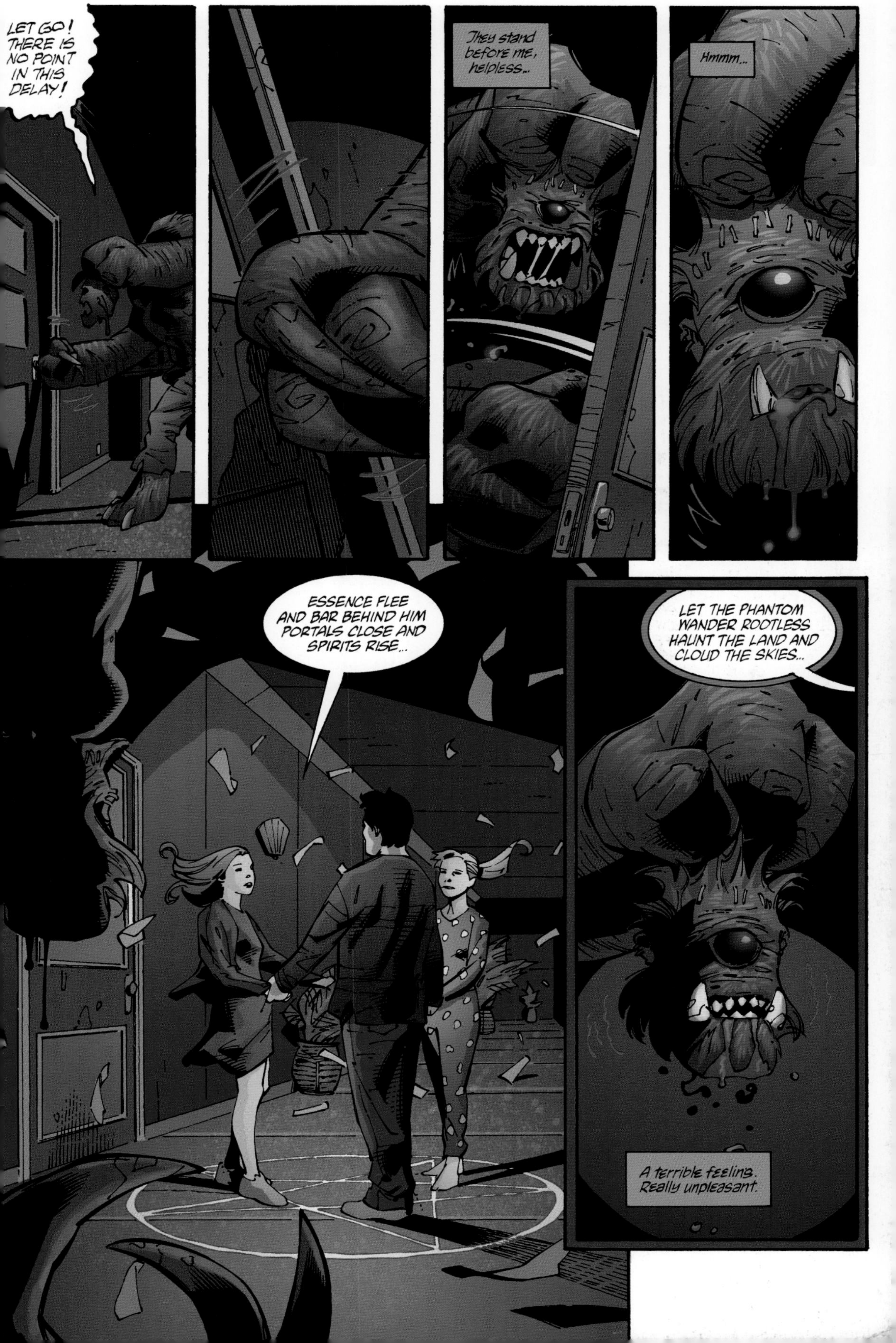

LET GO! THERE IS NO POINT IN THIS DELAY!
They stand before me, helpless...
Hmmm...
ESSENCE FLEE AND BAR BEHIND HIM PORTALS CLOSE AND SPIRITS RISE...
LET THE PHANTOM WANDER ROOTLESS HAUNT THE LAND AND CLOUD THE SKIES...
A terrible feeling. Really unpleasant.

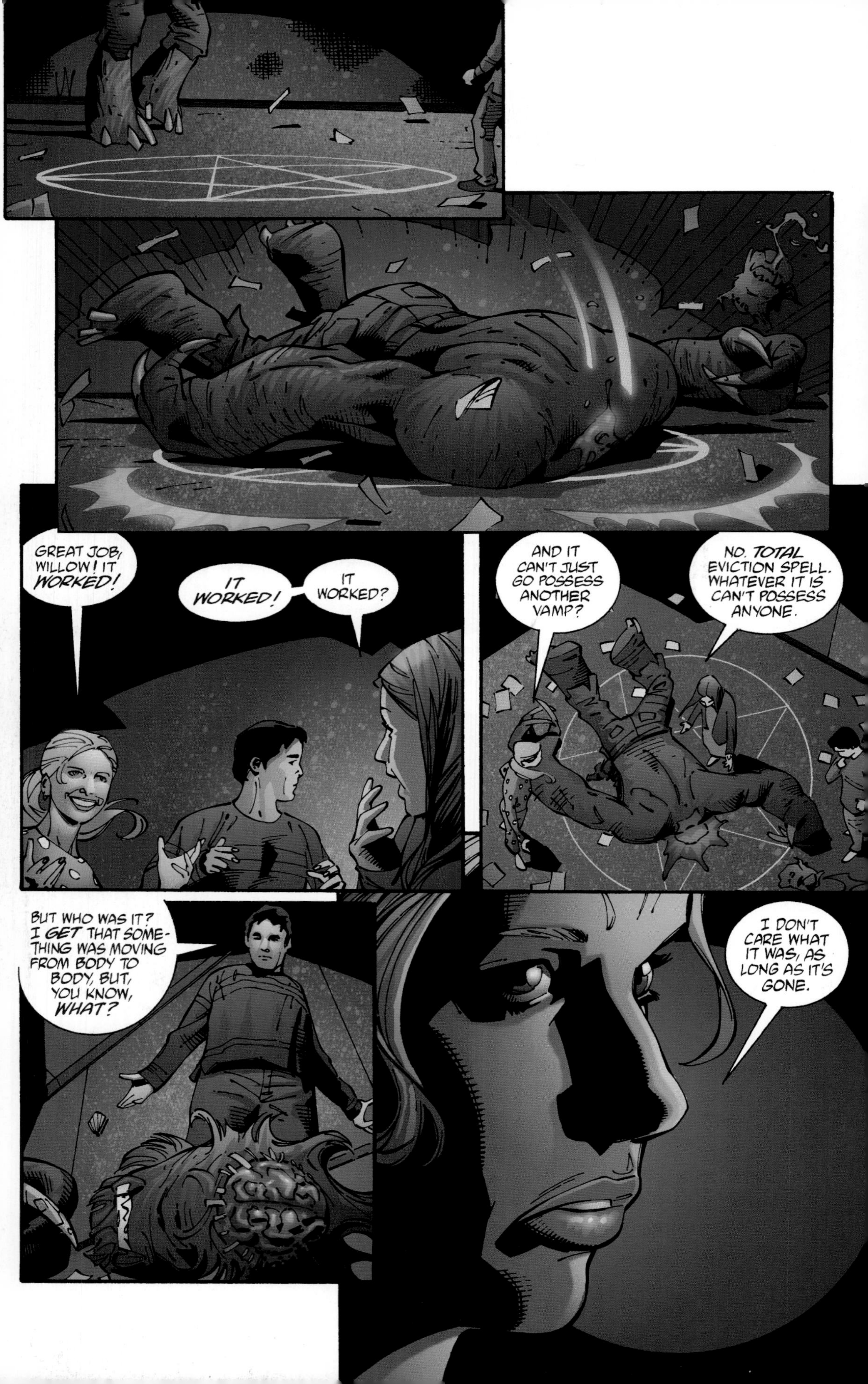
GREAT JOB, WILLOW! IT WORKED!
IT WORKED!
IT WORKED?
AND IT CAN'T JUST GO POSSESS ANOTHER VAMP?
NO. TOTAL EVICTION SPELL. WHATEVER IT IS CAN'T POSSESS ANYONE.
BUT WHO WAS IT? I GET THAT SOMETHING WAS MOVING FROM BODY TO BODY, BUT, YOU KNOW, WHAT?
I DON'T CARE WHAT IT WAS, AS LONG AS IT'S GONE.

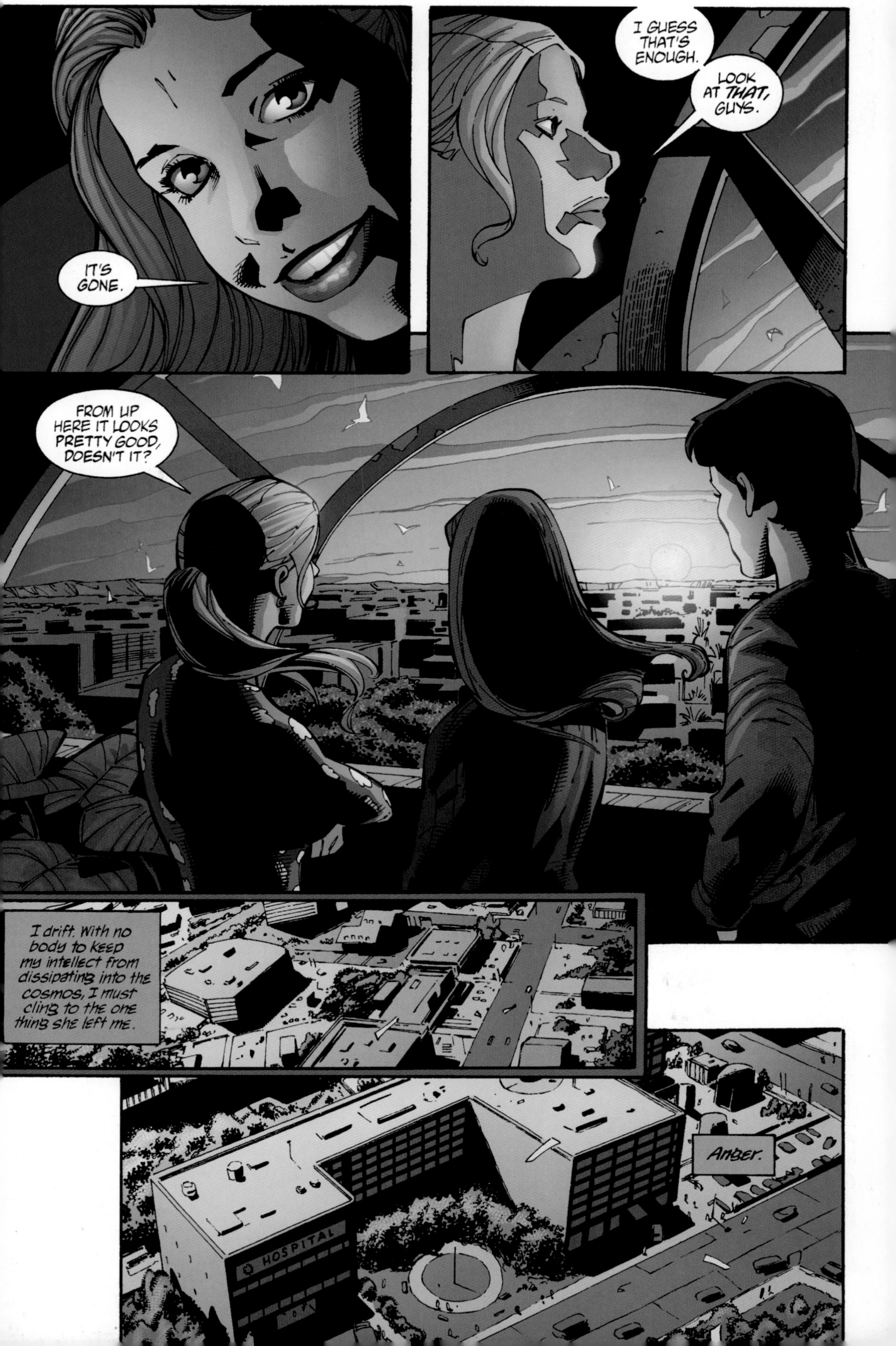
IT'S GONE.
I GUESS THAT'S ENOUGH.
LOOK AT THAT, GUYS.
FROM UP HERE IT LOOKS PRETTY GOOD, DOESN'T IT?
I drift. With no body to keep my intellect from dissipating into the cosmos, I must cling to the one thing she left me.
Amber.
HOSPITAL

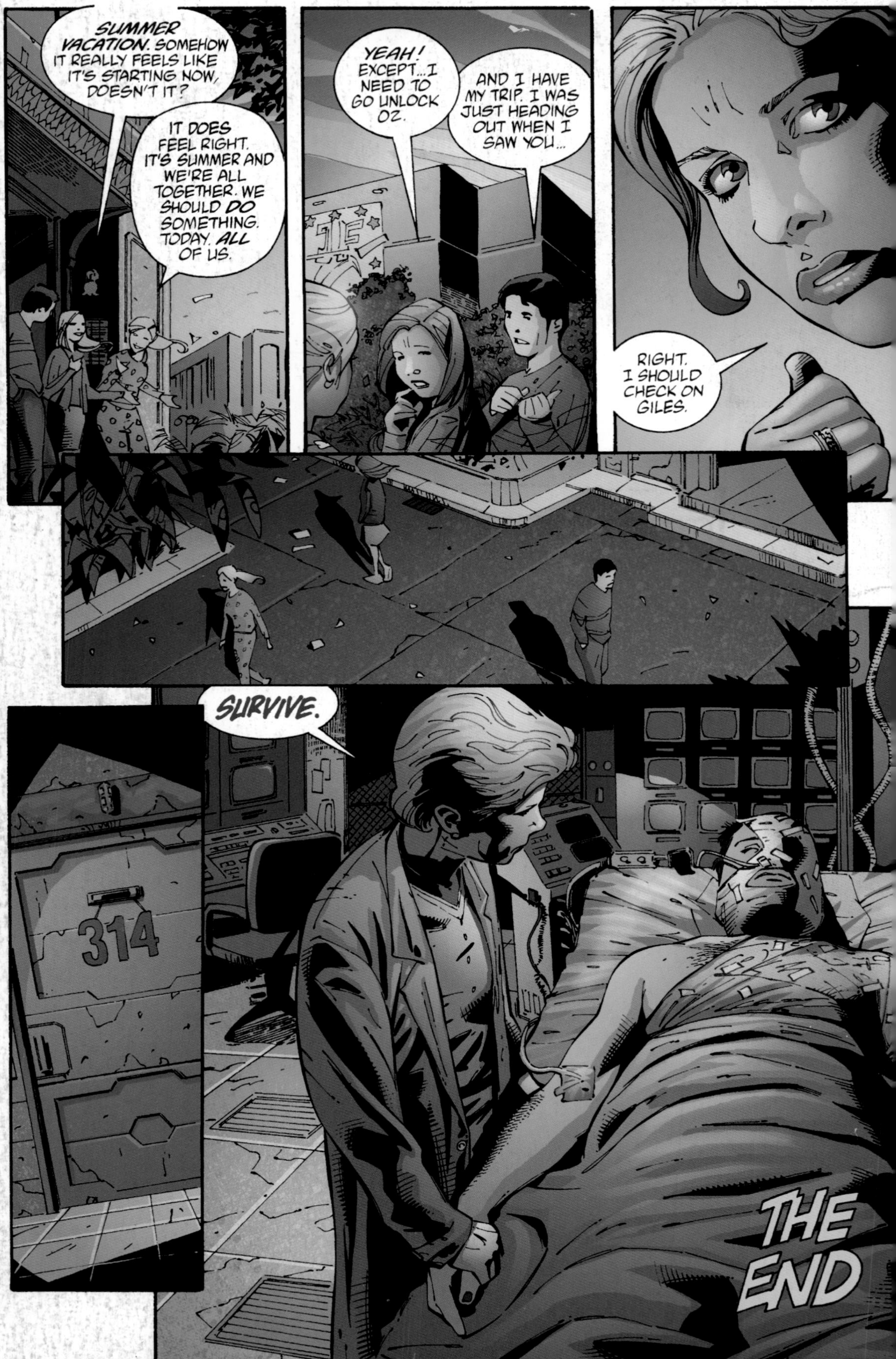
SUMMER VACATION. SOMEHOW IT REALLY FEELS LIKE IT'S STARTING NOW, DOESN'T IT?
IT DOES FEEL RIGHT. IT'S SUMMER AND WE'RE ALL TOGETHER. WE SHOULD DO SOMETHING. TODAY. ALL OF US.
YEAH! EXCEPT...I NEED TO GO UNLOCK OZ.
AND I HAVE MY TRIP. I WAS JUST HEADING OUT WHEN I SAW YOU...
RIGHT. I SHOULD CHECK ON GILES.
SURVIVE.
314
THE END